Whispers
THROUGH
THE
Trees

Whispers THROUGH THE Trees

SUSAN PLUNKETT &
KRYSTEEN SEELEN

GuidepostsBooks®
New York, New York

Whispers through the Trees

ISBN-13: 978-0-8249-4711-8
ISBN-10: 0-8249-4711-8

Published by GuidepostsBooks
16 East 34th Street
New York, New York 10016
www.guidepostsbooks.com

Distributed by Ideals Publications, a Guideposts company
535 Metroplex Drive, Suite 250
Nashville, Tennessee 37211

GuidepostsBooks, Ideals and *Mysteries of Sparrow Island* are registered trademarks of
Guideposts, Carmel, New York.

The characters and events in this book are fictional, and any resemblance to actual
persons or events is coincidental.

Acknowledgments
Every attempt has been made to credit the sources of copyrighted material used
in this book. If any such acknowledgment has been inadvertently omitted or
miscredited, receipt of such information would be appreciated.

All Scripture quotations are taken from *The Holy Bible, New International Version.*
Copyright © 1973, 1978, 1984 International Bible Society. Used by permission of
Zondervan Bible Publishers.

Library of Congress Cataloging-in-Publication Data

Plunkett, Susan.
  Whispers through the trees / Susan Plunkett & Krysteen Seelen.
    p. cm. -- (Mysteries of Sparrow Island)
  ISBN-13: 978-0-8249-4711-8 (trade pbk.) 1. San Juan Islands (Wash.)--Fiction.
2. Ornithologists--Fiction. 3. Bird watchers--Fiction. 4. Endangered species--
Fiction. I. Seelen, Krysteen. II. Title.
  PS3616.L89W47 2007
  813'.54--dc22
                                        2006021346

Cover illustration by Chris Hopkins
Designed by Marisa Jackson

Printed and bound in the United States of America

10 9 8 7 6 5 4 3 2 1

To our Father God for His unfathomable love.

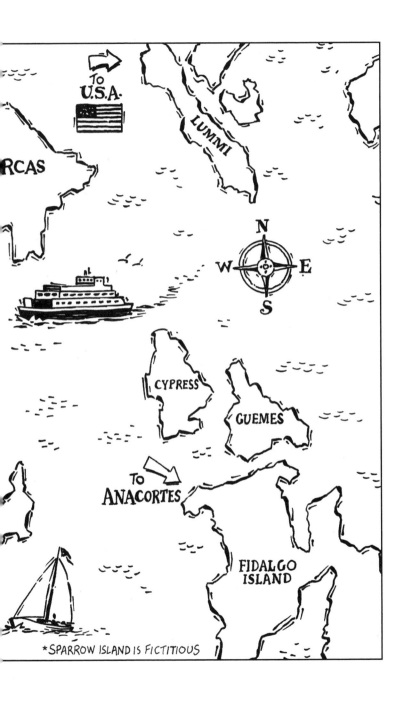

Prologue

I T'S GETTING BAD OUT THERE, Abby. Sure you won't stay the night?" A stiff wind blustered down the narrow street in front of Francine's house, rattling garbage cans, rustling branches and banging shutters.

"Thanks, but I need to batten down my place." Abigail Stanton collected the empty deli cartons from their dinner and deposited them in the trash along with their paper plates. "The weatherman said it's going to be an old-fashioned nor'easter."

"We'll probably lose power before morning." Francine walked with Abby out of the kitchen, into the living room and on to the foyer. She rubbed her arms and shivered as another chilly draft snaked around their ankles. "I'm glad you could stop by on your way home. I really appreciate your help moving that couch, and bringing dinner, to boot."

Francine looked around the cavernous living room. "You know, Abby, I often ask myself what I was thinking when I bought this old house. It's like living in an igloo. Especially on nights like this."

Abby retrieved her long wool coat from the closet in the foyer. "You were thinking about summer and lemonade on the wraparound porch. About watching from those fabulous up-stairs turrets as the maples turn red and gold in the fall."

"Oh yeah." Francine's self-mocking smile turned dreamy. "That's right. Thank heaven I have such a good friend to remind me I haven't completely lost my mind."

Abby laughed. Every winter they had this same conversation, although this year, it was long overdue. The leaves had already started to bud on the trees. Yet instead of welcome harbingers of spring, the early growth felt like a warning, like time was passing much too quickly.

Shaking her head, Abby shrugged into the heavy red wool coat and tried to banish this strange sense of regret that had crept in and had plagued every quiet moment of her day. Abby had been preoccupied as of late and, today especially, something was weighing heavily on her mind, as if there was some important business she had left undone. On top of that, she couldn't stop thinking about her sister Mary. Something inside her told her to get in touch with her as soon as she could.

She flipped up the collar of her coat, snuggling it close to the short brown locks that exposed her neck and ears. The storm from Newfoundland—winter's last gasp—was bearing down on Ithaca, New York, bringing more than a final blast of record cold. The turbulent winds seemed to scour the soul, swirling through the dust and detritus of the past, leaving in its wake a vague, yet distinctly uneasy sense of dissatisfaction.

A hand on her sleeve stopped Abby in her tracks.

"Are you all right?" Francine's warm brown eyes narrowed with concern. "You're a million miles away."

Abby felt her cheeks flame. She'd nearly walked out without saying good-bye. Not that she would have gotten very far. Her purse was still sitting on the bench by the door. "More like three thousand."

"Ah. Your family in Washington."

Nodding, Abby picked up her purse. "I've called Mary's flower shop three times today. It's so strange, so unlike her to take a day off in the middle of the week."

"That is unusual, but then again, you've told me your sister is a social butterfly." Francine reached into the closet. "You don't want to forget this." She pulled out a knitted white scarf—a gift from Mary—and draped it on Abby's head before twitching the ends over her shoulders. "Did you call your folks?"

"They're not answering either, though that's not unusual this time of year. Spring on the farm can get pretty hectic."

Her forehead puckering, Francine mused, "Well, it's still early there. Try Mary again when you get home. After you call me, of course, so I know this awful wind didn't blow you away."

"Sure, I will. See you tomorrow at work."

Blessing Francine for not discounting her concern, Abby said good-bye and hurried out to her car in the driveway. The three-hour time difference between the East and West Coasts might account for Mary's being unavailable.

Or something unforeseen had come up.

Yes. Of course there's a logical reason, thought Abby. *Mary's as busy as I am.* Rather than finding the reassurance she sought, Abby found the troubling feelings settling deeper into her heart. She and her sister were not as close as they used to be. Time, distance and differences in personality had seen to that.

Icy gusts pulled at the hem of Abby's skirt, stealing her breath and raising goosebumps on her legs. Shivering, she quickly climbed inside the car and started the engine. While she waited for it to warm up, she cleaned the condensation from her glasses and said a quick prayer for Mary and her family. Moments after she backed into the narrow street, icy needles of rain ticked against the windshield and stitched another layer of unease onto her taut nerves.

THE ORCHID GREENHOUSE was a tropical paradise filled with cattleya, cymbidiums, dendrobiums and phalaenopsis. Tiny buds as delicate as baby's tears shared the shelves with large showy bracts of elegant leathery-petaled hand-sized blooms. Tucked in a far corner, clusters of regal red, yellow and blue bird-of-paradise made a delightful surprise as did the dinner plate hibiscus blooms in shades of brilliant fuchsia and deep pumpkin.

The heavenly scents filling the glassed-in hothouse left tall, silver-haired Mary Stanton Reynolds gasping with delight. Not in her wildest dreams had she ever imagined finding such treasures on Sparrow Island.

"These are just fabulous, Goldie. You truly have a gift."

The shy, reclusive gardener smiled. "My plants have always

brought me joy. I'm just glad you talked me into finally sharing some of my flowers with the world."

Smiling back, Mary caressed a perfect fern frond. Goldie Landon was as charming and earthy as the plants she loved. Not only was her greenhouse full to bursting with exotic wonders, the grounds around her home in the remote area east of Oyster Inlet on the northern part of the island were packed with native varieties.

Mary had met Goldie on the ferry one day while the rustic septuagenarian was transporting some specimens she had bought on the mainland. Her hobby over the years had been growing orchids for her own delight. They got to talking and a business partnership—and friendship—was forged.

With these horticultural beauties under exclusive contract, Mary's flower shop, Island Blooms, would soon be the envy of every florist in the San Juan Islands.

Mary shook Goldie's hand to seal the mutually profitable deal. "I'll be back in about a week to collect the plants."

"Okay. Be sure to come on a day drier than today. You be careful driving home now."

With a hundred ideas for displays and marketing vying for her attention, Mary nodded distractedly as she headed toward her car. She tossed her yellow leather handbag onto the passenger seat of the silver sedan and climbed inside. Trying to keep her excitement at bay, she struggled to focus on her immediate surroundings.

She would really have to concentrate in order to remember

her way back here next week. Once, Mary had thought she knew every two-rut path on Sparrow Island. Yet without the orchid grower leading the way, Mary knew she would never have found the little dirt track off the main road. Fortunately, the rain had stopped and the sun was making a brief appearance before setting.

In a test of patience, perseverance and her car's shock absorbers, she bounced and jounced over the furrowed path cut into the steep hillside, rocking from one pothole to the next. Trees played hide-and-seek with the late afternoon sun, alternately dazzling her with glaring brilliance or plunging her blindly into deep shadow.

Even with her headlights turned on, she did not see the washed out gully until it was too late. The car pitched and shuddered as she caromed through it. Her new leather bag flew off the seat, spilling the contents onto the dusty floor.

"Oh no." With no place to pull over, Mary drove the car a few hundred feet more over the muddy path. The next thing she knew, she was back on the paved road.

Dismayed by the contents of her purse rolling around on the floor on the passenger side, she took a quick look up ahead and then reached across the seat.

No sooner had she done so than movement up ahead caught the corner of her eye. A black-tailed deer—brown and barely visible in the dappled light—stood right in her path. Large liquid eyes stared at her in frozen terror.

Mary yanked on the steering wheel.

Hit the brakes.

The tires skidded across the still slick pavement.

The car's rear end slid sideways to the left, over to the side of the road and then teetered at the edge of the embankment. Mary looked in horror at the deep plunge into the forest below. The steering wheel wrenched to the right and ripped from her grasp. Trees rushed toward the car, battering the driver's door and window.

Cracking, splintering and the sound of her own desperate cry rang in Mary's ears as the car tipped over again and again, tumbling down into the dark ravine.

"Abby!"

CANDLES FLICKERED ON THE MANTEL, throwing dancing shadows on the walls while the wind howled outside. Huddled on her couch, Abby drew the afghan closer. Rain pounded the roof and rattled the windows, yet it wasn't the storm's fury feeding her disquiet.

The grandfather clock in the corner bonged twice, the deep melodious tones announcing the wee hours of the morning. She knew she should go to bed. Tomorrow—that is, today—would be busier than normal, the ornithology laboratory filled with the innocent winged victims injured in the tempest.

She also knew climbing the cold stairs to her bedroom would be an exercise in futility. Sleep, in her unsettled state, was impossible. She stared at the telephone.

If only she could get hold of Mary. Through the long, dark

hours of the night, Abby had prayed for her parents, for her sister and for herself. *Please, dear Lord, heal this fear and doubt gnawing at my soul. Lead me back to Your peace.*

No matter how hard Abby prayed, she couldn't shake her feelings of dread. There was something wrong between her and Mary. An undefined something standing between them that needed to be resolved. Was it too late?

If only I could figure out what it is.

The telephone sat silent. Waiting. Beckoning.

Do I dare call again? Would I be mending fences or tearing them down?

She looked at the phone. *Brr-r-ring!*

Startled, she flinched, spilling lukewarm tea onto the front of her nightgown. The phone rang again and her heart pounded in her throat as a cold fear settled into her belly. Her hand shook as she picked up the receiver.

"Abby . . . It's Dad."

His voice was heavy with sorrow, gravelly with tears, and her insides congealed into an icy ball. "Is it Mom?"

"No. It's Mary."

Hot tears burned Abby's eyes and scalded her cheeks. *Dear God, no! Please. No.* "Is she . . . ?"

"We're at Harborview Hospital in Seattle." He choked. Coughed. Sniffed. "We don't know if she'll—"

"I'm on the way, Dad." Deep sorrow and remorse blazed in her chest. It couldn't end like this. "You tell her she can't die. She just can't!"

Chapter One

Six weeks later . . .

Abby Stanton hurried across the emerald lawn behind the family farmhouse to a familiar gravel pathway. Gray rocks crunched underfoot as she strode alongside the clapboard barn. Childhood memories peeked around its crisp, white corners, laughed from the loft under the rounded, sloping roof and called from the darkened interior.

Instead of answering their summons, she lengthened her stride. Yet now that the mental door had opened, a throng of reminiscences matched her pace. She had been five and Mary three years older when the Stantons left the mainland and moved to the farm in the San Juan Islands.

Green jewels set in the Pacific Northwest, the islands received only half of the rainfall that often shrouded Seattle and the Puget Sound region. The extra sunshine was only one of many reasons Abby and her sister fell in love with their new home on Sparrow Island. For them, it was a fantasy playland.

Initially, the rundown property was hard work for their parents, but for the girls, even their chores were an adventure. They had fields to run in, mysterious outbuildings to explore, hundreds of trees to climb and a private little beach for wading, until the cold water turned their toes blue.

In the summertime, the arrival of the huge orcas—swimming in pods and often visible from the beach—thrilled their little hearts. The sisters often spent hours watching and waiting, then squealing with delight when the magnificent killer whales breached the water in a splashing, crashing ballet above the waves.

Best of all, in Abby's estimation, were the birds. Eagles, falcons and hawks soared and dipped in a performance of aerial acrobatics that made flying look so easy everyone ought to try it. Under her father's tutelage, she learned birds were as peculiar as people. If she wanted to see herons and bitterns, the likeliest spot was near a body of fresh water. For terns and cormorants, her best opportunities were near the seashore.

Remembering how she had pestered her father with questions made Abby smile. She'd been like a hungry chick, demanding nourishment from his storehouse of knowledge. Only his enthusiasm had surpassed his patience.

Skirting the chicken coop, she marveled at how he had always made time for her. They had spent hours together poring over library books, learning to draw feathers, beaks and tails and practicing birdcalls. Recalling some of her first attempts at imitating birds, Abby laughed aloud. Her squawking and wheezing had sounded like she had something caught in her throat. Her mother had been certain her youngest was about to expire.

The downhill path made a hard turn to the right, taking Abby between velvety fields of alfalfa and filling her nose with the fresh clean scent. How many times had she and Mary run by these fields, with feet pumping and braids flying as they raced up to the house? Abby could almost hear the creaky spring on the old screen door screeching in protest as it stretched. When released, the door had slammed shut with a rattle that shook the frame. Funny how much she had missed that sound. Like background music in a movie, she hadn't really noticed it until it was gone.

Until I was gone, Abby amended. *I was the starry-eyed eighteen-year-old who left Sparrow Island. Was it really thirty-seven years ago? So little has changed, yet so much has happened.*

She and her older sister would never run anywhere together ever again. Mary couldn't even walk. The car accident had taken care of that. Abby stopped and took several deep breaths to quiet the emotions roiling in her chest.

Knowing she needed to spend time in prayerful meditation, she squared her shoulders and resumed walking. The dreaming rock was the best place for unburdening her heart.

Her time on Sparrow Island was drawing to a close. Soon, she'd have to return to the bustle of the life she had built on the other side of the continent. Here, island life ran on its own clock. Certainly, a more sedate timepiece than the one she had left in Ithaca, New York.

The breeze ruffling Abby's short, brown hair carried the rich zest of spruce, hemlock and cedar. Her feet moved faster around the final curve and into a seemingly endless stand of stately evergreens. A thick russet carpet of spent needles whispered a welcome with every step and she heaved a relieved sigh drawn all the way from her toes.

The spongy forest floor soon gave way to bedrock and Abby felt her pulse thrum with anticipation. She stepped into the clearing and there was the dreaming rock. The enormous, irregular boulder was worn smooth by wind, rain and time. More massive than a haystack, its undulating curves were as familiar as the palm of her hand.

From the moment she had discovered it, this was her special place, where she ran in times of joy or crisis, or just to dream about the future. Here, surrounded by majestic trees reaching for the heavens, she felt closest to God. The words from Deuteronomy 32:4 welled up in her heart: *"He is the Rock, his works are perfect, and all his ways are just. A faithful God who does no wrong, upright and just is he."*

Stepping carefully over the fractures in the underlying bedrock, she made her way to the far side where an ascent was easiest. A green plastic storage box sat right in her path. She stopped and smiled. How well her father knew her and her habits. Grateful, she pulled off the watertight lid and examined the contents.

A pair of thick foam cushions sat on top of a sweater she recognized as belonging to her mother, Ellen. Abby donned the sweater against the coming chill that would soon sweep through the late May evening.

Taking one of the sturdy pads, she climbed to the top of the boulder. Once again, her father had provided protection. He'd brought her up knowing the shelter of Jesus, the Rock. That lifelong faith sustained her. Without it, she never would have made it through this difficult period after Mary's car accident.

"Lord," she whispered, "please help me accept Your will. I don't know if I'll ever understand the reason for Mary losing the use of her legs. It seems such a . . . a bad thing. But I know You will use it for good. I don't know how. Yet.

"I'm struggling, Lord. I feel You have something more for me to do here. I trust in Your timing and that the plan You have for me will become clear."

Abby gazed upwards. In the little circle of sky overhead, golden light gilded the clouds. Drawing her legs close, she wrapped her arms around them, then rested her forehead on her knees and thought about Mary. What had happened to the closeness they once shared? Time and distance played a big role, but it was more than that. Their lives had taken very different paths.

The realization felt like part of an answer, but something was still missing.

These past six weeks had been the longest amount of time Abby had spent on the island since her career began. She had fallen back into the familiar patterns of island life, and liked it enormously. Yet something remained out of kilter whenever she thought of Mary.

Absorbed in her thoughts, Abby didn't notice the passage of time until a deep *whoo-whodoo-whoo-who* caught her attention. Surprised to hear that call while it was still so light, she adjusted her glasses, looked around and spotted her father at the base of the rock.

"Thought you heard a great horned owl, didn't you?"

"I sure did," she said with a grin. At a wiry five feet nine, with whitish-gray hair and dark brown eyes, he bore a closer resemblance to a snowy owl than the one he imitated.

"Good! Old Frank Holloway said you've been living in the big city so long you wouldn't know a horned owl from a barn owl."

"Old Frank is thirteen years younger than you, Dad."

"Guess that makes him a pipsqueak compared to me. Still, he'll have to eat his words while I'm enjoying an ice-cream cone at his expense."

"I thought you gave up ice cream."

"Once a year won't hurt. Besides, a man has to stick up for his girls."

Tickled, but not surprised by her father's loyalty, she said, "Are you sure Frank wasn't just trying to get a rise out of you?"

"Of course he was. That's why I'll be ordering a double-decker. It'll be a little reminder that I have two of the best daughters ever to grace the earth. I'll want sprinkles on the top too."

"For sticking up for me, you deserve them. By the way, thanks for the care box. The cushions are perfect." *I should have thought of bringing these down here a long time ago.*

"Are you ready to come down yet? I'm getting a crick in my neck looking up at you."

"Grab a cushion and join me."

"*Mmm*, better not. We'll be losing the light soon."

Abby scooted off the rock with a growing sense of awareness. At eighty-two and eighty respectively, George and Ellen Stanton had adapted to the restrictions of age. Yet her parents didn't let their aches or limitations stop them. Instead, they made adjustments, found ways to enjoy the things they loved. Hoping she'd be that wise when the time came, she put the pads on a lower outcrop and gestured to her father.

After they were sitting comfortably, he said, "You know, Abby, when your mother called you Mary earlier, she just got confused."

"I understand, Dad." Living in Mary's shadow was an issue Abby thought she had resolved long ago. To suddenly find a small feeling of resentment roosting on a familiar perch was an unwelcome surprise. "Really I do. I've seen my married friends confuse the names of their children."

"It's more than that. Your mother depended on Mary to chauffeur her to their knitting group, the book club. Everywhere. Now, she depends on you."

The weight of her long absences settled heavily on Abby's heart. Since coming home, she'd driven her mother's beloved old Lincoln as though it belonged to her.

At the time, Abby had been too overwhelmed with an endless list of tasks to consider why her mother handed over the keys so eagerly. Now it was clear that her mother was counting on her. "Mary's so thoughtful. You and Mom must be very proud of her."

"We're very proud of both of our girls."

With a shake of her head, Abby leaned back against the rock and squinted into the lengthening shadows. "I haven't been here for you and Mom. Mary has."

"Don't even go there, Abby," he warned.

"It's true. I've been on the other side of the country, while Mary's just a few miles away. She's always been right here, where you can count on her."

George nudged Abby's side. "A wise man once told me that children are like snowflakes. No two are alike. If you try fitting them into the same mold, you destroy what's beautifully unique in each of them."

Abby shrugged, unconvinced.

"Don't tell me you're having regrets about pursuing your dreams."

"I love what I do. It's been an incredible opportunity, but—"

"No buts. Not many people get a PhD at Cornell, then get to work at the ornithology research lab. Why do you think old Frank likes to razz me? Because he knows you did something special, Abby. Something you were born to do. Why, he's almost as proud of you as I am. Everybody feels that way. Most folks have big dreams. The sad truth is, only a few have the courage to live them."

"I'm beginning to understand I paid a high price for mine.

All those years Dad, coming home just for the holidays, I missed a lot."

"If you had stayed here, you would have missed your whole life. The way I see it, you're an eagle. You needed to soar. Mary's a nester like her mother. She needed to stay."

Abby grasped her father's message and because she didn't want him to hear the emotions crowding her throat, she simply nodded.

"Now if you look at Mary's children," he continued, "Nancy is a lot like her. She even looks like Mary did twenty years ago. We were all glad she came while Mary was in the hospital. But even Mary recognized that Nancy is a nester. Without her husband and children, she was miserable. It was a relief to send her back home to Florida."

In spite of herself, an appreciative giggle escaped Abby. Her father's insights were right on the mark. Like Mary, Nancy wore colorful prints and big chunky jewelry with a panache that turned admiring eyes everywhere she went. Even the cell phone constantly by her ear had a wardrobe of coordinating covers.

"Then you have Mary's boy, Zack," he continued. "We were happy to see him when he came to Sparrow Island after the accident, but he couldn't stay on here. He's an eagle. He needs to soar. He's like you and me, Abby. He has a dream and the talent to back it up. He also has the one, most important ingredient that sets us apart—passion for his work. His music is worth the sacrifices he makes. Now I wouldn't put in those kinds of hours to play jazz, or work in a laboratory, but when I was in the charter boat business—fishing and whale watching—the time just flew."

"It was your passion. I remember you coming home late at night, exhausted, soaking wet and grinning from ear to ear."

"Yep. It was a grand life. I think about it every now and then when I take my little fishing boat out."

"Why did you give up the charter business?"

"I was getting a bit long in the tooth and the Strait of Juan de Fuca is a hard taskmaster. Challenging it is a young man's game. The real reason, though, was that I was ready for a change. Life has seasons and they come at different times for all of us."

Thinking about Mary, Abby said somberly, "And sometimes change is thrust upon us."

"Yes, but your sister will handle what lies ahead. Jacob's death was a bigger blow for her than this. When you think about it, losing your mate is about the worst thing that can happen to a nester."

Abby straightened. "That's part of what I'm concerned about. After Nancy and Zack moved out, Mary and Jacob poured themselves into remodeling the house. Everything was right where they wanted it. Even the landscaping was perfect. And now, well, the operative word is *was*."

"So?"

The softly spoken question dug deep into Abby's fears. She'd overseen so many changes to Mary's house, from rerouting the plumbing to knocking down walls. "Mary is coming home tomorrow. What if she doesn't like the changes to her house? She loved the big rhododendron by the front porch. Now, that spot is covered in concrete."

"It was necessary. How else could they build a ramp?"

"Come on, Dad, you know what I mean."

"I'm afraid you're not hearing what *I* mean. What you did was a labor of love, Abby. Everything you put into or took out of that house was done to make life easier for Mary. How could she not appreciate your thoughtfulness?"

"Her tastes are so much different than mine," Abby answered bluntly. "And I didn't consult her on everything. I just authorized the changes as they came up. There wasn't time to run drawings back and forth to the Lifestyle Retraining Center. After we contacted the nonprofit group in Seattle and the Carpenters of Nazareth got involved, I had to make some snap decisions."

Abby fell silent, remembering how eagerly the Christian group of tradesmen had attacked the huge job, which included widening every downstairs doorway. The men came from all parts of the construction industry. Collectively, they considered themselves blessed and wanted to give back.

"Those Seattle fellows . . . the Carpenters of Nazareth . . . I had no idea all those tradesmen volunteered their time to step in and help others." George raised his eyebrows. "God bless them. They sure did a top-notch job, didn't they? You won't see workmanship like that on any of those television home remodeling shows."

"You're right, Dad. But remember, not everyone who gets a house makeover on those shows likes the end result."

"You're still not hearing what I'm saying, Abby. Must be that East Coast hurry-up thing short-circuiting your brain. Now, listen. You did a super job."

Her father slipped his arm around her shoulders. "Your mother and I together couldn't have made it happen as smoothly as you did."

Despite the heavy sweater he wore, Abby felt him shiver. "Let's head back to the house."

He kissed the top of her head. "Good idea. It will be dark soon and your mother will start worrying."

A quick glance confirmed his concern. Although the clouds still glowed in shades of gold and pink, shadows crowded the forest. Here on the island, without any city lights to distort the natural progression, darkness didn't descend, but rose from the ground up. After giving him an affectionate hug, she stowed the cushions in the box. "Shall I bring this?"

"No. I'm pretty fond of this place too."

To her surprise, he took a flashlight out of his back pocket, flipped it on and said sheepishly, "Your mother insisted. Just because she can't see well in the dark, she thinks I can't either."

Abby forced a nonchalance she didn't feel into her tone and said, "Better safe than sorry."

"One last word—and you have to trust me on this—I know your sister. She's going to love what you did."

"I hope so."

"You'll see."

Mulling over his words, Abby followed his circle of light through the maze of trees. In a matter of minutes, they were back on the gravel path, heading up the gentle slope to the house. Here on the path, she was relieved to see dusk had not yet deepened and her father felt confident enough to turn off the flashlight.

Halfway up the fields of alfalfa, he stopped abruptly and whispered, "Do you hear that?"

Turning slowly, quietly, she matched her movements to his until they both faced the same direction. Hoping whatever her father heard would repeat itself, she listened intently. As her concentration sharpened, a freshening night breeze caressed her cheeks, filling her with anticipation.

They stood silently, scarcely daring to breathe.

Waiting.

There!

A distinct series of high-pitched *keer-keer-keer* noises sounded from above the treetops at the bottom of the hill. Faint, yet growing closer.

Excitement pounded in her veins. It had been a long time since she had heard a call she didn't recognize.

Flickers of motion caught her gaze. She'd gladly trade a month's salary for the binoculars she usually carried. She cupped her hands around her spectacles. The professor who taught her the trick said it didn't work for everyone, but she found if she reduced her field of vision, clarity increased.

She spotted one bird, then another. Her heart rate spiked, thundering in her ears. During the few seconds the flying pair stayed in view, she ticked off a mental list of distinctive features. Even while the scientist in her cataloged her observations, the pure birder part of her wanted to tap dance with joy.

"Dad! Dad. Do you see them?"

"Not clearly. Short wings, rapid wing beat—probably a shore bird, something that dives for food. I haven't seen anything like those around here before."

"No," she said slowly, "I doubt you have."

George's forehead furrowed while he rubbed his chin and mused, "Definitely not a duck, not with that short, pointy beak. Too big to be a sandpiper, besides the coloring isn't right."

He shook his head. "Did you get a good look? Do you know what they are?"

"Yes to the first question and I'm not absolutely sure to the second."

"But that grin says you've got a good idea."

Barely able to contain her excitement, she clutched his arm. "If I'm right, Dad, this could be big. Really, really big."

His face lit up as he caught her enthusiasm. "Hot-diggity-dog! What is it? No, don't tell me. We follow the rules. But when you say this is big, you're talking about a rarity. Right?"

"I don't want to say." Her reputation relied on impeccable fieldwork. Speculation was for amateurs.

Taking her hand, he started back toward the house. "We've got to hit the books while the sighting is still fresh in your mind."

"We don't say anything to anyone about this, Dad."

"What? Why not?"

"I need to see these little guys up close, or at least through my binoculars. Before I hang my professional reputation on sighting something like this, I want to be absolutely sure I'm right."

Chapter Two

I F MARY IS EXPECTING a quiet homecoming, she's in for a major surprise," Abby said to her mother as they surveyed the party preparations. Crêpe paper streamers fluttered from the long wooden deck attached to the back of Mary's light blue house. Paper tablecloths in bright, flowery patterns covered three tables constructed out of sawhorses and plywood and set on the spacious lawn. On the first table, napkins, paper plates and cups in the same cheery colors clustered around gaily-wrapped bundles of eating utensils. The remaining space stood ready for the food sure to come in abundance with the guests.

Farther down on the recently mown lawn, an array of smaller tables awaited the arrival of folding chairs borrowed from Little Flock Church. Abby's gaze swept the weathered wooden fence separating the landscaped portion of Mary's large property from the woods that marched down to the shore. Sunlight glinted off the blue ocean, adding to the festive air. The gray boards of the fence were a perfect backdrop for the generous stands of lilacs, old-fashioned tea roses and alyssum perfuming the air with a sweet potpourri of spring.

Abby fiddled with a fern in one of the floral centerpieces adorning the tables. The bounty of Mary's green thumb was everywhere. Even the shrubs and flowerbeds seemed as full now as they were when Abby and her mother started harvesting what they needed. Any passerby on Oceania Boulevard could read the unmistakable, though nonexistent, sign: *Here lives a gardener.*

Ellen smoothed a lime-green apron embroidered with "I'm a Great-Grandma" across the bib. "You've done a beautiful job of setting this up."

"I had a lot of help, Mom, especially from you and Mary's friends." Thankful for the crew who had simply shown up earlier to help with the decorations, Abby met her mother's sparkling blue gaze. Seeing those loving eyes on the same level as hers still seemed strange. She always thought of her mother as so much taller than five feet three. "Everyone has been so thoughtful, so generous. When I'm in New York, it's easy to forget Sparrow Island does things in such a big way."

"Well, we did this for Mary because we love her so dearly. All her friends want to welcome her home and I know she misses them too." Ellen patted her beauty shop coif. Not a strand of gleaming gray hair dared to stray from the stiff hairspray holding the short curls in place.

Juggling two-year-old Toby on her hip, Patricia Hale placed a covered dish on the center table, stepped back and announced, "The chairs are here."

With a warm smile for Ellen and Abby, the wife of the Little Flock Church's pastor continued, "The McDonalds are helping James unload them. It's easy to see where they belong."

After giving Ellen a hug, she said, "I love the streamers and the 'Welcome Home' sign above the garage doors. Abby, you have talents we didn't know about. Mary will be so thrilled."

"I can't take credit for the ideas, just some of the execution," Abby said nervously, hoping Patricia was right about Mary's reaction. "Party planning is not my strong suit. There are so many creative people at Cornell, I've learned to borrow their ideas and tailor them."

"It certainly worked," said Patricia. "Everything is beautiful and cheerful."

The chairs arrived in a parade led by Pastor James. Behind him and the clattering armfuls he hauled, Sandy McDonald carried a huge layer cake under a glass dome. Then came her ten-year-old, Bobby, his short dark hair combed as though ready for Sunday school. Arms wrapped at impossible angles around two folding chairs, he moved with more determination than grace. Last in line, grinning fondly at his son, Neil McDonald easily toted two armfuls. The similarities between father and son prompted Abby's first real smile of the morning.

One day, she mused, Bobby would be a strapping young man as tall, or taller, than Neil's six feet. She hoped the two would be as close then as they were now. Just last week Neil had confided that his son's brilliant mind was already a challenge for a father who had barely graduated from high school.

Bobby's hazel eyes lit up when he spotted Abby. "Hey, Miss Stanton," he called, grinning.

A wave of affection swept through her. "Hey, yourself, young Master McDonald."

"He is that," said Sandy with a laugh as she placed the covered dessert dish on a table. "He told me this morning he's a master cake eater. You can't believe how I've had to guard this one from him and his father. A body would think I never baked for them."

"Yummy," said Patricia. "A Sandy McDonald Chocolate Wonder." She licked her lips. "Pure heaven."

"I want cake." Two-year-old Toby stretched toward the dessert table with enough determination to force a two-handed grip from his mother.

"After we eat," Patricia promised with a theatrical look upwards as she hung onto her wiggling bundle of energy.

"You can take him out on the lawn with Bobby and Neil." Shorter and curvier than the pastor's model-thin wife, Mary's neighbor Sandy shook her head, making her pixie-cut blond hair shimmer in the sunlight. "They'll keep Toby away from the desserts until we sound the dinner bell."

The knowing look between Sandy and the pastor's wife filled Abby's heart with thanks. Their easy fellowship and willingness to help one another bolstered her hopes for her sister. Mary's transition into a new way of life would be difficult. Yet she was blessed with loving friends looking for ways to help.

In that same moment, Abby realized that once again, her role was that of an outsider. Now she assisted where and when she could in the evolving community she had once called home.

"Here come the secretaries," warned Abby's dad. Carrying a folding chair and heading across the lawn to James and Neil, he winked at Abby and her mother. "I hope Janet brought her taco salad."

Abby shook her head. There was no point in reminding him to use the politically correct term, "administrative assistant." In his opinion, the secretaries weren't assistants; they ran the show.

Talkative, outgoing Janet Heinz worked at Little Flock Church. Margaret Blackstock, her blunt-speaking friend, was the administrative assistant at Sparrow Island's only school.

Watching the women and their husbands approach, Abby marveled at what a superficial study in contrasts they represented.

While Margaret loved bright colors and a bouffant coif, Janet preferred a subdued wardrobe in muted tones that brought out the reddish cast of her brown curls. Only Margaret's hairdresser knew the true color of her hair.

Despite their outward differences, the pair was as alike as two bees in a hive. They buzzed around local politics and the lives of the islanders, gathering information like pollen. Their intentions were always good. Often, they provided the verbal honey that sweetened the sourest of situations.

Margaret laughed at something her much older husband Joe said to Doug Heinz.

"The horde is right behind us." In a gesture as Brooklyn as his accent, Joe cast a thumb over his shoulder. "Are you ready?"

"As ready as we're going to get. This is a play-it-by-ear sort of gathering," Abby answered, glancing at her watch as her insides churned. Just about now, the ferry would be pulling into the Sparrow Island ferry dock.

Mary was coming home.

ABBY FELT A DEBT OF GRATITUDE to Dr. Dana Randolph. Her dedication to her patients not only included everyone on Sparrow Island, it had reached across Puget Sound to Mary at the Lifestyle Retraining Center. Saying she needed last minute instructions regarding Mary, Dr. Randolph had convinced George and Ellen it would be best to let her bring Mary home and save them the hours-long round-trip.

The doctor's van slowed to a crawl before turning into the driveway. Anticipation charged the afternoon air as family, friends and neighbors lined the asphalt and formed a line across the front of the yawning garage.

George and Ellen, with Abby in tow, moved toward the side of the van when the engine stopped. With a flourish usually reserved for the unveiling of royalty, George opened the passenger doors.

Although only a couple of days had passed since Abby visited with her sister, it felt like months. Anxiety, she suspected. Regardless of how often she reminded herself that Mary had approved the massive changes to her home, Abby remained unsure they shared the same vision. While she had the advantage of seeing the renovations occur day by day, Mary had to content herself with architectural drawings and photographs outdated the moment after the shutter snapped.

Now she was about to see the reality.

The lift mechanism whirred and Abby took a deep breath. What was done, was done. If it needed undoing, that would have to wait for another day.

Abby smiled when she saw her sister. The heart-stopping, head-turning beauty of Mary's youth had matured into a striking elegance. The new pageboy cut of her silvery hair looked terrific.

In her typical style, Mary was dressed beautifully. She wore a white skirt and sandals, with the polish on her toenails matching the vivid pink of the roses running along the lapels of her burgundy cotton jacket. A deeper rose-colored, open-collared blouse completed her fashion scheme. The silver chain and small cross she always wore hung around her neck.

A cloud of loss dimmed Abby's joy. Her sister would never dance with the waves again.

Undeterred by the wheelchair or the need to bend at an awkward angle, Ellen rushed to hug her daughter. "Oh, honey, I'm so glad you're home."

"I'm happy to be here." Emotion filled Mary's voice, reached across and lodged in Abby's heart. Manicured fingers clutched their mother's small shoulders. The gold wedding band Mary still wore ten years after her husband's death shone on her left hand.

"I've missed you terribly." For a moment, Ellen sounded all

of her eighty years and Abby realized how completely their mother relied on Mary.

George moved in to give his daughter a welcoming hug and his wife a moment to regain her composure. "I see you're dressed for a party."

Mary always dressed for a party. Wherever she went a celebration was likely to break out. Abby's smile faltered. *Please Lord, don't let that change. Help her deal with her new life in a manner that keeps her personality intact.*

George stepped back to make room for Abby, who moved forward, bent down and hugged her sister.

"Thank you," Mary whispered, holding Abby in a surprisingly strong embrace. "You made it possible for me to come home."

"Me?"

"Yes. I see the ramp you had installed. You can't imagine—"

"Oh, Mary." Abby hugged her tightly. "I hope you like what we did to the inside. If not, blame me. I made the decisions."

"It'll be fine whatever it is, unless you painted the walls a boring beige." Mary released her.

"Not to worry. I switched to an exciting ecru," Abby teased.

"Puh-lease!" Mary rolled her blue eyes. "Tell me you're kidding."

"You'll see." When Abby stood up, it felt as though the weight of the world had been lifted from her shoulders. "There are a lot of people who want to welcome you home." She squeezed Mary's hands. "What do you say to a party?"

"You know I love to celebrate. Coming home is reason for festivities in *my* book."

"Come on, then. All this party lacks is a guest of honor and you're it."

Mary hesitated and Abby felt her heart sink again. There was so much to learn about how and when to offer assistance. Even how to phrase things could be a challenge. "Do you need some help?"

"Only for getting my stuff out of the good doctor's van and into the house. I hadn't realized I'd accumulated so much until we began to pack it up. There is way too much for one person to handle alone."

"I'll take care of it," their father offered, stepping forward. "I want to. And I don't mind making several trips."

"Thanks, Dad." Spoken in unison, the words sounded like a chorus. Startled, the sisters looked at each other, then laughed. The sweet sound swept relief through Abby. Gesturing toward the crowd eager to greet her sister, she said softly, "Welcome home."

As though she'd been using the wheelchair for years, Mary gave the hand rims a hard push, flung her arms wide and called, "I'm ba-a-a-ack!"

With the floodgates open, everyone drew closer. Bobby, the most brazen of the group marched up and asked, "Are we going to plant a garden this year?"

Mary's laughter floated over the stunned silence. "If we do, you'll have to do most of the work."

"That's okay. My dad said it's a good way for me to build muscles while I earn my gardening badge. I want to be the first in our church youth group to get one from Pastor Hale. Mom helped me start some tomatoes and lettuce in foam cups. I've been watering them and putting them in the sun. They're coming up," he finished breathlessly then gave Mary a conspiratorial look. "We can have some of those garden sandwiches like last year."

"We'll make it happen," she promised, ruffling the boy's hair affectionately.

Abby noticed the gesture, so similar to their father's way of demonstrating "I love you."

As the crowd engulfed Mary, Dr. Randolph touched Abby's arm. "We need a few minutes."

Abby accompanied her to the rear of the van.

Dana Randolph smoothed a loose strand of her long blond hair into the neat bun crowning her head. "Let me reiterate what the counselors told you at the retraining center. As enthusiastic as Mary is now, she'll be that much lower later. The adjustments ahead are enormous. Her mood swings will mirror her accomplishments. And her frustrations."

"They warned me to stay calm and keep things on an even keel."

"This will be very trying for you at times. Your reaction is critical. Keep conflicts to a minimum. Don't take anything personally, especially if she blows up or has a crying jag." The doctor smiled sympathetically. "By all means, don't hesitate to call me *before* you reach the point of exploding with your own frustration."

"Thank you, I will." Whatever the cost, she would stand by her sister. "Let's join the others."

"I'd love to, but it would be best for Mary if there were no reminders from the medical field." Dr. Randolph glanced at her watch. "I think I'll indulge myself with a visit to the bookstore and find a novel I won't have time to read."

Abby matched the doctor's smile. "I won't keep you."

As the doctor drove away, a rather thin man with bushy brown hair and a mustache to match strode up. "Where are we setting up?" he demanded, his high-pitched voice cutting the air and startling her. "In the backyard?"

It took Abby a moment to place William Jansen, owner and editor of *The Birdcall*, Sparrow Island's weekly newspaper.

"I'll show you, Mr. Jansen."

"Good." He adjusted the bulging camera bag hanging from his shoulder and ordered pleasantly, "Call me William."

"Okay. William."

Abby caught Sergeant Henry Cobb's nod as she led the newspaperman through the knot of people. The deputy sheriff was an imposing figure, yet his tall, bulky frame was also solid and reassuring to those he protected. Judging from the way his attention focused on her sister, the secretaries just might be right in their speculation about him being sweet on Mary.

The question was—how did Mary feel about Henry?

Chapter Three

I'VE BEEN LOOKING FOR YOU," Mary said from the bottom of the ramp leading to the back deck. "Where have you been?"

"Helping William Jansen set up his camera tripod, showing everyone where the sodas are and," Abby held up a big plastic container full of water, "making more coffee."

Mary doggedly made her way up the ramp, the wheels of her chair thump-thumping on the weather-treated wood. "If you have a moment, how about showing me the house?"

"Okay." Abby finished filling the coffeemaker on the small patio table. The time had arrived. She felt at peace. She'd done her best, pouring her heart into the remodeling project. Now that she recognized the existence of the distance between her and Mary, Abby hoped that her efforts would somehow open a pathway to reconnect them. Whether the current circumstances drew them together or pushed them further apart was in God's hands.

"I can't even describe all the images running through my mind," Mary said with a mysterious smile.

"Are you a little anxious to see what shade of beige I picked?" Abby teased.

"You know, I learned a lot at the training center. I'm sure with a little practice I can wield a paint roller."

"Did you also learn the reason for putting me in charge of the color schemes? If so, I'd love to hear it." Abby had practically driven herself crazy trying to figure out the answer. She and Mary were so different, none of the reasons that came to mind made sense.

Mary nodded, her lips pressed shut the way they always were when she didn't want to reply to a direct question. Those lips twitched with the beginnings of a smile. "Shall we begin?"

THE DOUBLE-PANED sliding glass doors leading into the house from the deck opened easily. Frank Holloway had done a fine job of installing a miniramp so Mary could roll right over the jamb. Abby closed the sliding screen door behind them.

Abby stood in the living room and watched as Mary took her first real look. The honey-colored molding framing the white ceiling gleamed above walls shaded a deep rose. The hardwood floor that replaced the Berber carpet reflected the same warm tones. "We took out all the carpet down here," Abby said, breaking the promise to herself to stay quiet. "We didn't do anything to the upstairs."

"This is beautiful." Mary's wheelchair glided silently across the room. "And it's a relief to know I won't have to fight the carpet. Pulling it out must have been quite a job. And the walls. My goodness, they turned out even better than I had imagined."

Mary rolled slowly to the oak and glass showcase dominating a corner of the room. Three layers of interior lights shone on the delicate bone and ivory carvings that comprised Jacob's scrimshaw collection.

As Mary touched the glass door, Abby knew her sister was thinking about him. Not a day went by that she didn't miss him. He had been a true renaissance man who loved woodworking and carving, and had supported his family as a writer. "There isn't a chip or crack on any of Jacob's treasures, or the cabinet he made for you to show them off," Abby assured softly. "I took care of them personally."

Mary reached for Abby's hand and squeezed it. "Thank you."

"You're welcome. Come see what we did in the kitchen," Abby said, leading Mary through the dining room that separated the living room from the kitchen. "The Carpenters of Nazareth finished it just two days ago."

"I can hardly wait to meet them. When are they coming to the party?"

"According to the foreman, the parties are the best part of the job. Unfortunately, there was a glitch in their schedule. There's a little girl . . . "

"Who needs their help," Mary finished. "They sound like a terrific group. From what I'm seeing here, they do quality work at the speed of light."

Abby hung back and let Mary go into the kitchen first.

"Fantastic! You used my roosters to coordinate the colors." As though she had missed them, Mary rolled over to the wall where two large ceramic roosters stood guard on a shelf.

Abby silently congratulated herself. The hours spent finding just the right shades were paying off. The orange-red band near the white ceiling complemented the vibrant yellow walls. If the room was any cheerier, she'd have to do something silly, maybe even try yodeling.

"I love the new curtains over the sink."

"They're Rhode Island Reds, just like your cookie jar. I knew I couldn't miss with that pattern."

"This is so much better than what I had in mind," Mary said, surveying the area of lowered white countertops that gave the kitchen a stair-step appearance. She maneuvered her chair and rolled forward. It fit perfectly beneath the workspace. "This is great. Gracious! You even lowered the stove."

"Can you reach all the burners?"

Mary repositioned her chair a few times, then extended her arm. "Look! I can even reach the ones in back. Of course, I'll have to practice a bit before I'll be comfortable using them."

"Let me show you the rest."

Abby led the way through doorways widened to accommodate the wheelchair. "Except for widening the door, the guest bath is unchanged."

In the hallway, Abby straightened one of the pictures on the wall painted several shades lighter than the deep rose of the living room. She'd spent most of one night rehanging the photo gallery depicting Mary's life, her children and her grandchildren.

After giving her sister time to make sure all the familiar photos were present, Abby bypassed Mary's bedroom to show her the craft room first. She cautioned, "This room needs work."

Mary rolled through the doorway and gasped, her hands at her mouth.

"Hey, it's not that bad. I stacked the boxes."

"Wow, this is a crafter's dream."

"It needs organization. I didn't know where to put things." Abby's gaze roamed across the plastic and cardboard boxes brought down from upstairs.

"Eggplant and white . . . It's exquisite," Mary said admiring the walls. "So is the work space."

This time Abby did smile at the unusual dark purple walls. "I had my doubts about painting anything the color of a food best consumed breaded and fried."

Mary laughed. "Good idea, eggplant Parmesan. What a great way to try out my new kitchen." She rolled into the heart of the room. "I love having all the drawer space. I'll practically live in here."

"I have to admit, I like this a lot." Abby studied the room. "Maybe I'll try this color in one of the bedrooms in my house."

"Will wonders never cease? The woman who thinks ecru is exciting is actually entertaining the notion of moving beyond boring beige."

Abby shrugged a shoulder and smiled.

Mary gave the stack of plastic boxes a quick caress. The constant touching of every surface and familiar object seemed as intimate as it was revealing. She needed to reassure herself of their presence and start reclaiming what she missed.

"Now for the biggest change of all." Abby stepped back into the hall. "Are you ready?"

"Ready or not, there's no turning back," Mary murmured.

Abby lifted an eyebrow in silent admiration. Mary always found the strength to accept the things she couldn't change.

Abby stopped by the double doors. "Remember, we took out a wall here." She opened the doors, stepped back and let her sister enter.

Mary said nothing as she explored and for the hundredth time, Abby tried to see it through her sister's eyes. Against walls painted a rich seafoam green, the creamy white and gold of the long, low chest of drawers and dressing table gave the room a distinctly feminine air.

Abby had taken as much from the upstairs master bedroom as possible, hoping Mary would find comfort in the familiar furnishings. Yet, not even the pillow shams and bedspread in a pink and green cabbage rose print could disguise the stark reality of the hospital-like bed with the metal arm angled over the top. A triangular trapeze dangled from the end.

Mary examined the bed, raising, lowering and testing the angles and limits of the mechanism. "This brings me back to reality. While at the retraining center, so many things were easy to accept because they were a matter of course. Seeing this kind of bed here, in my bedroom, is just so . . . in-your-face undeniable."

"What can I do to make this easier for you?" Abby asked.

"Easy is not always the best way to go. You know, they asked me if I wanted an electric wheelchair."

"Do you?"

"It sounded good at first, then I realized I would come to rely on it." Mary glanced at the trapeze. "I want to be able to go to the bathroom by myself. It will happen sooner than you might think. Every time I push these wheels, I'm building the strength I need."

Mary was showing such remarkable courage and perseverance. *Thank You, Jesus,* Abby prayed.

"Seeing my home changed to reflect how I am now tells me my decision was right."

"When you set your mind to something, I know you'll do it. I'm glad you made that decision."

"Well," Mary said lightly, "I'm sure I'm the first on the block to have an orthopedic boudoir."

Rising to the hopeful challenge in her sister's voice, Abby responded, "Wait until you see your acrobatic powder room."

In the bathroom, cheery green and white hues in the tile matched the faux finished walls.

Mary's hand glided over the lowered counter and she glanced at herself in the mirror before rolling to the commode and testing the stainless steel support rails. Here, too, a triangular trapeze hung from strong supports in the ceiling.

Abby glanced at the third moveable trapeze and put her hands on the tub. "This is the latest in shower/bathtub combinations. Back up a little and I'll show you how it works."

She opened the side door on the shower-tub, slipped out of her shoes and stepped inside. "See, this is nice and wide. Once you have enough upper body strength, you'll use the trapeze to get from your chair to the seat.

"Then you close the door." She demonstrated. A tug and second click promised the seals were tight. "Now you can fill it and take a bath or you can shower." She jiggled the shower curtain.

"Where did you find this? I didn't know such a thing existed." Mary opened the tub door and glanced at the trapeze.

"The Carpenters of Nazareth brought it. A family had ordered it, paid for it, then . . . well, they didn't need it. Instead of returning it, they told the Carpenters to give it to a recent wheelchair recipient." *Oh, sometimes it was so hard to find the right words.* "That turned out to be you, Mary."

Mary's mouth opened and closed as though she had become so lost in the significance of the gift and the changes in her own life that she couldn't express herself.

Abby took a deep breath. How hard this must be. Everything, from the simplest task to the biggest, now required planning and accommodation. And some things, like climbing the dreaming rock, were gone forever.

"I don't know what to say. I can't thank you enough. You came when I needed you. And you did all this—" Mary's voice broke as her right arm arced in a sweeping gesture that took in the whole house. "I . . . Thank you, Abby. Thank you."

"You're welcome. You're my sister. You're part of me and I love you. That won't ever change."

Mary reached up and they exchanged a hug. "No, it won't, thank God."

Feeling the need to lighten the moment, Abby teased, "Does this mean you don't want to rearrange things?"

"I didn't say that," Mary quipped. A quivering smile accompanied the tears pooling in her eyes. "You know me. Every six months something has to change."

Abby laughed. It never ceased to amaze her how Mary could move a few pictures, make new throw pillows, switch an end table or two and create a whole new look. "You always needed rollers on your furniture," Abby said while handing Mary a tissue from the box near the bathroom sink.

"That's what Jacob used to say." Mary delicately dabbed her tears, then straightened her shoulders and wheeled toward the door. "I do believe it is party time. I'm certain half the people in the yard will want to see the marvelous things you did here."

"You're right," Abby agreed. "The other half helped get it done."

Mary halted abruptly at the bedroom door. "I'll need names. The least I can do is send thank-you notes."

"I've kept a list," Abby assured her.

"So have I," Mary said softly.

Abby couldn't help wondering what was on Mary's list and why she kept it.

Chapter Four

When they rejoined the festivities, Bobby McDonald and Patricia Hale were cutting into Sandy's Chocolate Wonder.

Friends called to Mary as she descended the ramp. Henry Cobb stood ready to help her across the grass. Confident he would see to Mary's needs, Abby gazed around the gathering and savored a warm sense of satisfaction and a deeper feeling of relief.

A hand callused by farmwork covered hers on the deck railing.

"Hey, Dad."

"Hey, yourself. She loved it, didn't she?"

"Yes. And bless you in advance for not saying, I told you so."

"You look a little peaked. Let's get you something to eat."

They walked down the ramp to the serving tables and as Abby began to fill a plate with small scoops from each dish, she saw her dad cut two large slices of Sandy's cake.

"Join me when you've got that plate full." He gave her a knowing nudge. "I've got your dessert."

"I'll do that," Abby promised, digging into Margaret's famous lasagna.

Before Abby made it to the table where her father had saved a seat, Marvin Sherrod waylaid her. The retired insurance adjuster had knocked on the front door of Mary's home the first day Abby arrived on the island. He introduced himself and said how he had heard about Mary's accident and wanted to help. He quickly earned her undying gratitude by stepping in to handle the mountain of paperwork associated with Mary's accident and medical needs.

"I set a couple of envelopes on the kitchen counter," he said while getting a better grip on a plate full of marionberry pie.

"Not more paperwork? I thought we were finished."

A soft chuckle escaped Marvin. "Paperwork moves the insurance business. About the envelopes, the small one contains two forms requiring Mary's signature. These are the new ones they require before they process her claim for lost wages. After she signs them, just drop them in the mail. The fat one is copies from the last round of forms you had Mary sign. File them with the rest of her records."

"Marvin, you are truly a Good Samaritan. Thank you, again, from the bottom of my heart for stepping in to help."

As though embarrassed, Marvin shrugged. "I know it sounds a little kooky, but for me that stuff is fun. Besides, it got me invited to the best backyard potluck I've seen in years."

Abby laughed softly as he went to join William Jansen at a table. Balancing her plate, napkin-wrapped utensils and a glass of fresh lemonade, she made her way to her father. At the next table over, Ellen sat between Mary and Janet. Candace Grover, the longtime employee and now manager of Island Blooms, the flower shop that Mary owned, also sat with them sipping a beverage.

Judging by their laughter, Mary was regaling them with humorous tales of life at the retraining center. Next to her, their mother positively glowed. Glad for both of them, Abby smiled and sat down at her father's table.

"Abby, honey, I want you to meet a good friend of your mother's and mine." He stood and assisted Abby with her chair.

Sharing the table with her father was a distinguished-looking gentleman of about sixty-five with snow-white hair and a matching mustache. His complexion gave him the appearance of a perpetual tan that accentuated his deep blue eyes. He rose and with a warm smile, extended a manicured hand.

"Abby Stanton," she said and took the offered hand.

"Hugo Baron." He released her hand and gracefully folded his tall, lean frame back onto the metal chair. "I've looked forward to meeting you for some time."

"Why?"

"After George told me you were an ornithologist—from Cornell, no less—I read the book you coauthored on migratory bird habitats and found it very helpful."

Abby's jaw sagged in amazement. She had no idea that anyone other than her father knew how many articles and books she had written, let alone read any.

"Uh, thank you, Mr. Baron." She unwrapped the napkin from around the utensils. The mention of the world where she lived and worked at a profession she loved reminded her that her vacation days were almost up.

"For what? I'm the one who owes you heartfelt thanks. Finding a book that explained so much in layman's terms broadened my horizons and taught me a great deal," he said. "And please, call me Hugo."

"There isn't anything Abby doesn't know about birds." Her father sat up straighter, his chest puffing with pride.

"I wouldn't go that far, Dad." Unaccustomed to professional recognition from islanders, Abby picked up her fork. "You two had a head start in the eating department. While I catch up, why don't you tell me about yourself, Hugo? How interested in birding are you?"

"Quite. Your article in one of last year's issues of *Living Bird* helped me organize a group of amateur bird-watchers here on the island. Their enthusiasm for birding and conservation convinced me to expand The Nature Museum at the Sparrow Island Nature Conservatory. I'm adding an ornithology wing."

"You're affiliated with the Sparrow Island Nature Conservatory?" she asked, filling her fork with lasagna.

"He *is* the conservatory," said her father.

Abby swallowed. Hugo Baron was turning out to be a very intriguing man. "How did you become interested in birding?"

"I'm a naturalist," Hugo said. "For years, my wife and I traveled the globe as advocates of conservation and preservation of endangered species. One of the most impressive sights we witnessed was the flamingos taking flight at Ngorongoro Crater in Tanzania, Africa. The beauty was indescribable."

"Yes, I agree." Abby laughed. Memories of her last field trip to the remote place flitted through her mind. Again, she saw tens of thousands of the big, pink birds rise from the lake and cast a huge shadow over the desolate land. "Wasn't the noise when they took off a big surprise?"

"It blew us away," Hugo said, grinning. His enthusiastic nod confirmed that they had each witnessed the wonder of one of God's incredible gifts. "We never expected anything so loud from the flapping of wings."

"What about South America?" George asked. "You've been there."

"Yes," Hugo replied. "We saw many unusual, colorful birds. My favorite was the Toco toucan."

Abby raised her eyebrows. "Wow, Hugo. I'm impressed. Most people go for the flashier, more colorful birds and overlook the Toco, which is indeed remarkable. What was it about the Toco that endeared it to you?" she asked.

"I think it was the big, yellow beak," Hugo said slowly. "It looks too big for the head. I kept waiting for the weight of it to overwhelm the poor thing."

"We saw the Toco in Brazil," George said. "About fifteen years ago I accompanied Abby on one of her field trips." His face lit up, though his eyes had a dreamy, faraway quality. "It was the adventure of a lifetime."

Abby sat back. The trip was a favorite memory of a special time shared. Since Jacob's death, her father had stayed close to home to keep an eye on Mary. Abby suspected the reason he declined subsequent invitations had more to do with being available for his wife and daughter than losing his taste for adventure.

They spoke of birding, traveling to exotic places and the devastating effects of poachers for several minutes before Abby changed the subject. "What brought you to Sparrow Island?"

"Globe-trotting lost its appeal after my wife died in 1975. Over the next four years, I went wherever the winds of need blew me. One day I woke up at Sparrow Island's magnificent hotel, The Dorset, a few miles down the road and realized the winds had stopped. Sparrow Island became my home. I opened the Nature Conservatory in 1981.

"I wanted a place where families could be with the animals and learn about nature—and where wildlife could be protected. We have a treasure of flora and fauna. But unless people learn to see it as such, they'll lose it to developers." He folded his arms. "Be careful. I might drag out my soapbox and go on a rant."

Abby smiled to herself, thinking she would enjoy such a display.

"In 1984, I opened The Nature Museum on the conservatory grounds as an interactive way for people to learn about nature. Since then, it has been improved and renovated and is now considered one of the best museums in the San Juan Islands."

"I can't wait to see it," Abby said. "I haven't been there in years."

"Hugo," George said in a low tone that caused his friend to lean forward. "We saw something very special last night."

"What was it?"

"Dad . . ." Everything in Abby stilled.

He turned to her. "We can trust Hugo."

The food in Abby's stomach turned into a lump. "We agreed," she countered firmly. They were supposed to keep the sighting between the two of them.

"Abby, Hugo can help us. We saw a strange pair of birds," George whispered. "Rarities."

"We don't know for sure," Abby said, casting another warning glance at her father.

"I understand your need for caution. I won't share what you tell me with anyone," Hugo promised.

Realizing that if she didn't her father would, Abby gave a brief description of the encounter, concluding with, "We didn't see the birds up close. This is the breeding season, so the plumage can be very deceptive."

"Go on," Hugo urged when she stopped.

"The birds were brownish, their heads and wings dark. Their compact bodies were a marbled brown and buff color."

"They had little, pointy beaks," George added enthusiastically. "Their short wings beat rapidly just to keep them in the air."

"It doesn't sound like anything I've ever seen." Hugo

stroked his mustache. "I certainly understand your hesitation. In fact, I find it admirable."

George turned to Hugo. "We think they might be marbled murrelets. They're almost as rare as the opportunities to see them. When they aren't nesting, they live at sea, and their plumage is a more dramatic black and white."

"You sure it wasn't a sparrow or a duck?" Frank Holloway asked with a note of derision in his voice.

Startled, Abby, George and Hugo looked up at the hardware store owner. Panic hit Abby like a fist. When she first came to the table, two people shared a secret. Then there were three. Now Frank made four. That was two too many.

"Where *did* you come from? And how long have you been standing there eavesdropping?" George demanded.

"Long enough to know you're chasing a figment of your imagination. For your information, I wasn't eavesdropping. I was getting a soda."

"Right," George shot back. "For your information, we saw what we saw."

Frank harrumphed derisively. "Keep it to yourself," he ordered. "We don't want the island inundated with a bunch of outsiders rampaging across the countryside in search of something that isn't here."

"We won't make any speculations, Frank," Abby said with more calm than she felt. "Can we rely on you to do the same?"

"I don't spread wild stories." With another harrumph, he stalked off.

"My goodness." Shaken by the encounter, Abby watched Frank snatch a soda out of the cooler. "He seems angry."

"Not with you, honey," assured her father. "I'll talk to him later. See what's really eating him and stress the importance of keeping this quiet."

Hugo turned to Abby. "How about joining a small group of amateur birders for a couple of hours this Friday?"

It would be wonderful to go out bird-watching. There had been no opportunity to take even a few hours for her favorite pastime since her arrival. "You know, I'd like to," she said slowly. "Thank you for asking. I'll have to see what I can arrange. Where do you go?"

"We stick to the conservatory's land." Hugo picked up his soft drink. "Speaking of which, the San Juan Islands Birding Society is enthusiastic about my expansion of The Nature Museum. They've set aside several boxes of books and papers. I haven't had an opportunity to pick them up yet. When I do, perhaps you'd like to go through them with me."

"It's always interesting to see what other people have spotted and the data they logged."

"Meanwhile, if you're right about the rarities on Sparrow Island, they should be located and protected. That's the purpose of the conservatory. So if there's anything I can do, call me."

Meeting Hugo's gaze, she realized she had found another bird lover as interested in the elusive, rare marbled murrelets as she.

Chapter Five

"YOU'RE HOVERING." Irritation clipped Mary's words.

On the other side of the craft room, Abby closed her eyes and searched for an appropriate response to Mary's dark mood. Before it came, laughter spilled out.

"What's so funny?" Mary rolled away from the work table. The disarray in the room looked as though a tornado had swept through moments earlier.

Abby uncrossed her legs and pushed to her feet. Bits of glitter fluttered off her denim trousers. Yesterday, they had spent the afternoon sorting out boxes and finding new homes for Mary's hobbies. For reasons Abby couldn't explain, she had never considered Mary's interests ranging beyond her flower business, her gardening and knitting in front of the television.

At least until today. She hadn't known manufacturers made eighteen kinds of glitter or that artist paintbrushes came in more shapes than the figures in an advanced geometry book. She'd even learned that with a glue gun and enough artificial flowers anything could be turned into topiary.

"Remember when we were little girls?" Abby asked.

The bewilderment on Mary's face stated she didn't understand what their childhood had to do with Abby's hovering.

"Those first years on the farm we practically lived in each other's pockets," Abby continued. "We couldn't wait to get up in the morning and explore the changes that had taken place during the night. Do you remember the tree house Dad helped us build in the big maple out back?"

"I remember when we came down with mumps and wanted to sleep there."

"Mom said no, so we slept together in your room so each of us could make sure the other didn't die." Abby grinned at the absurd logic of two little girls.

"We were so silly." A wistful smile touched Mary's lips. "We were hardly even sick."

"No, we were imaginative and dramatic."

With each nod of Mary's head, her smile blossomed. "That we were."

Opening her arms to encompass the room, Abby said, "Just think of what we would have done with all this stuff."

Mary surveyed her domain, then laughed as she rolled into the center and only clear space. "We probably would have made as big a mess as this one."

Mary's lightened mood gladdened Abby's heart. Some things the years didn't change, like the enjoyment of making her older sister laugh.

"I don't mean to hover or get on your nerves," Abby said as a way of apologizing while explaining. Knowing just how much to do, and when, was new territory. Most of the time, Mary required little or no real assistance.

They had handled the awkwardness of bathroom navigation. Once Mary developed enough muscle to use the trapezes and lift herself without help, true independence was within her grasp. The simple things caught them unawares, like getting the crackers off the upper shelf in the pantry.

"I know," said Mary. "And I'm sorry for being sharp. Having someone around twenty-four hours a day takes some getting used to."

Abby bit her tongue. She knew exactly what Mary meant. Suspecting the real source of her sister's discontent ran deeper, Abby chose her words carefully. "I guess the bustle of the hospital or the retraining center was different. You expected people to always be around."

"And I knew it was temporary. This is very strange. My home is . . . " Mary's voice trailed as her gaze turned toward the window.

"Safe harbor?" Abby thought of her place in Ithaca. Was Francine watering the plants? Was she filling the bird feeders? Abby mentally shook herself. Of course she was. *She's as reliable as the sunrise.*

"Safe harbor. That's a good description," Mary said thoughtfully.

Using her foot, Abby pushed away a plastic tote filled with colorful knitting yarn and gave Mary a clear path to the door.

"What do you say we take a break? Try out that herbal tea concoction Mom dropped off yesterday."

"All right," Mary agreed without enthusiasm. "Be ready to catch Blossom when you open the door."

Sure enough, the snow white Persian was outside the door when Abby opened it, and tried to slip past Abby's grasp. In a motion quickly becoming second nature she scooped the cat into Mary's waiting arms. Blossom made a halfhearted attempt to break free while Abby wheeled them into the hall and closed the door.

"Looks like she's still miffed over her banishment to the farm." Abby reached down and stroked the thick, silky fur. "Sorry, sweetie, but it was the best place for you. Now you're home again."

Just thinking about the first crazy days of construction still gave her the willies. Blossom, queen of her domain, would never have tolerated workers intent on remodeling her castle. It was asking for trouble. Fortunately, George and Ellen had been happy to come to care for her during that hectic time.

A pair of feline, sapphire-colored eyes pleaded with Abby before looking at the closed room. "Sorry. It's off-limits until we're done."

Mary settled Blossom on her lap. "She's used to having freedom to go anywhere." The yearning in Mary's voice said she was too.

A recurring sense of helplessness washed over Abby and she sent a prayer heavenward for strength.

In the kitchen, Mary opened cupboards and drawers as if planning to rearrange the contents again. Abby put on the teakettle and reflected on her sister's restlessness. *Dr. Randolph was right. This is harder than I thought it would be.*

Since the party three days ago, Mary had busied them both with one reorganization task after another.

Abby worked silently, pouring the boiling water into the teapot and putting it on the table to steep.

"The tea's ready," Abby said, hoping the cheeriness in her voice would prove infectious.

As Mary rolled toward the kitchen table, Blossom leapt to the floor and sauntered away. Mary took the napkin and clutched it in her hands.

Abby reached for Mary's arm. "What's bothering you? Can you share it with me?"

"I'm not sure I can put it into words." Mary gave a dismissive shake of her head.

Fair enough. Sorting thoughts and feelings took time. Abby sat back in her chair and asked, "Is there anything I can do?"

"Yes." Mary lifted her teacup. "Call Hugo Baron. See if he's having a bird walk. If not, take one on your own. Or go visit the conservatory. He loves to show it off."

Startled, Abby blinked several times. "There is a walk today." And she wanted to go, but her sister came first. "He invited me to go along during the party."

"So, go."

"Be reasonable. I can't leave you alone."

Mary set her cup down on the saucer with a loud clank. "Sure you can. I'm not an invalid." The conviction in her tone filled the room. "I'm a woman in transition. Learning a new way of living."

"But . . . what if you need help? What if you need something you can't reach?"

"I'll be fine. Frank said the grabber thingy would be in today. If you don't mind, you can pick it up for me while you're out." Animation returned to Mary's expression. "As for the other, well, we'll make a bathroom run before you leave. It's not as if you'll be gone forever, Abby. We're talking a few hours."

Torn between a strong sense of responsibility and Mary's desire to spend some time alone, Abby vacillated.

"I have a phone," Mary said confidently. "And, honey, I know how to use it."

"Who would you call?"

"You've got to be kidding. I have the numbers of half the island memorized. Plus, both Nancy and Zack said they were going to call today." Mary leaned forward and took Abby's hand. "Not to worry. Go. Please. I'll keep the cordless phone with me if that will make you feel better."

Abby heaved a sigh. "I'm beginning to think if I don't go you'll find a way to lock me outside."

"Now there's an idea."

"Okay. I give. We'll do it your way. And I'll stop at the hardware store, but what is a grabber thingy?"

"A collapsible pole with a claw-like apparatus on one end

and a mechanism to open and close it on the other. I can reach things in the cupboards and closets with it that otherwise I couldn't. Frank, bless his thoughtful heart, ordered it as a homecoming gift."

Abby glanced at the clock. There was just enough time to take care of things here and make the bird walk. There she might find answers to some of the questions that kept her awake at night.

ABBY TURNED INTO THE PARKING LOT of the Nature Conservatory and contemplated the challenges ahead.

Sparrow Island belonged to a loose cluster of more than one hundred and seventy islands situated just below the Canadian border in the northwest corner of Washington State. The five main islands were Orcas, Lopez, Shaw, San Juan Island and Sparrow Island. From the flatter pastures and fields of Lopez to the stone tower crowning lofty Mount Constitution on Orcas, each island offered a unique landscape.

If Frank breathed a word of the conversation he'd over-heard, she would learn of it here at the conservatory. The birders would be excited at the possibility of adding a rarity to their life lists. In that case, conducting a discreet, solo search would be more difficult, but one she had to pursue.

If she was right, a pair of marbled murrelets had made their home on little Sparrow Island. Unlike other alcids that nested in the craggy cliffs by the shore, these preferred the lofty upper branches in stands of old-growth trees. They would even commute almost fifty miles to feed. Talk about hunting for a needle in a haystack.

Abby grimaced. This was the kind of challenge she usually relished—when there weren't so many demands on her time. Drawing the clean perfume of evergreens deep into her lungs, she took a moment to savor the scent. Perhaps because it was the aroma of home—the undeniable security of love and the carefree innocence of childhood—nowhere on earth smelled or felt like Sparrow Island.

With the question of Frank's silence niggling at the back of her mind like an itch, she gathered her binoculars off the front seat of her mother's Lincoln.

As she headed across the lot for the conservatory, she tucked her notebook and the car keys into a pocket on her birding vest. While out in the field, the vest became an extension of her hands, which automatically went to the right place to retrieve whatever she needed.

She reached The Nature Museum. Taking time to survey Hugo's headquarters, she could readily see why he was so proud of it. A bigleaf maple dominated the garden plot at the heart of the circular drive. Brilliant, blue-flowering lithodora formed a formal border at its base. She walked down the long curved sidewalk toward the warm sandy toned building in the shade of several tall Sitka spruces. The entryway was a thoroughly modern mix of glass and chrome.

Dressed in hiking boots, brown twill trousers, matching shirt and a multi-pocketed vest similar to hers, Hugo Baron waved as he exited the building. She returned the greeting and thought he looked the part of a proper birder, although the fedora covering most of his white hair seemed a bit too fashionable for the practical purpose it served.

As a half dozen people filed out behind him, a sense of familiarity swept through Abby. East Coast, West Coast and all points in between, true birders bore an unmistakable stamp. Armed with binoculars, sketchbooks and a love for God's winged creatures, they came in all ages, shapes and sizes and wore practical, drab-colored clothing to blend in with their surroundings. This group of amateurs was no different. Most carried cameras and two even had tripods and long telephoto lenses.

Wondering if her secret was still safe, Abby closed the distance between them.

Hugo extended his hand in welcome. "Glad you decided to join us."

She gave a small shrug and an apologetic smile. "Mary insisted. I suppose we both needed a few hours apart."

A shadow of sorrow dimmed the dazzle in Hugo's smile. "For those of us accustomed to what youngsters call 'their personal space,' it is a major adjustment to have constant company."

Knowing he'd just spoken the understatement of the year, she nodded and glanced expectantly at the birders lined up behind him. "Are we all here?"

Hugo took a moment to make introductions and provide

the group with a glowing synopsis of Abby's career at Cornell. Every word increased her apprehension. It sounded as though he had researched her credentials via the Internet.

He finished his introduction with, "Are there any questions for Miss Stanton?"

Dread squeezed her insides. *What on earth is Hugo up to?*

If even a whisper of a rarity on the island had reached the group, this was the moment of truth. She braced herself.

Chapter Six

ABBY FIELDED A BRIEF FLURRY of questions about the birds the group expected to see today. Although the query she feared didn't come immediately, she worried that it might when they reached the privacy of the forest.

Hugo gestured toward the trees and began walking.

"What was that grand introduction and accolade all about?" she asked. "Anyone who didn't know better would think I worked here."

"Would you like to?"

Abby laughed at the absurdity of his jest. She had established her career—her life—at Cornell. Not in a million years would she consider starting over at fifty-five as a newcomer anywhere else.

A gregarious bunch of Steller's jays chattered in the bigleaf maple in the courtyard, bidding them farewell and bringing joy to Abby's heart. She loved being among the trees, playing visual hide-and-seek with the birds.

The small group quickly felt like one of her own and her

guard relaxed. Bright red berry clusters on red huckleberry bushes added a splash of color to the varieties of green in the forest. Presently, a herd of wrens hopped from bush to bush gathering the fruit.

Blackberry vines, their profuse white blossoms promising a bumper crop in late summer, snarled impossibly on the edge of a gully and gave shelter to several vireos impatiently waiting for the human intruders to leave.

The bird walk approached its second hour while Abby made notes on the birds she spotted, their habitat and behavior.

"Time to head back." Hugo's tone carried the same regret as that of a little boy who knows he has to stop playing with his friends and go inside.

"I do hope you'll join us next time, Miss Stanton," said Rebecca, a tall, dark-haired girl of about sixteen. "When I told Grandma I'd come with her today, I never expected to have fun." Color immediately filled her smooth cheeks. "I mean, I'd never gone bird-watching."

"And it sounded as boring as watching paint dry," Abby said as the group headed back to The Nature Museum.

Caught, Rebecca nodded with a grin that revealed the braces on her teeth.

"Exactly!" she said. "But Grandma loves it, so I figured I could live through an afternoon of traipsing through the woods with her."

"So now that you've done it, what do you think?"

"I've found a new hobby." The girl glanced over her shoulder and Abby did the same. Rebecca's grandmother was deep in a quiet conversation with Hugo. "And I've found something special Grandma and I can share. I had no idea that she knew so much about birds or that I'd find it so interesting. You made it fun, Miss Stanton. Thank you."

Gratified by the addition of a young girl to the realm of avian watchers, she chatted with the teenager all the way back to the circular drive. Abby could not recall when she had enjoyed an afternoon in the woods as much. Perhaps Sparrow Island itself made the difference.

"Abby, do you have a minute?" Hugo stopped at the front door of the museum. Talking amongst themselves, the rest of the group headed for the parking lot.

She checked her watch. "Walk me to the car. I need to stop by Holloway's Hardware before it closes."

"Maybe the next time you get away for a few hours it will be closer to dusk," Hugo said thoughtfully. "Even though nesting season has begun, we aren't likely to confirm your sighting during the day."

Abby lifted her eyebrows. No one would spot marbled murrelets during the day without first finding their feeding grounds. That required a boat and the time to inspect every inlet and cove.

"There are thousands of possibilities for feeding grounds," Hugo continued. "But there are only a handful of possibilities for nesting grounds with so few stands of old-growth timber left on the island."

"You certainly have been doing your research, first on me and now this. The question is why."

"In good time." Hugo reached into his pocket and withdrew a heavy, folded paper.

Despite her reservations and the fact he had not answered her question, Abby's curiosity grew as he unfolded the paper. "What do you have there?"

"A topographical map of Sparrow Island. I've marked the best possibilities. We'll have to get permission from the landowners to go out there." He handed the map to her.

"Are you sure you want me to have this?" she asked guardedly.

"Yes, I made it for you from the original in the conservatory."

"Thank you, that's very generous." Judging by the detailed and color-coded markings, Hugo had put a fair amount of time and effort into the duplication.

"I admit I have an ulterior motive I'd like to explain."

"And what might that be?" Abby gazed up into his twinkling blue eyes. "I'm all ears."

"I'm hoping to use it as a lure."

He had her full attention. "What kind of lure? For what?"

"To keep you on the island. I'm hoping you'll decide to stay here."

"You mean, not go back to New York?"

"That's exactly what I mean."

"Why would I do that?"

"Lots of reasons." Hugo leaned against the driver's door of

the Lincoln. "For one, finding the marbled murrelets' nest would not only be a big feather in your cap in the bird world, you are also uniquely qualified to study them.

"My life's work is conservation. If we confirm you sighted an endangered species, they'll need a champion. I want that person to be you. You would also be a tremendous asset to our expanding bird program. I'd like you to work with me as associate curator."

During the silence that followed, a thousand thoughts crowded Abby's mind. The implication was clear. If she walked away, Hugo would feel obligated to fill the role of champion, even though birds weren't his area of expertise. Staying on the island had far-reaching benefits. Sharing her parents' golden years and supporting her sister through this transition sounded idyllic. But it wouldn't be easy. She couldn't ignore the sad realization that there were unresolved issues between her and Mary that she didn't understand.

Although they were together most of the time these past few days, they avoided deep conversations. Abby wondered why. Their togetherness should have renewed the old closeness, the easy familiarity of thoughts and feelings. Yet they seemed to be drifting further apart.

How much was her fault? More importantly, how could she fix it?

With Hugo looking at her, waiting for an answer, Abby focused on the present. "I'm flattered you want me to work with you. However, my life is in Ithaca."

He opened the door of the Lincoln for her to get in. "Think about it, Abby."

She wanted to say there was nothing to think about, but knew that wasn't true.

"WHERE'S FRANK?" At the checkout counter, Abby looked across the cash register at Frank's tall, lanky grandson, Aaron. Judging from the way his long brown hair kept falling over his deep brown eyes, a visit to the barber was a month overdue.

"He had to go to the mainland," Aaron answered.

Yesterday the senior Holloway had stopped at the house to pick up the tools he'd left after doing some last minute work before the party. To her delight, he had joked with Mary, played with Blossom and teased her. From his upbeat conversation, he had planned to be in the store today. "Is he all right?"

"Just fine, Miss Stanton. He said there was something he had to do and left on the first ferry out this morning. He does that, but I reckon you know how he is."

Abby's head swam. At one time, she did know. Now, she wasn't so sure. Solid, reliable Frank Holloway going off to the mainland at a moment's notice didn't equate. Neither did his flash of anger at the party. According to her father, Frank was uncomfortable with all the changes newcomers had brought to the island. The last thing he wanted was to attract more.

Health issues often changed people, she mused. Perhaps he had received news he wasn't ready to share.

"Abby! Good to see you," called Joe Blackstock from the doorway. "Do you need help with anything?"

Joe's accent reminded her that people *did* move from New York. And when Joe had moved twelve years ago he was sixty-two, certainly older than Abby was now. She looked from Joe to Aaron.

"Frank said he ordered a grabbing apparatus for Mary. It was supposed to arrive today."

Aaron checked behind the counter before standing at attention in front of her. "We got deliveries this afternoon. They're in the back."

Joe joined Abby at the counter. When Aaron made no move to check the boxes, Joe asked, "Would you like me to go look?"

"We haven't inventoried them," Aaron said tightly.

Abby glanced at her watch. She needed to get home. She had already left Mary alone too long.

"Aaron?" Joe said in a gentle voice. "Do you know how to inventory a delivery?"

The young man studied the countertop as though some profound answer might be engraved there. "No, sir."

"I'll be glad to show you." Joe started around the long counter. "You go check on Miss Stanton's package. If it's there, we'll inventory it together, okay?"

Relieved, Aaron hurried to the back of the store.

When he was out of earshot, Joe said, "The kid tries hard. He just doesn't know a hex-head from a lug wrench. He's learning, though." He chuckled and shook his head. "The poor guy stepped into a strange world and now he has half a dozen 'uncles' telling him six different ways to do things. But we all want him to succeed. When Frank retires, he wants Aaron to take over the store."

"I can't imagine Frank retiring."

Holloway's Hardware was a fixture on the island. For as long as she could remember, Frank had manned the counter. For just as long, the covered front porch served as the gathering place for the townsmen to swap stories, trade fix-it tips and debate politics.

"Does Frank take off like this often?" Abby asked.

"Now that you mention it, he does every couple of months or so. Never wants any company. I know what you're thinking, Abby. Frank is in good health."

"You're sure?"

"Sure, I'm sure." Joe grinned. "Last time he went, I asked Doc Randolph. 'Course, she couldn't say much, but she let me know that Frank is in better shape than most of us. So whatever he has going over there, it isn't a health issue."

Abby felt better with Joe's reassurance, though she still considered Frank's behavior curious. "Funny how on this island we all feel entitled to know each others' business," she said, thinking of Hugo. Before she went off to college, that assumed privilege had irked her. Now it felt like genuine concern.

"This is it!" Aaron rushed forward with a long, rectangular box. "I'm sorry, Miss Stanton. While I was back there, I remembered Grandad said this is a gift for your sister. I don't think I need to inventory it." His brown eyes focused instantly on Joe for confirmation.

"No. You're good to go." Joe picked up the box. "I'll put it in your car."

"Thank you, Aaron, Joe." Abby waved farewell to Aaron as she headed toward the door. All the way home, she questioned Frank's strange behavior and his impromptu, yet seemingly regular trips to the mainland.

Early Saturday morning, while Mary slept soundly, Abby poured a cup of fresh coffee, then carried it and her Bible out to the back deck.

As was her habit at home in Ithaca, she settled into a wicker chair, sipped the fragrant brew and watched the world wake up. A faint sea breeze whispered in the tall evergreens in perfect counterpoint to a familiar chorus of birdsong. In the distance, a sailboat tacked with the wind.

Answers to the myriad questions she'd taken to God in prayer last night remained elusive. There had to be a way to remain on Sparrow Island until Mary was capable of living independently.

Abby opened her Bible to the bookmark holding her place. Solitude helped her concentration and soon she was deep in the Word, seeking guidance from the Psalms. Three times, she read Psalm 102, then prayed the first two verses aloud.

"'Hear my prayer, O Lord; let my cry for help come to you. Do not hide your face from me when I am in distress. Turn your ear to me; when I call, answer me quickly.'

"Show me the way, Lord. I need Your guidance." She closed the book and folded her hands on top of it.

Staying longer seemed the only viable answer she could live with. Mary still needed help with her transition. Their aging parents couldn't step in and take over. The farm and their animals required tending. Nor could Mary move out to the farm. There were too many stairs. Besides, her home was perfect for her.

A new option surfaced. With the end of her paid vacation a week away, she could request an unpaid leave of absence. With enough time, she and Mary could also work on mending the distance in their relationship.

The uncertainty of how the university would respond to a request for leave sat heavily on Abby's heart, and she wished she didn't have to wait until Monday to call.

Her thoughts returned to Hugo and his employment offer. The prospect of leaving her friends, her home and especially her church, cut deep. What about the career she loved? Too young to retire, too old to start over, the issue seemed to settle itself.

An image of Hugo in front of the museum formed in her mind. Abby shook her head. Goodness, she hadn't been inside the place in years. She had no idea of what the job entailed, or what it paid. Then, there were benefits like a retirement plan and medical insurance to consider. Those things were a given at Cornell.

Determined to stop dithering, Abby tucked the Bible under her arm and picked up her coffee cup.

Blossom sat regally on the other side of the screen.

"All right, you can come out," Abby crooned.

Tail lifted, head high, Blossom detoured on her exit to brush Abby's calf as though bestowing a special favor of contact.

"You've got personality," Abby said, watching Blossom walk across the deck. "And you picked your people well."

As Abby turned to go inside, she spotted a package wrapped in plain, brown paper and tied with string. Someone had nestled it beside the glass doors, between a planter brimming with geraniums and the house.

Assuming it was another of the many gifts left for Mary, Abby retrieved it, then nearly dropped it when she saw her name printed across the front. She glanced over her shoulder, wondering who might have left a gift for her and when. Strange that anyone would bring it to the back door instead of the front. *Why not put it in the mailbox?*

Seeing nothing unusual in the yard, she carried the package inside. As soon as she set down her cup and Bible, she carefully untied the string and unfolded the paper. An old leather-bound journal, dog-eared, water stained and smelling of mildew, filled her hands. Looking for a note, she sat on the couch, laid the book on the coffee table and opened the cover.

Age had yellowed the edges of the pages. On the flyleaf, she found an inscription that read: "Nature Chronicles of Sparrow Island." Below the words was a date more than sixty years old.

With each page she turned, her heart hammered harder in

her chest. Superb, detailed drawings depicted many of the native birds. Abby marveled at the accuracy of each feature. Meticulous handwriting filled page after page and begged reading. Sporadic maps and sketches of landscapes jumped out from the narrative.

"What a gem," she murmured, turning to the end of the book.

She could barely breathe when she realized the final pages described the fishing habits of the marbled murrelet. The last drawing showed a pair of birds perched on a branch and feeding a chick. Entries in the journal clearly indicated that the birds had nested on the island in the past. Their disappearance had coincided with the diminished stands of old-growth timber and the proliferation of predators.

She closed the book and reexamined the paper for any sign of the sender. *Who are you? Why give this to me?*

Only three people knew about her interest in finding the marbled murrelets. The book wasn't her father's. That left Frank and Hugo.

Hugo had openly given her help, the map showing likely places. Frank had made it clear he didn't want her looking for them.

The journal means someone else knows about my interest in the birds. Who? And how does that person know I'm looking for them?

Gazing at the book, Abby realized that Sparrow Island held hidden mysteries. Would she get to stay long enough to solve them?

Chapter Seven

MARY BLOTTED WATER DROPS from her chin and arms. "Who would have ever thought cleaning up after breakfast could be this difficult?"

"It'll get easier with practice." Abby mopped the floor with a handful of paper towels and tried not to think about the journal, which she had found earlier that morning, waiting upstairs next to her laptop. The minutes she had spent skimming the book before Mary awoke had only heightened a hunger to research the treasures inside.

Reminding herself of God's perfect timing in all things, Abby said, "You did much better today than yesterday."

"That's a relief. I was beginning to think I ought to combine bathing and pot washing. Make one less mess."

Abby chuckled as she discarded the wet wad of paper and washed her hands. "What would you like to do today?"

"Mary! Miss Stanton! Come see what we brought."

"Sounds like it's just been decided." Mary maneuvered her chair out to the deck. "Gracious, Bobby. What have we here?"

"Seedlings for the garden. Mom's bringing the rest."

Abby stepped outside to say hello and couldn't restrain a huge grin at the sight of Bobby McDonald. In a plaid shirt, overalls and broad-brimmed straw hat, he made an adorable little farmer.

"Hey, Miss Stanton! Look at these." He proudly held up a pair of tomato plants. "Want to help us put them in the ground?"

Taken with his enthusiasm, but not wanting to tread on Mary's territory, Abby glanced at her sister. Instead of the expected moue of disapproval, Abby found a warm smile of welcome.

"I think it'll be fun," Mary said.

"All right," Abby said, seizing the invitation. "Give me a minute to change my clothes, then we can grab our hats and get started."

Upstairs, as she hastily donned some of her birding gear, Abby made a point of avoiding the desk where the journal beckoned. Gardening with Mary offered an opportunity to grow closer. That wouldn't wait, the journal would.

Abby raced back to the deck, plopped a floppy hat on her head and gave another one to Mary before helping her maneuver the chair across the lawn. In the side yard, at the center of the fallow vegetable garden, Sandy McDonald leaned on her shovel while they exchanged greetings.

"Whatcha doing, Mom? I thought we were just going to dig holes." Bobby eyed the seedlings he had so lovingly tended.

"She's aerating the soil," Mary explained. "We want to make it easy for these beautiful plants to grow."

Hands fisted on his hips, Bobby nodded thoughtfully.

With Mary directing, Abby and Bobby lined up the contents of the garden cart along the rows and hills as Sandy fashioned them. Soon, four kinds of tomatoes, several varieties of bush beans, peas, lettuce, three kinds of peppers, a bouquet of marigolds and a whole flat of kitchen herbs were spread out on the soil, ready to plant.

Several seed packets staked a claim to three rows in the back of the bed and promised a salad bowl harvest that would put any store's spring mix to shame. Praying everything would continue to flourish long after she returned to New York, Abby said, "Wow, Sandy. You and Bobby have certainly been busy."

"I'm just the day labor." Laughing, Sandy waggled the shovel. "Bobby started the seeds, helped Neil make the stakes, then labeled everything. He also moved the seedlings in and out of the garage several times to make sure they didn't get nipped by the frost."

She draped her wrists over the top of the handle and smiled fondly at her son. "It's part of Pastor Hale's program for the kids. Bobby, why don't you tell Abby about it?"

"It's really cool." He carefully slipped a leafy tomato plant from its container. "We get to pick the things we want to work on. Then Pastor Hale gives us a list of things we have to do. When we finish, we get a pizza party and badges. There's blue and silver and gold. The blue ones are for the little kids. Big kids, like in high school, can get the gold ones, but their list is a lot harder."

While the youngster awkwardly tamped the soil around the green stem, Abby saw Mary's fingers flex. Clearly, she longed to sink her hands into the soil.

"So," Mary said too brightly. "Will you get a silver badge for this?"

Abby's heart ached for her sister. This was one of those times Dr. Randolph warned of. Mary's new reality was bumping hard against her old interests.

His forehead puckered. "Don't you remember? You and Pastor Hale worked on my list. You said if anyone could earn a gold badge in gardening it was me."

"Oh my goodness. You're right. I did say that. I'm sorry, honey. It just slipped my mind for a minute." Mary opened her arms, inviting Bobby in for a hug.

In typical boy fashion, he eluded her grasp, but deposited a quick kiss on her cheek before saying, "I heard older people forget things. But you're not *that* old."

Laughter bubbled out before Abby could contain it. A half second later, Mary joined in. Then Sandy's merry tones made a three-part harmony while Bobby looked at them as though they'd just lost their minds. Shaking his head, he went back to planting, muttering, "This must be one of those girl things Dad was talking about."

That set the women off again and Abby couldn't remember the last time she'd laughed so freely or felt such camaraderie.

The cleansing mirth was so much more than mere amusement. Thrice blessed for the sharing, it was a poignant, soul-filling affirmation of life.

Afterward, time seemed to fly and all too soon, the seedlings had new homes, complete with name stakes and a thorough watering. As Bobby packed up the last of the tools and foam starter cups, he gave Mary a hesitant glance.

"This certainly looks like a gold badge to me," she announced grandly. "We'll have garden sandwiches in no time."

Grinning hugely, Bobby rubbed his tummy and said "I can hardly wait."

"Honey, why don't you take the cart back over to the house?" Mary's next-door neighbor took off her gloves and set them on the top tray. "After you put everything away, you can have some of the brownies on the table. I'd like to visit with Mary awhile before your father comes home."

Taking the cue to leave the two friends alone, Abby put the gloves she'd borrowed from Sandy on the cart and patted Bobby on the shoulder. "As the Irish say, it's a grand garden, Master McDonald. Thank you for inviting me to help."

"Wait. Mom? Can Miss Stanton come with me? I want to show her my tree house. That is," he looked up shyly, "if you want to see it."

Abby saw Sandy nod. Silently blessing the boy for giving her such a graceful exit, Abby said, "I'd love to see your tree house. And please, call me Abby."

"Okay, Abby." Bobby smiled.

She collected the rake and shovel, then with Bobby pushing the cart, they headed for the woods separating his parents' property from Mary's.

THE PRIVATE AERIE was a masterpiece of love that took Abby's breath away. Made of discarded pallets scrounged from the grocery store, the sturdy platform seemed to grow naturally out of the spreading limbs of a bigleaf maple. Branches as thick as her wrists and pruned from the surrounding trees formed a safety railing and a ladder strong enough to hold a grown man. Leaves the size of dinner plates shaded the structure.

"Bobby, this is wonderful."

"Do you really think so?" He gave a pile of leaves a playful kick.

The hole in the toe of his sneaker reminded her that although both of his parents worked, they kept to a strict budget. The nursing home expenses for Sandy's father took most of the salary she made as a schoolteacher. The family stretched the wages from Neil's job on the ferry to cover everything else, including Bobby's college fund.

"It's the best tree house I've ever seen. Can I go up, or is it private?"

"It is, sort of. But, you're okay, Abby." He scrambled up the ladder and grinned down at her. "You just have to be careful."

Fit from a career of playing hide-and-seek with birds, Abby climbed to the top and paused to admire the view. Ten feet off the ground, in the lower story of the leafy canopy, she could see Mary's backyard, the rocky shoreline bordering the properties and the water beyond where a flock of gulls were feeding.

"Pretty neat, huh?" Bobby asked as he opened a hinged wooden box the size of a small trunk. "This is my treasure chest. And this," he pulled out a cardboard tube wrapped in tinfoil, "is my spyglass. 'Course it's not a real one, but Dad says I can still watch for pirates with it."

"Pirates and birds." Abby directed Bobby's attention to a woodpecker, then a robin.

"How do you tell which one is which?"

Tickled by his interest, Abby described how to look first at the general shape, size and color. The typically vivid summer breeding plumage made it easier to hold his attention, although hers kept straying to the journal in her room.

Bobby peered through his spyglass and described a sailboat just off shore as an encroaching pirate ship.

Abby heard a vehicle in the distance and glanced at her watch. Mary might need her.

"I hear my dad's truck."

"It must be time for both of us to go home. Maybe we could do this again sometime."

"That would be cool." He waited for her to climb down then quickly followed. "You can use my tree house anytime you want, Abby."

"That's very generous." Abby smiled at the boy. "I'll probably take you up on your offer."

Spending a few sunsets at that vantage point might prove opportune. The marbled murrelets didn't always feed at the same place, but they returned to their nest nightly.

IN HER ROOM LATE THAT NIGHT, Abby tried to find humor in the irony of her predicament. Yesterday, Mary had wanted solitude. Today, almost from the moment Abby unwrapped the journal, her sister seemed to crave her company, keeping both of them up well past their usual bedtime.

The words on the screen of the laptop computer blurred again and Abby reluctantly shut the machine down. Cleaning her glasses wouldn't help, nor would staying up all night surfing the Internet. Her eyes burned and she was simply too tired to absorb any more.

She finished getting ready for bed, slid between the sheets and carefully picked up the journal. The first time she had held it, the book had been exciting and interesting. Now that she had conducted an initial review, it was beyond precious. Written in fountain pen, in an old-fashioned hand, the painstaking entries matched both her knowledge and her research. With one notable exception.

She stroked the cover. The ornithological community said the first validated sighting of marbled murrelets occurred in 1974. The volume in her hands laid claim to a date a full thirty years earlier.

As a birder, the discrepancy no longer disturbed her. In her heart, she was convinced the writer had personally witnessed everything that was described. The truth of this person's deep and abiding love for all birds fairly leapt off the pages and was too powerful to discount.

As a scientist, she still had to reserve judgment. Abby put the book on the nightstand and turned off the light. Until she knew the giver's identity and purpose, keeping the gift a secret was imperative. If the donor had wanted it made public, he or she could have done so easily.

Perhaps she'd been given the journal as some sort of test. The last entry referred to another book and that only made sense. She couldn't imagine an avid birder abandoning this passion simply because the last blank page was filled.

After her prayers, she fell asleep wondering if she'd pass the mysterious test. And if the prize was the second journal.

Chapter Eight

CHIDING HERSELF FOR hitting the snooze button once too often, Abby hurried through her morning routine then rushed down to her sister's room.

"What took you so long?" Mary grumbled as Abby helped her from the bed to the chair. "I don't want to be late for church."

"I, ah, didn't know you were . . ."

"Going to attend? Of course I am." She snatched necessities from a dresser drawer, dropped them on her lap and wheeled into the bathroom. "Bring my blue dress, please. We have to make up for lost time."

Abby did as she was told, assisting when and where she could, yet her reservations kept growing. Thanks to strict adherence to an exercise regimen, Mary was getting stronger but it wasn't enough. "I don't mean to discourage you, but I don't think this is a good idea. Even with your help, I'm not strong enough to get you into and out of the car by myself."

"Of course not. Neil's coming over to help."

"I . . . didn't know."

"I told you yesterday." Mary's hairbrush flew through her silver locks. "I should have known you weren't listening. You were probably too busy making plans to get back to New York."

"Excuse me?"

"Don't use that indignant tone with me. All evening, you had that look you get when your mind is somewhere else. Well, if Ithaca is where you want to be, fine. Don't stay on Sparrow Island on my account." Mary tugged irritably at her hosiery. "I don't want pity. Especially yours."

"Good. Because you're not going to get it." Abby knelt and put the shoes that matched the dress on her sister's feet. *And while I'm down here, Lord, please forgive me. I was distracted last night.*

She looked up and met her sister's shocked gaze. "You have my concern, my admiration and my help. For as long as you need it, or . . . as long as you want it."

"I wish—"

The doorbell interrupted Mary and she sighed. "That must be the McDonalds. If you'll get the car, I'll meet you out front."

As Abby pulled out of the garage, she tried to guess what it was her sister wanted. If only the doorbell had delayed another second. But it was too late. The moment was gone. Praying there would be another opportunity, she put the car into park and pressed the trunk release.

The next second, Neil McDonald opened the passenger door. A ruggedly handsome thirty-eight, with sun-streaked brown hair and cinnamon-colored eyes, he had a muscular physique many men would envy. What Abby liked most about him was the way he looked at his wife—as if she'd hung the moon just for him.

As Mary shut the front door and wheeled down the ramp to the car, Neil stuck his head inside and said to Abby, "We'll follow you to Little Flock Church, then do this in reverse, okay?"

Without waiting for an answer, he effortlessly lifted Mary out of her wheelchair and put her on the seat. "No speeding," he teased. "I'll be watching."

Neil stashed the wheelchair in the trunk and closed the lid. Abby pulled out of the driveway onto Oceania Boulevard, heading for town.

"I've missed our little church and Rev. Hale's sermons," Mary said.

"I can easily understand why. He has a fresh way of looking at things that makes him more of a teacher than a preacher. And he gives me plenty to think about when I'm reading my Bible."

"I know what you mean. When he visited five years ago to interview with the elders for the position of pastor, most of us had doubts. He looked more like a surfer than a reverend."

"Mom told me about that. The blond hair and California tan really stood out in a crowd of pale-skinned Northwesterners." Abby smiled, recalling all the jokes about Washingtonians mildewing rather than tanning.

She slowed for a car turning into a driveway. "As I recall, Mom liked him after his first service. She's always been an excellent judge of character."

"I suppose it just shows that looks can be deceiving," Mary said flatly and shrugged a shoulder. "In more ways than one. I'm sorry for snapping at you earlier. I keep waiting for my life to get back to normal. Except there is no normal. And sometimes I feel like I'm just floundering."

"Jesus knows. Better than any of us." Abby reached across the seat and squeezed her sister's hand. "He'll help you define a new normal."

"My heart is steadfast, O God. My heart is steadfast." Mary turned her head to gaze out the passenger window, a gesture Abby recognized as the end of the conversation.

The weathered metal cross at the peak of the shingled steeple over the side entrance of the church came into view. Abby turned off Harbor Seal Road and onto a side street leading to the church's parking lot.

Built in the 1880s, the white building was narrow and tall with arches over the doorways and windows. Slender bands of stained glass bordered the clear panes. A line of rhododendrons spilled red, pink and lavender blooms over the white picket fence defining the formal grounds from the activity field.

Not until returning to the island this time had Abby noticed the ramp stretching from the walkway to the sheltered portico where parishioners gathered to greet one another before and after the service.

As she parked between a 1970s Volkswagen Bug and a bright yellow Hummer, she thought about the changes to the San Juan Islands. Islanders tended to drive their cars for years beyond their projected life. With the help of the mechanics at Al's Garage in town, many of those vehicles became classics while still in service. In contrast, the influx of wealthy people building remote getaway homes had increased over the past decade and their expensive autos were easy to spot.

Abby released the trunk latch and heard Neil remove the wheelchair. Within minutes, the five of them were ready to move toward the door. The group chatting at the bottom of the steps turned to go inside.

"I apologize if we're late." Mary glanced over at Sandy who shook her head.

"We're not late," insisted Neil, pushing the wheelchair up the ramp to the portico.

As though uncertain, Mary checked her watch, which prompted Abby to do the same.

"We're definitely not late," she assured her sister.

Bobby circled around and bounded up the two stairs that led to the door. He held the door to make sure it remained open while Mary entered. Sunlight streamed through the windows, softening the look of the age-darkened pews on an even darker hardwood floor. The polished wood gleamed as though stroked regularly by soft cloths in loving hands.

George and Ellen sat side by side in the last pew, which was shortened to accommodate a wheelchair without obstructing the aisle. Neil maneuvered Mary next to Ellen. As one, the congregation rose and began applauding until the sound filled the building.

"Welcome home, Mary Reynolds." Rev. Hale came down the aisle and took her hand. "Your church family missed you and prayed for you every day. The Lord heard our prayers and blessed us all with your return."

"Thank you, Rev. Hale." A tear trickled down her cheek. "My thanks to all for your prayers and warm welcome."

Looking around, Abby knew that if smiles could generate light, there was enough here to power the entire West Coast. She gave her sister's shoulder a parting squeeze before circling around the back of the pew and sliding in next to their father.

The service began with song. Filled with love, Abby thanked the Lord that she could make a joyful noise. With diligent concentration and His help, her ability to stay on key had improved over the years, though her voice had not. Still, she could not sit silently through the beautiful verses of praise and worship.

Rev. Hale spoke about God's purpose for His creations and struck a resonant chord in Abby's heart. After the service, as the church members came singly and in twos and threes to reconnect with Mary, Abby was content to wait outside in the sunshine and reflect on the teaching.

The whole situation with the elusive, little seabirds was beginning to feel familiar. God was using His creations to expand her territory. She didn't know how or why or even what He wanted her to do yet, only that He was moving in her life and there were lessons to be learned.

She watched the congregation mill about the portico,

greeting each other and catching up on the events of the last week. Had one of them left the journal?

Thanks to her father, there probably wasn't a soul on Sparrow Island who didn't know about her career at Cornell. Perhaps the donor selected her precisely because she had the training to understand the importance of its contents.

She looked around with a new interest. Was the sender also the author, or a relative, or a stranger who had merely stumbled upon the book? She was back where she started. Who else knew about her search for the marbled murrelets and how did he or she find out?

She rubbed her forehead. Anyone could have left the book, even a bibliophile who wasn't interested in the subject but couldn't bear to throw someone else's work in the trash. Yet, Abby couldn't shake a feeling of purpose. Things happened for a reason, whether she could immediately perceive it or not.

Sandy McDonald, with Bobby in tow, joined Abby on the walkway. "Are you coming to the baby shower?"

Unable to think of anyone she'd met since returning to Sparrow Island who was expecting a child, Abby shrugged helplessly. "I think I missed something."

"Can I miss it too?" Bobby gave his mother a pained look. "Showers are boring, Mom. There's no one to play with and nothing to do."

Sandy shook her head. "I'm sorry, honey. Your father and I are going to the Pierces' shower. So is Mary."

Feeling as trapped as Bobby looked, Abby said, "I've never

met this couple and I really wouldn't be comfortable attending. Suppose you take Mary to the shower and I'll take Bobby hiking." *And do a little birding.*

"Oh, please, Mom. Can I? Please?" The boy managed a pathetically pleading expression better than any Manhattan sidewalk mime.

AN HOUR LATER, Abby drove up the winding, two-lane road carved into the side of Mount Ortiz. Beside her, Bobby sat wide-eyed, staring out the windshield at the magnificent views around every curve in the winding road. Trees and a steep slope abutted the pavement on the passenger side, but on the driver's side, only the sparse oncoming traffic and a wooden guardrail stood between them and the postcard scenery.

"Wow," Bobby whispered, "the islands look like giant green gumdrops."

Keeping her hands on the wheel and her gaze on the road, Abby laughed. "I've heard them called many things, but this is a first for gumdrops."

"That's my favorite candy. Mom says they didn't have chocolate bars and gumdrops and stuff when Jesus was a boy. I think that's pretty crummy. I'm sure He would've liked them."

"I agree." Abby sent a sincere thank you winging heavenward. No wonder Jesus told the apostles to let the little children come to Him. To Bobby, she said, "I thought we'd go to the very top of the mountain and look around. What do you think?"

"Are there any hiking trails up there?"

"There didn't used to be, but there may be some now. It's been a long time since I drove to the top. On a clear day, like today, you can see the curvature of the earth."

"That's really far, huh?"

"Yes, it is."

"Can we see Seattle?" he asked enthusiastically.

"There are islands between the city and us. Besides, it's too far."

"The earth curves before then?"

"Afraid so," she said apologetically.

"Well, that's okay."

Gravel crunched beneath the tires as she pulled into the shady parking area. She picked up her gear from the seat beside her and offered the binoculars to Bobby. "Do you think you can carry these?"

"I'll be very careful," he promised solemnly.

Abby tucked the keys into her birding vest and checked the number of pictures available on the memory card of her digital camera.

"Lead the way, Master McDonald." She closed up the car, ready to pit her experienced climbing skills against the energetic inexperience of youth.

Holding on to the binoculars hanging around his neck, Bobby stayed beside her as they crossed the parking area. A foursome of tourists laughed as they made their way to an extremely long RV. Abby wondered how they got it around some of the sharper hairpin turns.

Bobby waved at them when they looked his way and Abby followed suit.

"You're in for a treat," called one of the women. "It's beautiful up there."

Bobby moved ahead of Abby when they reached the sun-dappled path leading to the peak. "Careful of the rocks and roots," he cautioned. "You could slip and fall really easy if your foot gets caught on one."

"Thank you for watching out for me," Abby said sincerely.

At the clearing on top of Mount Ortiz, they climbed a platform built out of native stone and looked around.

"Wow. You can see forever." Bobby adjusted the binoculars, then slowly scanned the horizon.

"Have you been up here before?"

"Sure, with my Dad. I didn't have binoculars to look through and it was usually cloudy or you couldn't see very well. What do you call the fog you can't really see?"

"Haze," Abby answered absently, unfolding the map Hugo made for her.

"That's right. I read about haze. Look." Bobby pointed across the distance. "That's Bellingham, right?"

"Yes. A little to the north is Canada." She checked the coordinates on the map. According to the markings, there should be a stand of old-growth timber right below and to the south.

"Canada is where the mountains with snow are?"

Abby glanced to the northeast. "Yes. I think those are part

of the Canadian Coastal Mountains and the ones farther east are the Kamloops."

She raised her camera, turned south, adjusted the telephoto lens and zoomed in on the spot targeted on the map in her hand. To her dismay, the area wasn't genuine old growth. She supposed by some standards, it might seem that way. Judging by the size of the trees, only about a half-century had passed since they sprouted.

When Bobby had looked his fill, they walked to a sturdy split rail fence and peered over. Below them, the cliff face plunged more than a hundred feet down to a fan of broken rocks.

He took her hand. "I don't think we ought to go that way."

"I saw a trail not far from here. What do you say we drive down there and see where it leads?" She ought to be able to see another of the sections designated as old growth and a perfect nesting habitat for the marbled murrelets.

Eager for the next adventure, Bobby sprinted to the path leading to the parking lot.

Abby laughed aloud when he stopped short as though forcing himself to wait for her.

"Go ahead, Bobby. I'm right behind you."

"I'll wait for you at the bottom, Abby."

"Give me a shout when you get there." She kept him in sight. As the afternoon wore on, she found herself indebted to him for his boundless enthusiasm.

He didn't complain when they stopped at every lookout facing a new direction. Or while she spent long minutes comparing the topography to Hugo's map, then took pointless pictures. Most of the island had been logged at one time or another and replanted.

As she grew discouraged, Bobby grew restless. To make up for the dull parts of his afternoon, after they descended Mount Ortiz, Abby drove him east to Arrowhead Hill and told him to pick a deer trail. They'd follow it and see what they could learn.

The tracks led them through thick brush and crowded clumps of slender saplings, across chilly rivulets and up rocky ravines. When they burst out of the undergrowth onto the southeastern flank of Arrowhead Hill, Abby could scarcely believe what she saw in the distance.

If marbled murrelets were actually nesting on the island, it was out there, in that magnificent stand of old-growth forest.

Chapter Nine

CAUGHT BETWEEN CONCERN and confidence, Abby hung up the telephone just as Mary rolled into the kitchen.

"Good news, I hope?"

"I'm not sure." Abby ran a hand through her short brown hair and winced inwardly. She still wore the sweats she had donned that morning to sit outside for her Bible study, whereas her sister, with a minimum of assistance an hour earlier, had not only dressed for the day, now her makeup was perfect and her silver pageboy gleamed.

Abby had wanted to catch Jerome Winthrop before he left for lunch, and as it turned out, the time difference on the East Coast was the least of her worries. "I've talked to four people and still don't have a definite answer."

She fetched coffee for her sister and herself, then took a seat at the table. "The head of my department is in transit, returning home from Beijing."

The corner of Mary's mouth twitched once, a sure signal she didn't like what she was hearing. "What's the problem?

Surely after thirty-five years you're entitled to a leave of absence."

"That may be, it's just not that easy. I need Jerome's signature on my request and someone has to take over the commitments I left behind. There is one bright spot. We have a graduate student in the lab, a very smart but shy young lady. I've been trying to get her to test her wings in the field. Now, she's agreed to take my symposium in Brussels."

"Brussels?" Mary's eyes widened. "As in Belgium?"

Abby nodded, enjoying her sister's incredulity. "It's a tremendous opportunity for her."

As if she had trouble getting her mental arms around the idea, Mary said slowly, "I, uh, didn't realize you'd be giving up a trip to Europe."

Abby laughed. "Believe me, it's not as glamorous as it sounds. Presenting at a symposium is a lot of work. And living out of a suitcase loses its luster rather quickly. In fact, I'm glad to be relieved of the obligation." Even as she spoke, she was amazed to discover how much freer she felt, as if she'd set down a large burden.

Mary's cup clacked as she set it down on the saucer. "So, what happens now?"

"I'll have to wait a couple of days until Jerome returns to the university and call again. Then, when Human Resources gets his okay, they'll process my request."

Mary rolled her shoulders as though preparing for battle and asked, "How about some breakfast?"

At the mention of food, Abby's stomach rumbled. "Breakfast sounds good. What would you like?"

"I'm going to fix cereal, toast and orange juice." Mary glanced at the pantry. "If you bring down the toaster, I can get everything else."

A reproachful meow immediately commanded Abby's attention. "Oh, Blossom. You need food, too, don't you?" The fluffy, white Persian sat regally on her haunches and waited for Abby to clean and refill the special ceramic kitty dishes.

While she worked, she wondered if she could interest Mary in her quest. To enter the property where the old trees stood, Abby needed permission and for that, she needed a name. A name she should be able to find on the tax rolls at the county seat on San Juan Island. "Do we have a ferry schedule?"

"In the top drawer in the phone stand. If you don't see it, check under the phone book too." Mary reached into the cupboard for two cereal bowls.

Abby retrieved the schedule and unfolded it.

"Where are you going?" Mary opened the refrigerator and took out the milk and orange juice.

"Friday Harbor. I'm hoping you'll come with me."

Watching the way the cartons teetered and tilted on Mary's lap, Abby held her breath. Half a gallon of milk made a big mess. When Mary had both containers safely on the counter, Abby exhaled and said, "There are some birds that nest in old-growth timber and I—"

"Friday Harbor? That's such a time-consuming trip. And

I have my knitting group this afternoon. We're working on projects for Warm Up America."

Crestfallen, Abby folded the ferry schedule.

"Hey, that doesn't mean you can't go. It's just that the sooner I get back into the routine of my life, the faster things will fall into place. And Mom's expecting me. After we eat, you can take me over there and then go catch the ferry. Dad and Sam can get Mom and me to the knitting group later on."

Mary pivoted the wheelchair and pulled placemats and cloth napkins from a drawer. "Come to think of it, today may be Mom's day to hostess. We rotate so it doesn't get to be too much for any of us. One of these Mondays you might consider joining us and learning how to knit."

Abby bit back a reminder that her leave request wasn't guaranteed. Mary was dealing with that uncertainty in her own way.

Shortly after breakfast, while Mary was on the phone, Abby finished getting ready. Just as she came down the stairs, the doorbell rang. She found Sam Arbogast on the front porch and invited him inside.

The Stanton's hired hand for the past eleven years was slightly taller than Abby and a few years younger. He had a stocky, muscular build that suggested tossing around hay bales didn't require any effort.

"Mary called. I'm here to help you get Mary in the car."

"Terrific. I was wondering how we'd manage by ourselves."

"Now you don't have to. Hello, Mary."

"Sam, you're an angel. I've missed you." She clasped his hand in both of hers.

"You've been sorely missed, too." Sam's blue eyes shone with sincerity as he shook her hands in both of his and released them. "The Lord surely answered our prayers when He brought you back to us." Sam swept a grayish-black lock of hair off his tanned forehead. "If you're both ready, let's get going."

Mary led the way into the garage where Sam helped her into the Lincoln.

Exiting the car at their parents' farm went even smoother.

Abby noticed her mother on the porch and wondered how many times she had stood there waiting for Mary to join her.

"Will you look at that," Mary cried out. "Oh, Sam, you built a ramp."

"Me and George knocked it out in a day and painted it the next." Sam patted Mary's shoulder. "We couldn't have you shouting at us from down below when you came visiting, could we?"

Abby and Mary greeted their mother and they all went inside. Familiar baking aromas filled the kitchen. "Gather around the table," said Ellen. "I've made lots of food for the knitting group. Sam, you absolutely cannot go back outside until you've eaten. You too, George."

Although dressed for farmwork, at the mention of food, Sam and George went to the sink to wash up. Abby's father threw her an amused glance and asked, "Are you taking up knitting?"

"No. I'm going over to Friday Harbor." Regular phone calls

had kept him up to date on her progress, or the lack thereof, with the birds. The fact that his curiosity about the murrelets still burned brightly felt as good as a hug. "Does anyone need me to pick up anything while I'm off island?"

"Not me. George? Sam?" Ellen queried over her shoulder to where the men dried their hands on paper towels.

"Can't think of a thing," her father said firmly.

Sam shook his head.

"That settles that. Come on now, Abby. Sit down and eat. It's a long trip."

"Mom. We just had breakfast."

"You'll be hungry soon." Ellen opened the cupboard and started taking down plates. Serving food and caring for her family's needs were some of the many ways she showed her love.

"You're not going to let me out of here unless I eat, are you?" Abby asked with a laugh.

"Not unless the sun starts rising in the west," Mary chimed in, adjusting her chair at the kitchen table. "Accept it and eat something."

Abby glanced at the clock on the wall. "Suppose I take a lunch bag of goodies? If I leave in a few minutes, I can catch the next ferry." The sooner she reached the courthouse, the quicker she could find out who owned the last stand of old-growth timber on Sparrow Island.

And after that . . . On an island where people prized their privacy, she didn't even want to think about the possibility that the landowner might deny her access.

Abby left her mother's Lincoln behind Island Blooms, Mary's flower shop, and walked down Shoreline Drive. Lined with businesses on both sides of the street, the little commercial district possessed a charming old-world flavor. Flower boxes full of bright red geraniums and white alyssum adorned the shop windows. Wooden baskets crowded with petunias hung from light posts and trailed purple and white lobelia in the breeze.

Lighthearted, she swung her canvas tote bearing a Cornell logo onto her shoulder and waved at the men already gathered on the front porch of Holloway's Hardware. By the time she turned right on Primrose Lane and heard the distinctive clack-clack of tires rolling across the loading plank onto the ship's deck, she figured half of Sparrow Island assumed she was on a shopping excursion and that was fine with her.

She did not intend to correct the misperception. Instead, she quickened her pace. The ferries prided themselves on punctuality.

The *Takima*, one of the smaller boats used for inter-island runs, had only one deck for cars. Walk-ons and any drivers who cared to get out of their cars, rode in the enclosed lounge upstairs or walked out on the deck. On windy days with rough seas, she preferred traversing the Strait of Juan de Fuca in one of the bigger vessels that also made the runs to Anacortes, Washington, or the port in Sidney, British Columbia.

At the sound of her name, she looked down the rows of

cars and saw Neil McDonald in blue coveralls and an orange vest with a reflective stripe. Smiling, she returned his wave before opening the heavy stairwell door and climbing up to the passenger deck.

Within minutes, the big engines moved them away from the dock. Abby hitched the hoops of her tote bag higher on her shoulder and went to the bow of the boat where she could stand outside and drink in the beauty of the islands. The engine noise seemed to trail away with the white, frothy wake.

She rested a hand on the rail, turned her face to the sky, closed her eyes and drew a long, slow, cleansing breath. For the first time in over six weeks, at least for a few hours, she had no responsibilities, no schedule and no demands. The air smelled a little sweeter. The morning caressed her skin with the heat of the warming sun and an appreciative hum collected in her throat. By Northwest standards, today would be hot; it might even reach eighty degrees. Abby walked around the deck enjoying the ferry trip and her sense of freedom.

About forty-five minutes later, an eagle cried and Abby was drawn out of her reverie. The ferry was making the turn to dock at Lopez, the flattest of the five main islands and most suited to cultivation.

Abby remained at the rail and watched ferry workers choreograph the unloading and loading of vehicles and passengers. Soon they were bound for Shaw, then on to Orcas. The final stop was Friday Harbor on San Juan Island. There, the cycle reversed, with the ferry making its first stop at Orcas.

On her return trip, she would see all the islands again before the ferry finally docked at Sparrow Island.

Though her thoughts had raced ahead, the boat sailed slowly through the channel between the islands. Steep cliffs cast a shadow on the water where a dozen shy harlequin ducks fed near the rocky shore. On her first trip to Sparrow Island after the tragic day of the accident, she had seen several of the magnificent gray whales who took up residence in the Strait of Juan de Fuca and had found a simple comfort in their ability to adapt.

As she watched the shoreline, large, rustic homes peeked through the trees, others perched on the top of sheer cliffs. Hugo's assertion that they needed to preserve the wildlife and habitat might be right, she conceded. People didn't mean to encroach. Most newcomers only wanted to share in the beauty of the islands and the richness of the wildlife.

The breeze freshened and she went inside to sit at a table during the last stretch of the trip. When next she ventured to the front deck, the ferry was rounding Brown Island off the coast of San Juan Island. As they entered the shelter of Friday Harbor, a cluster of buildings dominated the hillside on the right. The complex belonged to the University of Washington Marine Laboratories. The serious research conducted there drew scientists from all over the world. To the left were small shops selling gourmet coffee, books and clothing. Straight ahead was a small deli where many locals bought their breakfasts before boarding the ferry.

After the ferry docked, passengers crossed the bow and walked up the pavement to Front Street. Abby turned left on Spring Street, then turned right on First Street. The courthouse was two blocks down on her left.

The first of the answers she needed was up the stairs and through the glass doors.

"Abby!"

Startled, she turned to look for the source of the masculine voice calling her name and spied Sergeant Henry Cobb descending the courthouse steps.

She waited for him to come closer and thought about the numerous phone calls he had made to Mary since her return. From his serious expression, Abby surmised that the deputy sheriff's morning had not been pleasant. "Henry, how nice to see you."

"It's real nice to see you too, Abby. Especially now that I'm done in there." He cocked his head toward the doors, started to say something, then shrugged it off.

Suspecting it had to do with a depressing court case, she asked lightly, "Are you heading back to the station?"

"Not before I buy you a cup of coffee and we visit a few minutes." He gestured toward the sidewalk. "That is, unless you have an appointment inside."

"No, no one is waiting for me." Abby checked the time. "Although I suppose everyone I need to see is out to lunch now."

A smile flickered. "They are."

"How about if I take you up on your offer of coffee and we

find a place to sit? I have enough food in here for several people." She raised her tote. "Mom was certain I'd starve to death on the ferry."

The tension in Henry's features fled. "An Ellen Stanton lunch is an offer I can't refuse." He said the last part in a perfect imitation of Marlon Brando as Don Vito Corleone.

The waggle of his eyebrows made Abby laugh. "It's settled."

They walked down to Memorial Park and found a bench near two great elm trees. The nearby plaques said they were planted in 1921 to honor the soldiers and sailors who made the ultimate sacrifice in WWI.

"What brings you to Friday Harbor?" Henry removed the plastic lid from the coffee he'd bought at the Front Street Café.

"Professional curiosity." Abby opened her tote bag and withdrew a brown sack of sandwiches, which she offered to Henry. "I want to find out who owns a piece of land."

"I hope this means you're planning to buy it and stick around. Mary could use the company." He bit into a sandwich and closed his eyes for a moment. "This is great."

Rather than divulge the real reason for her interest in the land, Abby said proudly, "Mary is adapting much faster than the counselors at the retraining center predicted. And they say they're optimistic because of her strong determination and positive attitude."

"That's Mary. She takes the worst disasters in stride. She's quite a woman."

The mix of admiration and wistfulness in his voice caused

Abby to give him a sideways look. If she read the longing on Henry's face correctly, he was definitely smitten with Mary.

"Do you favor my sister?" The question popped out of Abby's mouth and left her appalled for asking.

Henry finished his sandwich before speaking. He took so long Abby feared he was insulted by her audacious prying. "I'm sorry, Henry. That was inappropriate and it's none of my business."

"I was the first on the scene of Mary's accident," he said solemnly. "But it wasn't the first time we'd met."

Abby gave him the dessert bag. He took out a homemade granola bar. "Tell me about it."

He glanced around as he sipped his hot coffee. "A little over a year ago, I was on Sparrow Island for a briefing with my men. Hal Niven's wife just had a baby, so I stopped in at Island Blooms to get her some flowers. That's when I 'met' Mary. Although I knew her before that, it was only vaguely."

Henry finished off the granola bar and wiped his fingers on a napkin. "I tell ya, Abby, I've bought more flowers in the past year than all the rest of my life put together."

She laughed with him, all the while admiring his honesty and willingness to reveal his feelings. "I had no idea she was dating anyone," Abby mused. "But then, Mary and I never discuss such things."

"Why not? You're sisters. You're friends. Why wouldn't she tell you we went out a few times?"

"I don't know, Henry. I'm trying to figure that out." *And*

I'm beginning to think the problem is mine. "How did you find Mary after the accident?"

"I was at the Sparrow Island Sheriff's Station when we received a call about headlights shining out of a ravine. It had been a busy afternoon for the deputy on duty, so I went to investigate. It took a few minutes to recognize her car even after I put the spotlight on it. She was pinned inside."

"Was she . . . was she conscious?" Abby asked, remembering the place on the rural road her father had pointed out. He had taken her there the one time and had avoided the route since. Mary consistently refused to speak about the accident.

"Yes. Fact is, by the time we got the Jaws of Life in place, she was reassuring me." He closed up the dessert bag and offered it to Abby.

"Keep it. The sandwiches too." Ellen would be delighted to see the way Henry savored the bag lunch.

"No argument from me." He set them on the bench. "Mary knew she was seriously hurt. She told me she couldn't feel her legs. While we were waiting for the helicopter to arrive and take her to Harborview Medical Center down in Seattle, she and I prayed, talked and prayed some more. As they were wheeling her to the helicopter, she asked me to come see her if she lived."

Henry snorted and shook his head. "She was counting on me. That's when I decided there was more going on here than a few casual dates. She has such fire."

"Did you go see her very often?"

"Every day I had off. It was better when she transferred up to the retraining center in Bellingham."

"Yeah," agreed Abby. "That's an easy boat trip in good weather, then a short cab ride." Mary's boating friends had shared the task of ferrying Abby to Bellingham more than a dozen times. Each time, they claimed they had business on the mainland.

Nodding, Henry continued, "But now, I'm back to square one. Maybe even square zero."

"What do you mean?"

"I was making progress with her before the accident. Since then, she's more resistant to my charming ways."

Abby joined him in a grin. "I can't imagine why."

"The wheelchair. She thinks I'm sticking around out of pity. For a smart woman, she can sure be thickheaded."

On that, they agreed, though Abby would never say so aloud. "Patience and persistence work with Mary. Or at least they did when we were growing up."

"Sort of like the water torture of a dripping faucet?"

"Exactly."

He finished his coffee and turned slightly on the bench. "This land you're checking up on at the courthouse—you didn't say if you were interested in buying it."

"I'm just curious to know who owns it."

"I'll walk you back. Ask for Laura and tell her I sent you. She's an encyclopedia when it comes to land ownership." Henry picked up the lunch bags and stood.

Abby took his offered hand, rose to her feet and swung the considerably lighter tote over her shoulder. "Thanks for the tip about Laura. I'll take all the help I can get."

At the door of the courthouse, they said their farewells and Abby went inside. She found Laura in the Assessor's Office and introduced herself.

In her late thirties, Laura grinned delightedly when Abby related Henry's glowing description of her. "Now," the youthful-looking woman said with a blush, "all I have to do is live up to all his praise. How can I help you?"

"I'd have to see the plat map, which shows the ownership boundaries, to give you the exact location," Abby began, then gave a general description of the property.

"Oh no. That's too easy." Laura sat at her desk, wrote out the name and post office box of a corporation in Delaware and offered her the slip of paper.

Her stomach lurching, Abby took the address. "How, uh, did you know I was coming?"

"I didn't. This one I memorized. I've been working here for eight years and not a month goes by that I don't get at least one or two inquiries."

"From who?"

"Developers, dot.com millionaires, realtors, even an oil sheik. Anyone who can afford to buy an unspoiled piece of paradise." Still grinning, she shrugged. "Personally, I hope Whale Riders, Inc., whoever they are, never sells."

So did Abby. The marbled murrelets and all the other

wildlife wouldn't stand a chance against a fleet of bulldozers. "How long has Whale Riders owned the property?"

"About ten or eleven years."

"That's all? Who had it before them?"

"It belonged to a family named Bowditch for at least a hundred years. The last Bowditch died in 1995. In his will—and this is public record, so I'm not gossiping—David Bowditch left his entire estate to Whale Riders, Inc."

"Now why would anyone leave a hundred-year legacy to a corporation?" Abby mused.

"Beats me." Laura shrugged. "Who knows why people do some of the things they do."

Abby gazed down at the Delaware address. "Do you have a phone number for them?"

"No, it was disconnected years ago. If you're planning on contacting them, good luck."

"What do you mean? Isn't the address valid either?"

"Oh yes. However, nearly everyone I've given it to comes back requesting another way to contact them. But this is the only address I have. We send the tax statements there and we receive payment. They're never late."

"So they aren't interested in any unsolicited correspondence?"

"Judging by what people tell me, Whale Riders just ignores it."

Another person came in. Aware of the line forming behind her and with no more information to be gained, Abby said farewell and left the Assessor's Office. Her mind whirling, she headed for the ferry dock. She could understand why Whale Riders didn't respond to offers to purchase the property. Her mission was different. Surely, they would respond to a request for permission to pursue the marbled murrelets.

Or would they?

Chapter Ten

At the heart of Green Harbor's tiny business district, the gift shop in the Springhouse Café drew women from all over the island and struck terror in the hearts of men. For the first time, Abby understood why and sympathized with the masculine gender.

It wasn't the overwhelming femininity of the graceful swags cascading from the tops of the windows, or the artful arrangements of countless lotions, bath powders and glycerin soaps. It was the vulnerable uncertainty of being surrounded by a fortune in breakables.

She pretended to be interested in a display of cut-crystal toiletry articles and tried to look inconspicuous while she waited for her sister to catch up. Mary had fiercely insisted she wanted to navigate through the gift shop and into the restaurant on her own. If she needed assistance, she said baldly, she would ask.

Yet the urge to go back and steer Mary's chair through the obstacle course of fragile froufrous grew stronger by the second. Abby tightened her hold on her purse strap and on God's word—"be not anxious."

As Mary drew near, Abby's heart quieted. She approached the hostess's podium to claim their lunch reservation. Then she waited at the table with an encouraging smile while Mary jockeyed her wheelchair into position and set the brake.

Delight glittered in her eyes as she leaned over and whispered, "I did it! Slower than a snail maybe, but all by myself. And I didn't break anything."

"You were fabulous," Abby said softly, meaning every word.

"I'll get better. And faster." Mary turned toward the kitchen and sniffed. "Just smell those fresh-baked herb scones. That's what I call incentive!"

Abby spied Janet Heinz and Margaret Blackstock entering the restaurant section and waved. Mary's close friends had showered Abby with warmth, support and friendship from the day she arrived.

Janet took the seat across from Abby. Margaret settled her full-figured frame on the chair to Abby's right.

"Good afternoon, ladies." A young waitress with a name tag that said "Ida" appeared immediately. "I know at least two of you are on a lunch schedule. May I get something for you to drink while you check out the menu?" A pen with a pink rose fastened to the blunt end stood poised above her order pad. "Let's see, Janet and Mary take Earl Grey Breakfast Blend. Margaret wants coffee." She turned to Abby. "And you'll have . . . ?"

"Make mine coffee too." Abby smiled.

The waitress recited the luncheon specials before adding, "People are raving about the cheese and broccoli quiche."

"That's what I'll have, then." Abby set the menu aside.

"I'll have the quiche too," Mary said.

After a quick visual exchange between Janet and Margaret, they made the selection unanimous.

With the orders in, Mary, Janet and Margaret launched into a flurry of conversation.

Abby tried to listen with interest as they caught Mary up on recent events and their plans for the summer. Abby knew the people under discussion only by name and her thoughts kept straying to Janet and Margaret.

They were fixtures on the island. Between them, they knew any news worth knowing—and sometimes more. One or both of them might know about Whale Riders, Inc.

Abby adjusted the heavy flatware with tiny roses around the handles and wondered how to bring up the subject without giving away her secret.

The meal arrived and shortly after, Janet turned to her and said, "My, but you're quiet today."

"Just a little preoccupied," Abby responded.

Mary settled back in her wheelchair, her eyebrows knit with concern. "You've been quiet all morning. What's going on in that terrific brain of yours?"

Abby smoothed her napkin. She might not get a better opening. "Have any of you heard of Whale Riders, Inc.?"

"Do they do whale watching tours?" Mary grazed a tiny pat of butter onto her scone.

Abby shrugged. All she knew was that the corporation was the official owner of the old-growth timberland.

"Let's back up a little." Janet cut into her quiche. "How did you hear about this company and in what context?"

"They own a piece of land—"

"And you want to buy it and move back to Sparrow Island," Margaret interrupted. "How wonderful. I know a talented architect who will build—"

"Don't get carried away, Margaret." Janet's hazel eyes narrowed thoughtfully. "That isn't what she said."

Margaret and Mary exchanged a disappointed glance. "Well," Margaret sighed, "we can hope."

The earnestness in their faces sparked a new awareness in Abby. *They really want me to stay.* The realization surprised her with a sharp tug at her emotions. "One thing at a time," she said as much to herself as to the others. "Let's eat before it gets cold."

Moments later, Janet said, "Tell us about this land and why you're interested in it." She raised her fork with a steamy piece of quiche on the end. "Between bites, of course."

"I was hoping to get permission from the owners to do a little birding on their property," Abby began, choosing her words carefully. "There isn't much old-growth timber left in this part of the world, but there is a patch here on Sparrow Island. I found out yesterday it's owned by a corporation named Whale Riders, Inc."

"Where on the island?" Margaret asked.

Abby described the location she had marked with a big X on the map from Hugo and added, "The previous owners were a family named Bowditch."

"Bowditch." Mary finished off the crumbs from her scone. "Why does that name sound familiar?"

"Because it was the great tragedy of our youth." Janet put down her fork. "Only I don't think any of us paid attention to it at the time. We had more important things to think about, like boys, dances and who was going to Vietnam."

"You've been holding out on me." Margaret's Brooklyn accent became pronounced. "There was drama on Sparrow Island and you kept it a secret?"

"I haven't thought about it in years. I only remember the incident because it upset my parents so." Janet poured tea into Mary's cup, then refreshed her own. "In the 1960s, the Bowditches were to Sparrow Island what the Kennedy family was to Hyannis Port, with one notable exception."

"That being?" asked Abby.

"David Bowditch only had one child. I think his name was Jonah. There was a horrible boating accident and Jonah didn't survive. After that, David became a recluse. He died about ten years ago. We, that is my husband Doug and I, figured some relative back east inherited the estate. Since nothing ever came of it, at least nothing I've heard, their lack of interest was fine by us."

"I most definitely agree," Mary said with conviction. "No

one wants bulldozers showing up to level more trees for houses or condominiums."

"If the owners know what they have here, it still might happen," Margaret lamented. "Sparrow Island is like a little Garden of Eden. That's what brought Joe and me out here when he retired. Naturally, now that we're here, I want to close the door."

They ate and talked a little while longer. Then, their lunch hour over, Janet and Margaret took their leave to return to work.

"Let's go over to the newspaper office and check the archives," Abby suggested.

Mary shook her head. "Do you mind going without me? I have some paperwork of my own."

"You do? I'm sure Marvin took care of the insurance."

"Not that. My business." Mary grinned. "Candace has been handling everything for the last couple of months. We have a lot to go over and I'm itching to see how we're doing."

"I'm sure you are." Abby laughed softly. "If all the flowers you received in the hospital and while you were at the retraining center came from Island Blooms, I'd say you have nothing to worry about on the ledger sheet."

Mary checked behind her and rolled her chair back. "Hey, I'm the only flower shop in town. I better have the market cornered or figure out why not."

ABBY ACCOMPANIED MARY to the flower shop, stopped in long enough to say hello to Candace, then retraced her steps on

Shoreline Drive. After passing Holloway's Hardware, she turned left, climbed the hill and cut through the park to Kingfisher Avenue. Half a block down on the right sat *The Birdcall* newspaper office.

An old-fashioned bell attached to the door jangled when she entered.

"Nice touch," she murmured, looking up at the bell.

"I'll be with you in a moment," William Jansen called from the back.

Intrigued by a pair of large picture frames showcasing two five-year-old pages of *The Birdcall*, she said, "Take your time."

She studied the headlines on the front page and the editorial section. Neither carried any earthshaking news and she guessed they were William's first edition as owner and editor-in-chief.

Last night, in preparation for a visit to *The Birdcall*, she had researched William C. Jansen on the Internet and learned a great deal, most of which puzzled her. Why would a successful tycoon come out to Sparrow Island and run a weekly newspaper? Surely, it had been a drastic change to go from being the CEO of Jansen Essentials—producers of baby products—in dynamic, fast-paced Chicago to running a newspaper in sleepy Green Harbor.

To fill in the blanks Abby had phoned her father and learned that William had always wanted to be a reporter. He'd even worked at the *Chicago Tribune* in his youth. His talent hadn't matched his aspirations, so he went to work in the family business.

When he turned fifty, he sold everything, retired to Sparrow Island and bought *The Birdcall*. The tone of the newspaper immediately improved. A businessman, he knew the importance of keeping islanders informed not only of local interest stories, but also state, national and world events.

The former editor, a retired librarian with cataracts, had favored lengthy articles full of arcane research that few readers appreciated. Her father's complaints echoed in Abby's mind and she suppressed a smile. William's ability to proofread copy virtually eliminated the typographical errors that used to frustrate most of the readers.

She moved to the long counter and recalled her father's assertion that few people knew what they really wanted to do and of those, even fewer risked actually doing it. It gave her a new admiration for William Jansen. He might be a little eccentric, but he had a dream and he followed it instead of continuing to labor in a field he didn't love.

"Miss Stanton," he said as he entered the front office. "I apologize for keeping you waiting. My staff took a late lunch. What can I do for you?"

"I'm hoping you can help me with a little research."

He approached the high counter, his brown eyes bright with curiosity. "Do I sense a story here?"

She hoped not. Her worst nightmare was for the cold eye of the press to scrutinize her every move. "It's a bit more personal." Seeing his interest wane, she hastily added, "Although it could have real importance if things work out the way I hope."

"That's very nice, but—"

"I thought you'd be interested in an exclusive."

"An exclusive?" he asked, his voice an octave higher than his normally high-pitched tone.

"Yes, providing my research corroborates my initial investigation."

"Can you tell me what it's about? A teaser I can use in the paper?"

Abby considered his request for a long moment before answering, "Old-growth timber."

William blinked twice. Each sweep of his short, thick eyelashes wiped another level of excitement from his face. "Timber. You're talking about conservation. Environmentalism."

"Possibly a great deal more." She paused, trying to figure out how to get what she needed without revealing anything. Yet, there was only one choice. Honesty. "What I really need is a LexisNexis link. I thought, who better than William Jansen to have access to such a powerful search tool.

"After all, you *are* the newspaper. You check out your stories and you run a column on separating facts from factoids, which is excellent by the way. I'd love to see it syndicated so I can continue to enjoy it when I return to New York."

The sincere compliment repaired some of the damage done to his hopes for a juicy headline. "Well, I don't just let anyone who walks off the street use my computers, Miss Stanton. I have confidential information on them. Opening them up for public use—"

"I'm not just anyone. My interest has a professional bent. Remember, if things work out, I am going to give you an exclusive. In the meantime, you can think of me as a volunteer reporter on a matter you have neither the time nor the interest to pursue."

She watched him decide whether to give her a flat refusal, bluster a bit or open the gate that allowed her access to the computers. Hoping to nudge him in the right direction, she said, "I already know how to use LexisNexis. We have it at Cornell."

"All right," he said after a long moment. "But keep this to yourself. I don't want half the islanders flocking in here for computer time. Next thing you know, they'll want to send e-mails to their kids on the mainland and their folks in Florida."

"I appreciate your concern and promise to keep your generosity quiet," she assured him.

He unlatched the swinging gate and held it open for her. "Come to the back so people walking by won't see you behind the counter."

Once Abby tapped into the enormous database for company data, public and government records, she maximized her efforts by checking the list she had made the night before.

Even with all the preparation and the information she gleaned from the computer, her searches took her from one dead end to another. After an hour, she took off her glasses and rubbed the bridge of her nose in disappointment.

Whale Riders, Inc., wasn't a real business. It was a dummy corporation, a legal construct that concealed the names of the true owners of the property.

What were they hiding? And why?

"Who are you?" she whispered at the computer screen.

The cursor blinked in silence.

Chapter Eleven

I<small>N THE FLOWER SHOP</small>, carnations, lillies, freesia and jasmine perfumed the air and filled Abby's senses. On her left, pink asters, purple larkspur, blue delphiniums and yellow-gold daisies overflowed their decorator pot, a riotous garden feast for the eyes.

On the right, a refrigerated case held delicate vases of roses, tulips and irises sprigged with baby's breath and lily of the valley. Next to the case, dracaena, schefflera and philodendron in various shades of green created the look and feel of a mountain glen. Near the front desk, stair-step bonsai trees accented a magnificent arrangement of African violets. Colorful foil, ribbons and balloons festooned the display rack behind the counter.

"Mom called," said Mary as she wheeled out around the counter.

"Is everything okay with her and Dad?"

"Yep. She wants us to stop by."

"Let me guess—for dinner."

"My, my, my. You're developing a gift for prophesy."

Laughing, Abby asked, "Did you get your paperwork all done?"

"We got it started." Candace Grover came out of the back room carrying a flower arrangement nearly as big as she was and placed it on a low table beside the counter. An inch or so shorter than Abby, the store manager looked like she needed to carry an anchor in a strong wind. The strawberry-blonde hair shimmering to her waist would make quite a sail.

"Frankly, I think Mary is dragging the paperwork out so she has an excuse to return to work." Candace's teasing grin lit her pale brown eyes. "She misses this place. And the customers and I miss her something fierce."

Abby hadn't considered the prospect of Mary returning to Island Blooms. But why shouldn't she? After she adjusted to life in a wheelchair, the greatest obstacle was transportation. With the Lord's help, they could find a way to handle that.

"You're the manager, Candace. The only way I'll be coming back full-time is if business triples and you move away."

Candace stepped back, tilted her head and gave the arrangement a final examination. "What if I quit?"

"I'll hunt you down and drag you back," Mary said, then laughed with Candace.

"Sounds like you have a job for life," Abby chimed in.

"That it does," she agreed. "You two had better get over to the store and buy the ice cream your Mom wanted."

"Ice cream?" Abby pretended to be horrified.

"Frozen yogurt. We'll be saving Dad a trip to town and

the temptation to buy the real stuff." Mary wheeled to the back of the shop and emerged moments later with her purse. "I'm ready."

LATER, AS THEY LEFT The Green Grocer on Kingfisher Avenue, Mary said, "Ah, this sun feels good."

Abby hung the heavy grocery bags on the handles of Mary's chair to free her hands for pushing. "It sure does. I was beginning to get frostbite in the frozen food section." They headed toward the car.

"Hey, ladies," Joe Blackstock called cheerfully. "Do you need a hand?"

Abby thanked God for always sending help when it was needed.

"Thanks, Joe. I'm getting better at this, but I have a ways to go before Abby and I can do this easily."

"*Whoa.* You are one strong lady, Mary," Joe exclaimed after helping her into the car. "What have you been doing? Lifting weights?"

"That's precisely what I do. It's also a great incentive not to gain a single pound."

"I get it. You gain it, you lift it." He closed the door then stowed the chair in the Lincoln's trunk.

"Thanks again, Joe," Abby said.

"Any time." He waved and headed into The Green Grocer.

Mary waited in the car while they stopped at the house and Abby unloaded their groceries.

On the way to the Stanton Farm, Abby doubled back through Green Harbor. As they passed the post office, Mary cleared her throat. Abby recognized the agitation in that sound. "What's on your mind?"

"What's going on, Abby? The trip to Friday Harbor yesterday, the questions at lunch today and the time you spent over at *The Birdcall* have my curiosity humming."

It was a good question and deserved an answer. Despite her sister's interest, Abby had held on to the discoveries she made at the courthouse. *Why?*

A lack of trust.

The realization that she was the problem in their relationship made Abby's heart skip a beat.

How can that be? Mary has trusted me with everything—the remodeling of her home, her finances, the insurance and her friends. What's the matter with me? Why don't I trust her? When did I stop?

"What are you looking for?"

Faced with the choice of jeopardizing her search for the murrelets or compromising the fragile relationship with her sister, Abby chose to step out in faith.

Taking a deep breath, she provided a detailed account of spotting the birds, the follow-up actions she and her father did to identify them as marbled murrelets and her subsequent research.

"Professionally I can't claim the birds are here on the flimsy evidence of a single sighting. It was dusk. I didn't have my equipment with me. Not even my binoculars." She shot a nervous glance at Mary. To her surprise, her sister was listening intently.

"So professionally, it would be a disaster if news got out and you're wrong."

Her heart in her throat, Abby nodded. "Hugo gave me a map with the old-growth timber spots marked on it. Only one of the sites turned out to be genuine old growth."

"Hugo Baron knows?"

"Yes."

"Who else?" Mary asked, her eyebrows drawing together in concern.

"Frank Holloway overheard Dad, Hugo and me talking at your welcome home party." Turning into the driveway of the Stanton Farm, Abby slid her gaze back to her sister. "And now you, Mary. I'm trusting you to keep this to yourself."

"You say that like you *don't* trust me. You should know better. I would never repay your kindness with an act of betrayal." Mary's chin hardened into a familiar expression of stubbornness. "That's what it would be if I divulged your secret."

"Yes," Abby agreed as she parked the car.

"There's more you haven't told me," Mary urged.

"Only because I want to discuss it with Mom and Dad too. I'm hoping they might know something about the Bowditches or Whale Riders, Inc. I'm running out of rocks to turn over."

The door of the Stanton home opened and Ellen, George and Sam came out to greet them.

"Let's go inside." Mary gave Abby's arm a reassuring squeeze. "And don't worry, I'm on your side."

"After Sam leaves, we'll put our brilliant Stanton minds and memories together and see what we actually know."

"Right. Remember what Bobby said about my memory . . ." Mary let her voice trail as they shared a knowing grin.

"Dinner's almost ready," Ellen announced as Sam retrieved Mary's chair, then Mary.

While Abby collected their purses, her father opened her door and asked, "Did you bring the ice cream?"

"Sorry, Dad. It's frozen yogurt. And it's melting in the trunk."

"Better than nothing."

After dinner, Sam left for his apartment in Green Harbor and it quickly became apparent that their mother knew about the bird sighting. "Your father leaves the house every night just before twilight and stays out there until dark," said Ellen. "He carries his binoculars and the big camera with a telephoto lens. That means only one thing to me. He's looking for a specific bird."

"Nothing I do escapes your mother's notice," he said with a wry smile. "As for our birds, I'd hoped they would fly this way again, Abby. If I could get a picture, you'd have concrete evidence to substantiate their presence. No luck so far."

"Me neither," Abby mused while refilling the ice water pitcher.

"What do you mean?" her father asked.

"Yesterday," Mary said to their parents, "when Abby went to Friday Harbor, she was doing research."

"On what?"

Abby explained her visit to the courthouse to find the name of the owner of the old-growth timberland. "So, Dad, Mom, unless one of you have heard of a corporation named Whale Riders, Inc., I'm looking at another wall."

Her father shook his head. "It doesn't sound familiar. What do they do?"

"That's part of my problem. I don't know. In fact, the absence of information about the company is mind-boggling. As near as I can tell, and I checked and triple-checked as much as you can when the only address available is a post office box in Delaware, this company doesn't do any business."

"What do you mean?" Ellen asked.

"It makes nothing. It sells nothing. It has no board of directors, no officers." Saying aloud what she knew added to Abby's puzzlement. "And it is so insulated, there isn't any way to find out who actually owns it or controls the land and the fortune David Bowditch left."

"Wait!" Her father set his water glass down with a thud. "What does David Bowditch have to do with it?"

"The land was his," Abby said slowly.

"Go on."

"According to public records, he left the property and his entire estate to Whale Riders."

George leaned against the backrest of his chair. "Well that's a twist I never would have expected."

"You knew him?"

"Not really. When we first came to the island, everyone in the Northwest knew who he was. Some people loved him, some feared him and others wouldn't have crossed the street to pull him out of a mud hole." George turned to his wife. "It's been what, Ellen, thirty-five years or more since David closed the door on everything? And everyone."

Abby's pulse quickened as her mother nodded.

"Good grief, Dad," Mary interjected. "Why wouldn't people pull him out of a mud hole?"

"David was . . . a difficult man. Wealthy, powerful, he served several terms as a state senator down in Olympia. He had his own ideas about how things should be run and he was pretty high-handed putting them into practice. He really knew how to use the media to win support. I don't know if he believed it or not, but around here he acted as if a man's mea-sure was the size of his bank account. His was plenty big."

Ellen covered her husband's hand with hers and said, "Folks either liked David Bowditch or they didn't. And either he liked you or he didn't. With him, there was no middle ground and he didn't bend. He even had a falling out with his son and publicly disowned him."

"That's awful. Why would he do such a thing?"

Rather than answer Abby's question, Ellen looked at her husband.

"No one knows," he said. "It happened right before Jonah died in a freak boating accident. David never got over losing his son. I think he blamed himself and that's too heavy a burden for any man to carry. Especially alone.

"I tried to bring him God's comfort. He called the law on me. David said he'd have me arrested if I trespassed again."

Ellen said, "You ought to talk to Hugo Baron, Abby. If anyone would know anything about that land and Whale Riders, Inc., it would be him."

"Why Hugo?" Abby asked. "He wasn't even on the island when David went into seclusion."

"No, he wasn't." George stroked his wife's fingers. "But Hugo knows more about the history of the people and this island than most natives."

Hugo already knew about the birds and her search. What did she have to lose?

Chapter Twelve

Biting her tongue and praying for patience, Abby flipped the French toast in the electric skillet. Sometime during the night, the cranky bug had bitten Mary again and nothing Abby did seemed to please her. They had even changed her clothing three times before she finally settled on her first choice, a lovely teal print shirtwaist.

Abby rolled her shoulders to ease a lingering twinge and checked the bacon in the microwave. Deciding it needed a little more time to reach perfect crispiness, she pressed the extra minute button and asked lightly, "What's on the agenda today?"

"What makes you think I have an agenda?" Mary retorted.

Because you have always had an agenda. Wishing for an end to the mood swings, Abby stole a look at her sister. Until Mary's emotions leveled out, delving into the volatile trust issue that separated them would only make things worse. "Are you feeling okay?"

"Just jim-dandy fine," Mary said as Blossom jumped down from her lap.

It sure didn't sound like she was fine. Even the cat knew to make herself scarce during her mistress's turbulent times.

Mary bumped into the wrought iron garden stand holding a large pot of kitchen herbs and muttered something under her breath. Earlier, she had irritably insisted Abby move the stand from its new, safer location in the corner, back to the spot it had occupied for the last ten years.

Certain it would prove inconvenient, and just as positive Mary would have to find that out for herself, Abby had quietly complied with the request. Since then, she found herself wondering if her sister regretted having turned so many of the remodeling decisions over to her. *More to the point, why did Mary trust me with all this in the first place?*

Abby put the butter and syrup on the table. Twice she had posed that very question; once at the beginning of the project and again at the welcome home party. Both times, she received vague nonanswers.

Her desire to identify and resolve the problem between them made those specifics more important than ever. Yet, her sister's current mood made asking again too risky. The last thing they needed was an emotional explosion.

The microwave dinged and Abby removed the bacon. She stacked the slices of French toast in the skillet before transferring them to the breakfast china. As she carried the food to the table, she tried to remember the last time she'd eaten breakfast in her own home.

Looking forward to the meal, she took her place across from

Mary, bowed her head and said a prayer of thanksgiving. Almost before she finished, Mary pushed away from the table, went to the linen drawer and withdrew placemats and matching napkins.

Abby's hopes for a pleasant meal sank. She had forgotten Mary's preference for a proper table setting. Once their plates were on the placemats, Abby smoothed her linen napkin over her lap.

It seemed such a small faux pas, yet they ate without speaking, Mary preoccupied and Abby feeling chastised for her oversight. Rather than stew in silence, she decided to "turn from evil and do good; seek peace and pursue it." Psalm 34:14 was one of her favorite signposts on the road of life.

She got up, fetched coffee and returned to the table. "Let me take your plate." Abby set down the cups on their saucers and gathered the empty dishes.

"Breakfast was very good." The edge in Mary's voice lost its sharpness. "Thank you."

Accepting the compliment as conciliatory, Abby said, "You're very welcome."

Smiling inside and out, she made quick work of the cleanup chores and returned to the table to enjoy her coffee.

"It's past time for your department head to phone you, isn't it?"

"Soon." Abby glanced at her watch. "I don't expect him to call for another five minutes or so."

"Maybe you ought to call him now, while you're having your coffee."

"I could, but he won't be in his office." She assessed the anxiety pinching the faint laugh lines around Mary's eyes. "He's just returned from China, so I'm sure he's coping with a tremendous time shift."

"I forgot about that." Mary toyed with her coffee cup.

"Knowing Jerome, he tried to get on New York time immediately, but overslept. It's a standard joke around the office. We all try to bounce back like we did in our twenties, but we've lost some of our spring."

"And here I thought you were procrastinating because—well, never mind."

"Let's get something straight, Mary. These people are my friends. They understand the importance of family. Some of them are sacrificing time with their loved ones to pick up my commitments. I'm going to ask them for more time. At the very least, I owe them the consideration of an explanation."

The phone rang, interrupting Mary's response.

Abby pushed away from the table. "That's probably Jerome now."

She answered the phone and nodded an affirmative to Mary. "How was China?"

Jerome's excitement was contagious. In his enthusiasm Abby heard the siren call of her life at Cornell. Her work, her friends and the special energy that seemed to flow from the graduate students she supervised tugged at her heart.

In her practical mind, she realized that as much as she would have loved the fieldwork in China, she was far more comfortable with the slower pace of island living. Yet the very idea scared her. She wasn't ready for the seasons of her life to change.

"We miss you around here," Jerome said. "What's this about you staying out there?"

"I miss you, too, but my family needs me here a while longer."

"How long do you need, Abby?"

"It's difficult to say." For so many reasons, the main one being the complex relationship with the woman watching her and barely taking a breath.

"Give me something to work with at Human Resources."

Therein lies the rub. Abby switched the phone to the other ear. She could not leave until she was confident in her sister's abilities to live independently. If determination alone were sufficient six weeks would be enough. But progress, like life, was seldom a straight line. The mountains Mary was climbing were bound to have even bigger valleys than the one they walked through this very morning. "Two months or so," Abby answered vaguely.

"You don't sound certain."

"I'm not." In fact, she felt torn. Even two months might not be enough.

"All right," Jerome said, exhaling audibly. "Suppose we try a different tactic. Can you think of any professional reason for you to stay on Sparrow Island? Something I can use to avoid a leave of absence and still justify shuffling your students if you need more time?"

A sudden dryness in Abby's mouth sent her reaching for her cup. "As a matter of fact, there is just such a reason." As she gulped her coffee, her reluctance to reveal the secret of the marbled murrelets vanished. God worked all things for His purpose. If the appearance of the rarities bought her more time with Mary, He had made it happen.

"Don't keep me in suspense. Tell me."

With fresh optimism, Abby detailed the sighting and the steps she had taken to track down the little brown birds. When she finished speaking, the silence on the other end of the telephone line was deafening.

"Are you there, Jerome? Or did I bore you into a nap?"

"I'm here. Just thinking."

"Care to share?"

"My first impression, after recovering from my excitement over the return of a species on the rarity list, is that what you have is flimsy."

"I agree. That's why I was hesitant to say anything."

"Well, I know you, Abby. If anyone can prove those birds are nesting there, it's you. Let me digest this and come up with an authorization plan for a study grant."

"A study grant?" Her pulse pounded and the phone felt slippery. "Are you serious?"

"Absolutely. Meanwhile, keep looking. If we can work this out and find funding, when you're ready to go public it might be possible for us to buy the nesting grounds."

Abby put down her empty cup and patted her chest to calm

her racing heart. When God blessed, He blessed abundantly. "All right. I'll do that."

When she hung up the phone, she felt positively giddy.

"I heard your side of the conversation, but not his." Mary twisted her napkin in her hands. "I'm on pins and needles here. Quick. Fill in the blanks, please."

"Jerome is going to do everything he can to help me stay here as long as I need to. On salary."

"Because of the birds?" Mary asked incredulously. "I'm surprised you told him about them."

"When God opens a door, the best thing you can do is walk through. If we can find the nesting site or evidence that the marbled murrelets are actually here, we'll have something to take to the university. Jerome will back me for a study grant. That will let me stay—" She shrugged her shoulders. "Who knows how long?"

"Who is 'we'? Do you have a mouse in your pocket?" Mary ran open palms across the armrests of her wheelchair.

"No, I've got Dad, Hugo and you!"

"Me? How? I wouldn't recognize a murrelet even if it knocked on the front door and introduced itself."

Abby got up, dropped the phone back into the charging cradle, plucked a pen from the drawer and took the calendar off the wall. "You know your schedule," she said, sitting down again. "I don't. We're going to put all your commitments on this calendar so I know where to be when. That way, I can schedule my search accordingly."

"What I need is a car," Mary said wistfully.

"I know Marvin has filed all the insurance paperwork. I imagine you'll get the settlement check for your lost wages pretty soon."

"Ah, another lesson in patience." Mary gave an exaggerated roll of her eyes and pursed her lips.

"Those are the toughest ones."

When Abby returned the calendar to its place on the wall, she marveled at the number and variety of activities that filled Mary's life.

"We have half an hour before I need to be at the library for my reading group." Mary wheeled down the hall to her bedroom. "Would you like to join us?"

Although the reading group did sound enticing, Abby was eager to get to the conservatory. "Not today, thank you. I'm going to take Mom's advice and talk to Hugo Baron. Let me know what book you pick for the next meeting."

"Seeing Hugo is a great idea. Take all the time you need. After the discussion ends, the group goes over to the Springhouse Café for lunch."

A couple of hours should be enough to look around at the conservatory and museum and ask Hugo what he knew about Whale Riders, Inc. "Okay, I'll pick you up there."

"Not necessary. Patricia Hale has a van and she'll bring me home. Go find your birds."

Feeling liberated, Abby followed Mary down the hall. "That'll be great."

For an instant, it seemed that Mary cast a look of consternation over her shoulder.

Abby dismissed it as a figment of her imagination. Her mind raced with possibilities. A grant was the answer she'd been looking for. With it she could stay on the island long enough to help Mary through this time of transition and not lose her standing at Cornell.

Jerome, the potential grant, everything was falling into place so perfectly. Why, then, did she feel as though she was trying to straddle two worlds, serve two masters?

Chapter Thirteen

Aꜰᴛᴇʀ ɢᴇᴛᴛɪɴɢ ᴅɪʀᴇᴄᴛɪᴏɴꜱ to the back room where Hugo was working, Abby strolled purposefully through the exhibits at The Nature Museum. Against meticulous backdrops, there were displays of animals that looked so real they seemed alive: an eagle clutching a salmon in its talons, a stealthy red fox poised to pounce, a harbor seal basking on a rock and wading herons eyeing the fish caught forever in a pool of glass. With each display, her admiration for the man and his considerable talent grew.

Several tourists huddled around a cutaway model of Mount St. Helens. Equipment hidden inside projected a computer-generated hologram of the May 18, 1980, eruption onto the plastic covering, giving the viewers an exciting visual lesson on the power of a pyroclastic flow and the resultant ash fallout.

Leaving them to *ooh* and *aah* over the spectacular special effects, she walked slowly past dioramas of extinct and endangered species. The contents were as impressive as the authenticity of the displays and the skill of the taxidermists.

Clangs, bangs and giggles drew her to the practical science room where several children and their parents played with the hands-on exhibits. She loved these interactive displays where learning about the laws of nature was so much fun. A smile stretched her cheeks as a young mother joined a pair of twittering four-year-olds running their palms over an enormous plasma ball to spark the electricity trails inside.

Near her destination in the back of the museum, Abby noted a mural featuring dozens of birds, the most prominent being eagles, owls and ducks. A sign on a large leaf in the mural said, "Coming soon: The Wonderful World of Wings."

Delighted with the title, she turned and looked back. Although small by big city standards, Hugo's museum was a true gem, a diverse and accurate teaching tool. He had a right to be proud of it.

She found the door marked "Private," knocked, then entered. Instantly, she felt like she'd stepped back in time to her first days as an intern. Cardboard boxes in every shape and size crammed the shelves lining the back wall. More boxes made a maze on the floor around the tables. Displays in a state of change or creation filled the corner.

"Abby!" Hugo's delight to see her was so obvious it made her smile. "I need your help."

"So I see." She eyed a stack of journals, files and books teetering on the nearest of two long tables. On the floor sat another carton filled with zippered plastic bags of tiny bird bones. "Rule number one—if it's at all questionable, fumigate. Rule number two—fumigate again."

Hugo chuckled. "Sounds like you had an *experience*."

It was her turn to laugh. "You could call it that. Very early in my career I came across a specimen riddled with nits. It was the only time in my life I seriously considered bathing in bleach." She shuddered. "I itched for days."

"I hope that didn't turn you off to the thrills of the hunt."

"Not a chance." She swept her arm out to include the room. "You call this the hunt. I think of it as kind of an ongoing birthday party . . . except you never know if the box you're opening is full of garbage or goodies."

"You're absolutely right. And speaking of goodies, I think I have one here."

He wove his way around the boxes on the floor until he stood in front of her and offered her the book he had been examining. "What do you think of this?"

She studied the book for several minutes. "It's a first edition and probably quite valuable. Where did you find it?"

"In one of the donation boxes Frank Holloway brought over from the San Juan Islands Birding Society."

"Frank?"

"Yes. He wanted to make amends for his outburst at the party. Not that he's changed his mind about all the newcomers to the island, but he likes what I'm doing here."

"I'm glad to hear it." Abby returned the book to Hugo. "It's surprising the society gave this away."

"I'm surprised by a lot of the stuff they sent." He put the book on an old rolltop desk and went to a closet. Opening the door, he said, "I'll ask them about it later. Right now, let's get you suited up."

"Sure. I'd love to help."

She put her purse on the shelf, exchanged her blazer for a smock and donned a pair of disposable gloves. "What do you mean, you're surprised?"

He led her back to the table. "Look at this. There are several more books just like it."

Inside the box he'd been working on was another book, begrimed with hardened layers of dust. The tape on the flaps was yellowed and brittle. "My guess is that no one has been through these in decades."

"Interesting." The sharp whine of an electric saw prevented her from saying more.

He hurried over to a bank of windows and closed the two that were open. "Sorry about that. Construction."

Abby looked outside. "My goodness! When you said you were expanding, I had no idea you meant an addition. I thought The Wonderful World of Wings would be in here."

"This isn't big enough for even a fraction of what I want to include. And we'll still need a workroom." He gave her a meaning-filled look. "Of course, we'll have formal offices too."

Obviously, Hugo didn't do anything small or haphazardly. Deciding she could talk and sort, she moved to another box on the table.

After a brief rundown on his system for categorizing the donations, he asked, "Have you made any progress with the murrelets?"

"Yes and no. Mostly no." She brought him up to date on her search for the stands of old-growth timber marked on his map and on her father's sunset vigils. "Mom says you're an expert on the history, land and people of Sparrow Island."

"I hope she doesn't regard me as a big mouth." Hugo placed a water-stained book so torn and wrinkled that it was unreadable on the discard pile.

"No. She speaks very highly of you." Abby opened a yellowed folder. The articles ripped out of magazines were nearly twenty years out-of-date and she added them to the discards. "In fact, Mom suggested I ask if you know anything about Whale Riders, Inc."

A thoughtful expression graced his patrician features as he put a picture book on terns in the save pile. "Whale Riders. Now there's a story. But something tells me you already know it."

"Partly. I'm hoping you can fill in the blanks."

"Okay. I'll begin at the beginning, then. When I was looking for a place for the conservatory, a beautiful piece of land caught my eye. With a little prying, I learned it belonged to David Bowditch and the only way to contact him was through the mail.

"He wrote 'Return to Sender' on my letters so I took to hanging out by his mailbox. Back then, there was one at the roadside on the edge of his property."

Hugo shook his head. "He was a strange man. Looked like a backwoodsman and spoke like a college professor. I gave him my best pitch but he was adamant about not selling. Even while apologizing for ordering me to stay off his property, he made it clear he would shoot any trespassers."

Hugo discarded a handful of mildewed papers. "After David died, I erroneously presumed he left the property to a relative. When the will became public record and I learned Whale Riders was the new owner, I made them a generous offer, one I was sure they wouldn't refuse. After all, what does a company on the East Coast want with a parcel of land on little Sparrow Island?"

Abby's hands stilled. "You found out who owns Whale Riders, Inc?"

"I hit a wall. The same one you did, I suspect. No one returned my phone calls or my letters. I couldn't even get a meeting. Worse, the paper trail ran cold."

"So cold, you would think the Ice Age returned," Abby grumped.

"I'm persistent. I had an offer to buy the land drawn up and sent it by registered mail to their post office box. When it didn't come back right away, I got excited. But two months later, the offer showed up in my mailbox with a big N-O in black marker across the back. The envelope had never been opened."

Hugo handed a spiral-bound notebook over to Abby. "Worth keeping? I already have a large collection of life lists."

She gave it a quick look. "Maybe. So that was the end of your attempts to buy the Bowditch land?"

"I'm afraid so." He picked up the next book and rested it on the corner of the cardboard box. "Although there is one thing that has gone around and around in my mind all these years."

"What?"

"The packet containing my rejected offer had a Seattle postmark."

She stopped what she was doing and met his gaze. "With a return address in Delaware?"

He nodded. "The same post office box I sent it to."

"How odd," she said, mulling over the anomaly. "Why would something mailed to Delaware be remailed in Seattle?" Nothing in the scanty information gleaned from William Jansen's LexisNexis had even hinted of a Seattle connection. "I wonder if I've been looking in the wrong places."

"What do you mean?" Hugo put the discard pile into the box he had just emptied.

"Well, if the Seattle postmark is significant . . . "

"Companies from all over the country incorporate in Delaware because of the favorable tax laws." He tucked the cardboard flaps into one another. "For all we know, the owner could have been on his way to the Orient, remembered the packet and dropped it in the mail at the airport."

Abby sighed. "I suppose you're right."

"Mr. Baron," said a soft voice from the direction of the door.

Startled because she thought they were alone, Abby looked up quickly and saw the teenager who had accompanied them on the bird walk last Friday.

"Hello, Miss Stanton," the girl said with a grin that showed off her braces.

"Hello, Rebecca." Abby glanced at Hugo.

"She's my newest employee." Hugo tilted his head toward Abby. "She's eager to work on the addition of The Wonderful World of Wings."

"I just started this week," Rebecca said. "Mr. Baron hired me for the summer and I love it. What's really cool is that Grandma is a docent two days a week. She's teaching me how to be a guide too."

When she paused long enough to take a breath, Hugo asked, "What can I do for you, Rebecca?"

"One of the men from the construction site wants to speak with you. I told him I'd see if you were available."

"Probably the foreman. Excuse me, Abby. I'll be back as soon as possible."

"Take your time," she said to his back as he closed the door behind him and Rebecca.

Abby dug into the box in front of her. How she had loved the early days of her career when she had time to pursue a single goal and see it through to the end. Whether sorting through grimy boxes or sitting in the same spot for hours documenting the nest building habits of various species, she had been fully engaged.

As the years progressed, she climbed the ladder of success and gained expertise. The university valued the recognition her name garnered and pressed her to do more symposiums and fundraisers. Each foray in that arena took time away from her true passion of studying the birds in their natural habitats.

If she had not fought to keep graduate students in her schedule, she would have spent the last few years giving speeches and attending conferences. She sighed. Her father was right. There was a season for everything.

Not wanting to deal with that uncomfortable issue while in the midst of something she enjoyed, she focused on the remote possibility of finding another treasure like the one Hugo unearthed. With an expert eye, she scanned dozens of books, folders and drawings.

Except for a large picture book with remarkable photographs, most items went into the discard pile.

At the bottom of the box, beneath a cluster of old pamphlets describing programs and events, Abby discovered one last item, a leather-bound journal. Expecting another life list, she opened it to the middle.

Her breath caught in her throat.

The old-fashioned script was almost as familiar as her own. The fountain pen had a new nib and the letters were crisp and clean. Shaking with disbelief, she sidled over to the chair at the desk, plopped into the seat and turned to the front of the book.

Her pulse played a John Philip Sousa march as she leafed through the pages. This was the second journal, the follow-up to the one in her room.

With each new drawing, her spirits soared higher. The

entire volume was dedicated to the marbled murrelets: their nesting habits, flight patterns, growth from chick to adulthood and the devastating effects of the loss of their habitat.

She leaned back and took several long, calming breaths. This was the kind of documentation invaluable for an on-site study.

"It looks like you found another treasure."

The sound of Hugo's voice startled her. She glanced up and saw him standing beside her. "You have no idea."

She closed the journal and hugged it to her heart. The book wasn't hers, but at this moment she could think of no other possession she wanted more. She had to make him understand. "There's something I haven't told you."

As soon as the words left her mouth, she realized that sharing the secret of the first journal was an essential first step. Watching for his reaction, she told him about finding the first journal and its amazing contents. "You and I are the only ones who know of its existence. And this picks up where the first one ended." She tapped a finger on the journal clutched to her bosom.

"It's easy to see why you want to keep it," Hugo said. "It might provide the key to the nesting grounds."

"I don't expect you to part with it permanently. It will become even more valuable once the presence of the marbled murrelets is established. I'd like to borrow it for a while. Perhaps you'd allow me to photocopy it." *Anything except take it back with a resounding no.*

Hugo crossed his arms. "I think we can work something out, but I want a couple of things in exchange."

"Tell me." If they were within her power, she'd give them to him.

"First, when you go hunting for the nesting grounds, I go with you. This little island looks tame from the vantage point of Green Harbor. You and I know how unforgiving the deep forests can be. One misstep or wrong turn . . ." His voice trailed away, underscoring the impact of his words.

She did know, and she understood the first condition came out of concern for her welfare. "All right. That's doable."

"The second is a bit less altruistic. I want to give you a complete tour of the buildings and the grounds. Show you my short-term and long-range plans. Last but not least, I want to cover all the details of the position I'd like you to accept here at the conservatory."

Abby took a deep breath. The journal pressed to her chest seemed to quiver as she slowly exhaled. "The tour and your plans . . . I look forward to both. As to the position, I can't make any commitments."

"You'll listen, though."

"Yes, I—"

The desk phone rang.

Hugo paused with his hand over the receiver. "You'll hear me out?"

He had no idea how he was complicating her life. Her plate was already full of difficult choices. She didn't need any more. Yet this wasn't a choice. It was an ultimatum. If she gave her word, she'd live by it. "Yes Hugo. I'll listen with an open mind."

He answered the phone, then offered it to her. "It's your father. It sounds urgent."

Chapter Fourteen

SPEED WALKING THROUGH the museum to the parking lot, Abby prayed for God's favor upon her parents. Despite her father's reassurance that everything was fine, his unheard of summons in the middle of the day incited the worry he had tried to quell.

She opened the car door and slid inside. Not until she switched on the ignition and reached for the steering wheel did she remember the journal clutched in her hand. With a sigh and a mental promise to finalize an arrangement with Hugo later, she tucked the book beneath the seat and put the Lincoln in gear.

Right now, nothing mattered beyond getting home to her parents. Fortunately, the farm was a short distance from the conservatory grounds. She strummed her fingers on the steering wheel as she waited for Frank Holloway's pickup truck to pass before she turned onto Primrose Lane.

A few minutes later, she pulled into the long driveway leading to the Stanton house. A sleek green automobile sat next to a plain vanilla sedan at the end of the drive beside her father's pickup truck. Confusion joined her concern.

The white car was familiar. The green Jaguar didn't belong to anyone she knew.

Abby dashed from the car, up the porch steps and into the house. Male voices sounded in the living room.

"Dad. Mom," she called out. "I'm here."

In the living room, she stopped short at the sight of Marvin Sherrod on the couch. Seated next to him was a man whose name she couldn't recall. Across from them, in their favorite chairs, her parents looked comfortably relaxed.

"Abby dear, I'm so glad you're here," Ellen said happily, rising to her feet. "Let me get you something to drink."

"No, Mom. Please." Abby reined in her anxiety. "What's happening?"

"Abby, you remember Victor Denny, don't you?"

The distinguished looking dark-haired man adjusted the horn-rimmed glasses on his long, straight nose and stood. Easily the tallest person in the room, he wore the distinct air of one accustomed to power.

A meeting, over a decade ago, took shape in her thoughts. With a warm smile, she shook hands with Mr. Denny.

When he resumed his seat, she greeted the man sitting next to him, "Hello, Marvin."

The grin enlivening his features grew wider. "Hi, Abby. Sit down and join the party."

"Here. Take my chair," her father offered.

Abby shook her head and settled on the ottoman. For a moment, no one spoke. "So what's up? I'm bursting with curiosity."

"It's about Mary," Marvin said. "Your parents had me come over because they know she's asked me several times about the insurance settlement for her car. She wants to use it as a down payment on a vehicle. She's talking about taking out a loan on her home to cover the rest. When Mary gets something in her head . . ."

"It doesn't end until she accomplishes it," Abby finished for him. "What's that got to do with me?"

"I need you to help me stall her," Marvin said.

"Why would I want to do that?"

"Let me explain." Victor Denny visually canvassed the others. "My wife Sherry and I owe your parents a debt of gratitude. Thirteen years ago, our son Kevin fell in with the wrong crowd. We tried everything we could think of to help Kevin change course, but we failed. He went into full rebellion against us and all the beliefs we hold.

"Then one night, he ran away. We didn't know where he went. He just disappeared." Victor laced his fingers and dropped his hands to his lap. "We prayed. We searched. Sherry and I hired private detectives, worked with the police. We nearly went crazy the first year, expecting a phone call that . . . expecting the worst."

Well aware of the rebellion far too many youngsters embraced during their first year of college, away from the steadying roots of home, Abby murmured, "The not knowing is the hardest."

"We were blessed. Thanks to your parents, our son returned. When Kevin came up the walk, I felt the same as the biblical father who ran out to greet his wayward boy. It didn't matter that he'd left, what he did while he was gone, just that he was home where I could see him, talk with him and touch him."

Racking her brain for a connection between Kevin Denny's running away and Mary's purchase of a new vehicle, Abby sat silently, hoping someone would enlighten her soon.

Color filled Ellen's cheeks. "Kevin was the young man who answered the ad we placed in *The Birdcall* for a farmhand. He told us he was eighteen and his name was Tom Smith."

"Oh, now I know who you're talking about. Tom was a sweet kid," Abby said. She recalled a Christmas he spent with the family and his questions about college life.

"When he came to the door asking for a job, I knew he was a troubled young man," George said nodding at the memory.

"He ate for days," Ellen added with a wistful look. "I don't know how long it had been since he'd had a real meal and a warm bed."

"He didn't start out as a happy camper, did he?" Victor asked as though he already knew the answer.

"George mentored him while they worked the fields together," Ellen said softly, as she looked at her husband.

"And you mothered him. Only the hardest of hearts wouldn't respond to you, honey."

Ellen scooted forward onto the edge of her chair. "We didn't know his real name until the day he said he was leaving and we took him down to the ferry. All the time he was here, God was at work in his life. Trusting us with his identity and making the decision to go home had to come from Tom. I mean Kevin," she corrected immediately.

Victor shook his head as though telling her not to worry. "Sherry and I are grateful beyond words for what you and George did for our son. You gave him shelter, meaningful work, guidance, direction and self-confidence—all the things he refused from us but needed desperately."

"Nothing affects us like our children," Marvin said thoughtfully. "They hold the power to be our greatest joy and our deepest heartbreak."

"Kevin came home eleven years ago. He lived with us while attending the University of Washington and graduated with honors," Victor said with an obvious mix of relief and parental pride. "He went on to medical school. Today, he's a doctor at Harborview Medical Center.

"That brings me to the purpose of my visit. Kevin recognized Mary's name when she was in the ICU at Harborview. He went to see her several times before they transferred her to Bellingham."

"You know," Ellen said slowly, "Mary mentioned being visited by a young doctor named Kevin Denny as though I should know who she was talking about. Truthfully, I didn't. I thought it would come to me. I still think of your son as Tom." She shrugged an apologetic shoulder.

"Back then, George, you wouldn't accept any compensation

for turning my son's life around. Sherry and I understood what you did wasn't for reward or gain and we honored your position."

Victor pulled a briefcase from beside the couch and placed it on the coffee table in front of him. Thumbing open the latches, he lifted the top. "Now, we'd like to return the favor."

Abby leaned closer for a better view of what he had in the briefcase. As though to satisfy her curiosity, he pulled out a heavy, glossy brochure and gave it to her. The advertisement showed a full-sized van with the side doors opened to reveal a wheelchair lift and a plush, modified interior.

"Of all the things Mary is coping with these days, there are two she shouldn't have to worry about: transportation and how to pay for it. Sherry and I want to make it as easy as possible for Mary to drive again."

Ripples of disbelief ran up and down Abby's insides. "Are you saying you want to buy this van for her?"

"We already bought it," Victor said with the kind of authority that brooked no argument.

"It must be very expensive," Ellen murmured as she looked at Abby on the ottoman.

"It is. For us, money is not an issue. Sherry and I have plenty, but it didn't help with our son. You did." Victor's voice cracked slightly.

Abby shifted on the ottoman. "Make no mistake Mr. Denny, I'm thrilled for your family and overwhelmed by your generosity. But I don't understand why I'm here and Mary isn't."

"As I said before, we need your help. Sherry and I want this to be a surprise for Mary. We need you to keep her from buying something before this van is ready.

"You see," Victor said, leaning forward, "we *know* this is the right vehicle for her. With it, she'll have total independence."

He pointed to a picture in the brochure George and Ellen were reviewing. "She won't need anyone to help her get in and out or deal with her wheelchair. Sherry loves hers."

A profound silence settled in the room as the truth behind the simple statement sank in.

"Your wife is in a wheelchair?" George asked.

Victor nodded. "The year after Kevin left us, she was in the middle of a ten-car pileup on Interstate 5. Her condition is the reason Kevin went into medicine."

Abby grasped the Dennys' motives. Mary wouldn't reject a gift from the heart. Not when it was forged in the twin fires of understanding and experience.

For a moment, Abby saw her parents through the eyes of a stranger. While she had built her life and career three thousand miles away, they changed their world one heart at a time through their love and living faith.

Chapter Fifteen

A<small>BBY EXAMINED</small> her limited wardrobe and wished she hadn't been so discombobulated when she accepted Hugo's invitation to dinner. As she selected the blazer she wore yesterday, then rejected it for that very reason, she wondered what she could have done differently. Nothing came to mind.

In truth, she had been so overwhelmed by her parents' and the Dennys' generosity she forgot Hugo was waiting for word on the "emergency" at the Stanton Farm. She didn't remember her promise to call him until she was heading for Mary's.

Abby had stopped at the end of the driveway, put the car in park and used her cell phone. Once she reassured him everything was fine, Hugo reminded her of the second journal and suggested they meet for dinner the next day to coordinate their search plans for the marbled murrelets.

With the secret of the Dennys' surprise gift thrumming through her veins, Abby realized she was rapidly running out of reasons to stay on Sparrow Island. Once Mary received the van and learned to drive it, she would no longer need chauffeuring.

It wouldn't be long before she could handle dressing and bathing alone either. She had already conquered the other private necessities of everyday life.

Hoping there would be enough time to establish the birds' presence on the island before her services were no longer required, Abby agreed to Hugo's invitation without giving his choice of restaurant a second thought.

Now, she wished she had. Winifred's was Green Harbor's most upscale dining establishment. Abby paired an embroidered sweater with her best birding shirt and checked her appearance in the mirror. The ensemble blended nicely with the twill trousers that mostly concealed her hiking boots. It would do, she decided, though Mary wouldn't approve.

Abby shook her head and fluffed her hair. Time away from her sister, even a few hours, was essential. Mary's mood had been so contrary today; the little progress they had made was in danger of vanishing altogether. She thought of Psalm 62:5: *Find rest, O my soul, in God alone; my hope comes from him.*

And from Mom and Dad, Abby thought wryly. Thank heaven they are coming over later for dinner and a movie with Mary. If anyone could put her in a more mellow frame of mind, they could.

Abby's gaze drifted from the mirror to the bed. Last night, sleep had been as elusive as the precious little birds she sought. Her thoughts, like homing pigeons, kept returning to her parents and every time she closed her eyes, she relived the dreadful feelings that had come with her father's unexpected phone call.

During the few minutes it took to race from the conservatory to their living room, her life priorities began a subtle, sideways shift.

The shift continued until long after midnight, when she knelt beside the bed, baring her questioning heart to the Lord and seeking His guidance. Inspired to look within, she made a stunning discovery. The trust issue dividing her and Mary stretched back to their teenage years and had colored her entire life.

Even now, fifteen hours later, the revelation still had the power to make her knees tremble; Abby moved to the bed and sat on the edge. The painful betrayal she thought she had forgiven four decades ago had not healed. Instead of cleaning the wound with openness and honesty, she'd covered it with denial. Hidden from the light, the injury continued to fester.

She folded her arms and hugged her middle. Back then, as a vulnerable teenager, she'd been too hurt and ashamed to share the secret of her broken heart. That was the day trust walked out of her relationship with Mary. Its absence cut between them, the space growing deeper and wider with every passing year, becoming a chasm that separated them.

Oh, Mary. Is it too late? After today, it certainly seems that way. Every time I try to open up, you shut me out.

Although a true reunion with her sister seemed further away and more impossible than ever, Abby refused to give in to a gathering cloud of doubt. Yes, the problem was too big for her to handle, but not too big for the loving God Who chose her before He laid the foundation of the world.

The faint click of the wall clock announced the hour.

Her troubles were in His more-than-capable hands. Determined to wait on His timing, she rose, picked up her tote bag and purse and left.

When she arrived at the restaurant, Hugo was waiting in the foyer. Abby silently conceded Mary was right. This was definitely a case of Land's End meets Neiman Marcus. In his Ralph Lauren tweed sports jacket, twill trousers and a soft cotton polo shirt, he was the picture of a perfect gentleman.

"Where we can see the water," Hugo told the hostess, then turned to Abby. "I hope that meets with your approval."

"My preference exactly." Smiling, she took his offered arm. She wouldn't worry about her attire. They had a great deal to discuss over dinner and even more to do afterward.

The hostess led the way through the empty restaurant to a choice spot with a spectacular view. "Dinner service doesn't begin for another five minutes so you'll have plenty of time to decide from our menu."

Abby and Hugo gave their beverage orders as they took seats on opposite sides of the table. Inside the embossed leather folders the hostess offered, the evening's entrees were inscribed in a calligrapher's hand on parchment. Somewhat surprised by the added formality, Abby quickly made her selection and looked around while Hugo decided between honey-grilled wild salmon or shrimp scampi over angel hair pasta.

"They've made some changes since I was here last." She especially liked the profusion of greenery.

Hugo set the menu down, his choice apparently made. "Have you had an opportunity to study the second journal?"

"I read it last night and both of them again today. The one we found at the museum is definitely the sequel to mine. The dates match up perfectly. So does the continuation of events. I'd like to photocopy both volumes to limit the wear on the originals. With your permission, of course."

"We have an excellent photocopy machine at the museum."

She reached into her tote bag and withdrew the folded map Hugo had given her several days earlier.

A waiter brought their beverages and left with their dinner orders. When they were alone again, Abby unfolded the map. "I've marked the areas I checked out on Sunday with Bobby. Along with what I learned about the Bowditch property boundaries, I've narrowed the area of probability to this grid. The timber stand we want is in the center."

She turned the map around and spread the section in front of Hugo. Tapping her finger on the heart of the old Bowditch land, she said, "There must be some way we can see into this area without trespassing." The temptation to just cross the boundary and conduct the search burned hotly. Finding the birds in their nest would give her a solid reason to stay without forcing her into a premature decision.

"Being lowered by helicopter would be the way to go," Hugo said with a teasing smile that turned solemn after he directed her attention to the map. "Look at these gradient lines of elevation. This is harsh terrain, Abby."

"True. But, we have to start somewhere. Until we obtain legal access, the periphery is all we have." She looked at Hugo's attire. Wondering if he'd mind shedding his dapper persona for a few hours and risk getting a little dirty, Abby continued, "I hoped we could start tonight. My parents are visiting Mary and they're bringing a movie."

Hugo's smile turned into a pleased grin. "Excellent. We'll begin our explorations after dinner."

Their meals arrived and they got down to the business of eating.

Half an hour after leaving the restaurant, Hugo took several back roads to the trailhead they agreed provided the best access. Hugo shed his jacket and changed from his Prada loafers into the hiking boots that he kept in his car. The day still held enough light for them to hike all the way to the barbed wire fence marking the old Bowditch property.

"Will you look at that," Abby said amazed.

"This?" Hugo tilted a metal "No Trespassing" sign hanging from a new strand of barbed wire.

"Yes. The small print says 'Private Property of Whale Riders, Inc.'" Puzzled, Abby exhaled her frustration in a loud sigh. "How do you suppose a company with no product and no business offices can send people out here to put up signs without anyone realizing there are strangers in town?" Most islanders were keenly aware of the presence of land developers. Surely, Janet or Margaret would have noticed.

"Excellent question." Hugo leaned close to the sign before

moving to the side and examining the fence repair at both posts. "See the way the wire is twisted? This was done by someone working from the other side of the fence."

Another mystifying complexity wasn't what she'd hoped to find. "Hugo, let's walk along the fence."

Their footfalls thumped and the sword ferns rustled, marking their passage through the underbrush. Just as the map indicated, the rugged terrain made for slow going. Abby gazed longingly at the other side of the fence. Somewhere in the heart of the prohibited land, an ancient treetop held a very special bird nest.

A faint, persistent beeping caught her attention. "What's that?"

Hugo touched his watch. "An alarm. It's time to go back. We're going to lose the light."

She scrutinized the steep slope ahead. Already the shadows were thickening. Soon, darkness would rise from the land even though the sky would be bright. Much as she yearned to keep going, they did need to return to the car.

"Next time, we'll bring ropes and climbing gear." She patted a big Sitka spruce. "I'm sure if we climb this tree we'd see a lot more."

Hugo gave her a skeptical look. "I've climbed my share of trees, but not recently. Frankly, I'd rather not require any medical services."

"I suppose you're right," Abby said thinking she'd have to start pulling together some climbing gear and show him how easy and safe it really was.

They hiked back to the trail and quickened their pace as the light faded. With the aid of flashlights, they arrived at the car a bit breathless and exhilarated.

"I haven't gotten this carried away and stayed out almost too long since I don't know when," Abby said, laughing.

"Probably not since your last hunt for a rarity," Hugo retorted with a grin.

"You're right. It was Brazil when Dad went with me." She rounded the car and opened the passenger door. "When was the last time you stayed out too long?"

"Africa, 1975." Hugo opened the door and slid behind the steering wheel. "Just before my wife died."

"I'm sorry. If you'd rather not talk about it, please don't. I had no idea one was related to the other."

"I don't mind. It has been thirty years." He put on his safety belt and met her gaze. "Clarissa was a unique woman."

"Was she with you when you stayed out too long?"

"In a manner of speaking, you could say we both stayed out in the Kenya brush too long. The rains had started. She caught malaria. The political situation turned nasty. It took days for us to get out. By then, we were out of medicine and Clarissa was out of time. The fever killed her."

"I'm sorry for your loss, Hugo."

"It took a while to accept. I'll never understand why Clarissa died of malaria and I didn't contract the disease. We were together all the time."

He started the car and pulled out. "Her mission here was

finished, mine wasn't. So, I keep expanding what she and I started and trust God to guide me."

Abby couldn't agree more. She knew God was guiding her on her own quest. The question was: What was she going to ultimately find?

Chapter Sixteen

"WHERE HAVE YOU BEEN?" Mary's icy demand frosted the air with anger.

Abby froze with one knee raised and her fingers entwined in the laces of her hiking boot. Her confusion grew as she studied her sister in the harsh glare of the laundry room lights. Hair askew, mascara smudged and shoulders rigid, she looked utterly frazzled.

Lowering her foot to the floor while racking her brain for the reason behind Mary's mood, Abby said slowly, "Hugo and I were looking for the birds. We need to—"

"You said you were going to dinner." Mary shoved a stray lock of hair behind her ear. "We expected you hours ago."

Praying for the soft words that turned away wrath, Abby went down on one knee and finished untying her bootlaces. The right words were nowhere to be found and, in what she knew was a feeble attempt to diffuse the situation, she asked, "Did you and Mom and Dad have a good visit?"

"No, thanks to you. We thought you were going to watch

the movie with us, like we used to do. They even brought popcorn. But, no, you were too busy gallivanting around. We expected you no later than seven. It's ten-thirty and you didn't even bother to call."

Astounded that, at their ages, Mary would even think of imposing a curfew or try to direct her activities, Abby struggled to hold her tongue.

Mary pointed an accusing finger at the floor in front of the washing machine. "At least clean up the mud you tracked in. I'll phone Mom so she and Dad can quit worrying about you lying on the side of the road."

"Why would they—" The words turned to dust in Abby's mouth. Of course, an accident would be their first concern whenever someone was late or stayed away longer than expected. "You're right, Mary. I'm sorry I caused such worry. I should have cued you in on all of my plans for the evening and called when it got dark."

Mary backed up slightly. "Yes, you should have done both. You have no idea what it's like to be trapped inside an overturned car, not knowing whether you're going to live or die before someone finds you. Nor do you know how it feels to have Henry Cobb carry that news to Mom and Dad."

Mary jerked her wheelchair into the kitchen. "Your comings and goings are not all about you, although you seem to think so. We were worried sick." Turning abruptly, she headed in the direction of the phone.

Abby stared at the mess on the floor until the sounds of her sister's conversation in the other room broke through her stunned inertia. Belatedly, she understood she had unwittingly caused the people she loved the most a great deal of unnecessary distress. Intense worry often turned into anger. Mary's fury was a measure of her fears.

After stripping off her remaining boot and cleaning the forest debris from her shoes and the floor, Abby went to the kitchen to wash her hands. The late hour fueled her remorse. Her parents were early risers, like the cows and chickens that expected to be fed on schedule.

"Were Mom and Dad still up when you called?"

"Do you think they'd go to bed while they were worried about you?" Mary opened the refrigerator and removed the orange juice. "Of course they were up."

"I should call." Abby turned off the water.

"And keep them up later than it is? That's not very considerate."

Abby didn't think her parents had gone to sleep in the last five minutes, but for the sake of harmony, she said, "I'll call in the morning. Obviously, this situation is my fault. I'm not accustomed to someone needing to know where I'm going and how long I'll be gone."

"I know," Mary snapped, pouring juice into a glass. "You answer to no one."

"In New York, that's true." Abby's schedule was her own business. As long as she showed up when promised, no one cared where she went or how long she stayed.

"This isn't New York."

"I've noticed. There, when someone wants to get in touch with me, they call me on my cell phone. You could have done that, too, and saved everyone the worry."

Mary slammed the juice carton onto the countertop. "Oh, now it's my fault."

"We're not talking about fault," Abby persisted with all the patience she could muster. "We're talking about communication. It flows both ways."

"That's easy to say when you're on the receiving end."

Mary seemed determined to extract a pound of flesh as punishment for an oversight Abby freely acknowledged. "What do you want from me, Mary? I've apologized. In the future, I'll make sure I call you and/or Mom so you won't be concerned."

"Will you also ask permission before you scribble on the fence?" Mary snapped.

Justified or not, the discussion grew more convoluted by the moment. "The fence? What are you talking about?"

"Nothing. Never mind. I'll scrub it off tomorrow." Mary closed the juice carton and put it back in the refrigerator.

"Someone wrote on the fence?" The very idea of an intruder in the backyard while Mary was home alone sent a chill of horror through Abby. No wonder her sister was so wound up.

"I thought you did it." Mary picked up the juice glass and wheeled over to the table.

"Me? You can't be serious."

"Why not? I don't know you anymore, Abby. I've tried to include you in my life by inviting you to my reading group. You were too busy. You don't want to learn how to knit and that's fine. Crafts don't interest you. All you can say about that is that I have too much stuff."

"I never said that."

"You didn't have to. Your 'I don't want to get involved' attitude says it for you. I'm beginning to think the only common ground we have is our parents, and then only when you come to visit. All I'm asking of you is to consider them while you're here.

"You live too far away to help out when one of them is ill or there's a crisis in their lives. When you leave, once again it will be up to me to handle the things they can no longer do. You miss out on the responsibility, but you also lose out on the joyful times."

Abby bit her lip to hold back a soul-deep groan. Much of what Mary said was true and was a resounding echo of the troubles Abby had poured out in prayer only last night. Certain this was the time, God's time, she collected two pens and a notepad and took a seat across from Mary.

"Okay, let's clear the air." Abby tore off the top sheet of paper and put the pad and second pen in front of Mary. "Make two lists, one for grievances, the other a wish list of things you want me to change so we can have a positive relationship. We're sisters. Family. We need to resolve our differences and live in harmony."

"This isn't some academic exercise—"

"No, it sure isn't. This is our lives, our future. You're not only my blood sister, you're my sister in Christ."

With a sigh, Mary reluctantly picked up the pen. "You only have one sheet of paper."

"One is all I need." Abby bowed her head and prayed for guidance and mercy. With God's help, they'd turn this situation into something good. She wrote two words. The past was where they needed to start. She waited for Mary to finish.

"All right. I'm done." Mary ripped off a third sheet from the notepad. "You haven't started."

"I'm quite finished." Abby sat back.

"May I see it?" Mary reached for the paper. "Please."

Her heart in her throat, her palms damp, Abby handed over her list.

"Roger? Good gracious. You don't mean Roger Harris, do you?" Color crept up Mary's cheeks.

"How many males named Roger did you convince to dump me? You could have dated any boy you wanted. You were Miss Popularity. I was your sister, the bird geek. I had half a dozen real dates in high school. Five of them were with Roger. It wasn't Roger's dumping me that hurt so much. It was that my own sister betrayed me.

"You'll notice the second item I wrote, on my wish list, is forgiveness," Abby said, her heart hammering wildly. For too long she'd kept the truth hidden so it couldn't be used against her. Bringing it into the light was an enormous risk, but unless she did, true healing couldn't happen.

"I only recently realized I hadn't completely forgiven you for hurting me, Mary. I thought the pain of that particular betrayal was behind me, but it isn't. Perhaps if you explain it, I'll be able to put it to rest."

Mary's color deepened. "It was forty years ago."

"I know." The acknowledgment made Abby feel small for allowing such an old hurt to dwell undetected for so long.

"Roger Harris." Mary combed her hair with her fingers and looked everywhere but at Abby. "I presume you mean the time I asked him to the Ladies' Choice Dance."

Abby nodded.

"But you never said a word. You acted like it meant nothing."

"What else could I do? Wear my broken heart on my sleeve because the beautiful, popular sister took the ugly duckling's boyfriend? I figured if you knew how much you hurt me, you would steal every boyfriend I ever got." The words sounded trite and shallow now, but the wound had cut deep into the trusting, self-confident part of her heart.

Abby continued, "I was fifteen and couldn't envision life beyond Sparrow Island. You were eighteen and so sophisticated. I know it sounds petty. But at the time, it fractured my world and filled me with self-doubt. I felt like a shadow around you. I couldn't compete with your vivaciousness so I stayed in the background, where shadows belong. Silly, huh?"

Mary turned her juice glass round and round for a long time before she said, "You weren't silly. *I* was. Silly and mean. That is . . . You were the smartest kid in the whole school, on the whole island. While I struggled to earn passing grades, you were an academic star. I couldn't compete with your brainpower and I didn't want to lose my spot in the limelight."

Abby's chin dropped and, for a moment, she thought it hit the table. "You felt like you had to compete with me?"

"Oh yes. That's why I asked Roger to the dance. He was the best looking boy in the senior class and, instead of being proud of my little sister, I was afraid she'd show me up by arriving on his arm."

Mary touched her knuckle to the tears on her cheek. "If it's any consolation, I felt so guilty about what I did, I had a terrible time. In fact, he brought me home early. When you were so blasé about it, I was relieved. I honestly thought you didn't care."

Abby could scarcely believe what she was hearing. They had each envied the talents and abilities the other possessed. "That one incident changed my life. I see now that it colored how I saw things. What I thought and felt."

"I'm so sorry, Abby. For Roger, for the betrayal, for breaking your trust. For everything."

"At least you didn't sell me into slavery like Joseph's brothers did."

Mary snorted through her tears and Abby laughed. "New York isn't Egypt, my boss at Cornell isn't the Pharaoh and I'm definitely not a patriarch, but God still used what happened for good. I don't think I would have found the courage to follow my dream any other way."

Mary pulled a tissue from her pocket and blew her nose. "Are you saying you would have stayed here? Now I feel even worse, like I ran you off."

"Only because I let it happen. We both made mistakes. I'm just very grateful God is moving in our lives and we're finally dealing with them. So, can I see your list?"

Mary spread her left hand across the pages she had written. "I've always known there was something unsettled between us, but not what." She crumpled the papers into a ball. "You knew of my perfidy all these years and still dropped everything when we, *I,* needed you."

"You're my sister."

Mary took the papers over to the garbage and deposited them. "After the accident, when I was waiting to be found, my greatest regret was the distance between us. I prayed for God to let me live, for us to find a way to reconnect." She wheeled back to the table. "I just didn't know how to go about it."

"Because you didn't know how it happened?"

Mary nodded. "I thought of a thousand things, but not Roger Harris." She rolled her eyes before her gaze settled on her sister. "You know, he was crazy about himself."

Mary placed her glass in the top rack of the dishwasher. "Can you ever forgive me for breaking your trust?"

"I already have. Can you forgive me for not dealing with it when I should have?"

"Of course I do. But you know, that incident changed my life too. If you hadn't gone to Cornell, I might never have met Jacob. He was on the ferry the day we took you to the airport." Love sparkled in Mary's eyes. "Have we made a start we can build on?"

Understanding the importance of the question, Abby went to her sister, knelt beside her and hugged her. "An excellent start, don't you think?"

She felt Mary heave a quiet sigh as she returned the hug. "Yes. And I owe you an apology about the fence. My alligator mouth overran my pint-sized restraint."

"I'll go look at it."

"No. Please. It's dark out there. I don't want to be alone and I don't want you out there alone, either."

"All right. I'll look at it in the morning. Let's get you ready for bed. It's almost midnight."

Once Mary was tucked in for the night, Abby brought her pillow and a blanket down to the living room and cozied up on the couch.

If someone was prowling around the yard, he would have to go through her to get to her sister.

Chapter Seventeen

SHORTLY AFTER DAWN, Abby rolled off the couch, put on her glasses and went to check on Mary. As she drew near, her sister stirred.

"Hush now," Abby whispered. "It's just me."

More asleep than awake, Mary mumbled, "It's too early."

"I know. But I'm up and I don't want you to worry if you hear me moving around."

"Ka-ay." The word trailed into the rhythm of contented breathing.

Abby returned to the living room. As she donned her terry cloth bathrobe, a sharp twinge ran up her back and she gave the silk damask couch a rueful glance. They definitely weren't made for each other.

Reining in her eagerness to see whatever was on the fence, she spent several minutes stretching, bending and twisting to work the kinks out of her spine. As her stiffness abated, her curiosity intensified. When she felt reasonably limber, she hurried to the sliding glass doors and peeked through the vertical blinds.

The shocking image on the fence amazed and repulsed her at the same time. She jerked her hand away from the fabric-covered window slat and stepped back. *No wonder Mary was so upset.*

This wasn't just graffiti. At best, it was an invasion. At worst, it was a threat. *Who would do such a thing?* she wondered. *What could possibly be gained by frightening a woman in a wheelchair?*

Righteous indignation surged through Abby. She cinched the belt of her robe and whisked open the blinds. The last thing she expected was to find the drawing less offensive on a second look.

But it was.

Perplexed, she went back to the couch, picked up her pillow and blanket, and hurried upstairs. While racing through her morning routine and getting dressed, she tried to make sense of what she had seen—what she could still see outside her bedroom window.

Even from that distance, the drawing of the bird was exquisite, and much larger than life. The wing size matched the body; the pert little tail pointed upwards at an appropriate angle. The belly, legs and feet were all in perfect proportion. But why, she asked herself for the hundredth time, didn't it have a head?

She grabbed her digital camera and returned to the window. Artistic works were often meant to be viewed at specific distances. Too close meant a loss of perspective; too far and the details disappeared.

She decided the best way not to miss anything was to err on the side of caution. Using the graduated steps of the zoom lens and adjusting her viewing angles, she snapped one shot after another.

Identifying the bird might help her figure out who had drawn it. At the same time, she had to admit that without knowing the size and shape of the eyes, or the structure of the beak, she was left with only speculation.

She stuck the camera in its special pocket on her vest and went downstairs. The first and most important task was a careful survey of the grounds and the exterior of the house. What she found there would determine her next move.

As she slid open the glass door to step onto the deck, Blossom darted out first. Obviously proud of besting a human with her speed, she sat on her haunches, preening her whiskers and waiting for Abby to close the door.

"Too bad you aren't a guard dog," Abby murmured as she turned her attention to the framework of the glass doors. A careful search with her fingertips proved it was as smooth and unblemished as always. Thankful, she headed for the shed that stored the yard tools and garden supplies.

She doubted any of the island's teenagers were responsible for the drawing on the fence. From what she'd seen at the university and suspected was true everywhere, kids out for mischief seldom had much patience. Still, she couldn't discount the more likely possibilities of vandalism and theft.

She tested the lock on the shed. Satisfied it was securely fastened, she unlocked it and opened the door. The leaf blower, lawnmower and weed whacker were right where she and Neil

McDonald had put them last week after they finished tending the lawn. With mixed feelings, Abby closed and secured the door. *If teenagers weren't the intruders, then who was?*

Moving on, she circled the house, inspecting the windows, screens and doors, and looking for anything suspicious or out of place. Again, she found nothing amiss, no sign that anyone had even thought of breaking in. A feeling of relief swept over her and she hoped it wasn't premature. She couldn't take chances with Mary's safety.

Abby hiked down the long expanse of lawn to the little grove of junipers near the water. On the way, she kept a sharp lookout for anything out of the ordinary. There wasn't even a candy wrapper, let alone a footprint.

Driven by the need to investigate every possibility, she followed a short flagstone footpath through the gnarled trees to the beach. The shore was too rocky to hold footprints. If there had been any other clues, the incoming tide had already scoured them away.

Abby retraced her steps and when she came to the chalk drawing on the fence, she pulled out her camera. "Who are you," she asked, clicking the shutter. "Why did you come? What do you want?"

After changing the view to wide angle, she set up another shot and stopped cold. Through the lens, she saw a chalk-line so faint it was almost invisible. She stuffed the camera in her pocket and started forward. An angry buzzing forced a hasty retreat. The alyssum border in front of the fence was full of bees.

Undeterred, she leaned across the fragrant blooms and studied the faint line. Then, taking great pains not to touch the chalk, she traced the line in the air. Once. Twice. The third time she was convinced. The bird wasn't actually headless. It was simply unfinished.

Her stomach rumbled as she pushed away from the fence, a cue she was almost out of time. Mary would need her soon. Afraid the damp breeze or a sudden shower might erase the evidence before she could get back, Abby retrieved the camera, took several more pictures, then jogged up to the house.

INSTEAD OF TAKING her usual spot at the table, where she could enjoy the view, Mary rolled to the other side and sat with her back to the window. "I know you slept on the couch last night."

Unsure of what her sister was up to or how to respond, Abby shifted the table settings to accommodate the change in the seating arrangement. Part of her wanted to keep quiet, but a stronger part, the one liberated by overdue honesty, took charge. "Yes, I did. I hope I didn't disturb you."

"Disturb? Hardly. You made me feel special, cared for, loved. It meant the world to me. What I'm trying to say is thank you."

"You are very welcome." Abby poured milk over the cereal and bananas in her bowl.

"I also want to thank you for going out this morning, checking the windows and the doors. It may seem like a little thing to you, but to me, it's huge."

"Stop right there. Please." Abby caught her sister's gaze and held it. "Over the last four decades, you and I have built up a lot of bad habits and negative expectations. The things we said just now are good examples.

"I automatically assumed you'd be upset because I slept on the couch. You assumed your concerns are a little thing to me. The reality is that both assumptions are wrong. I don't want us to live like that anymore."

Mary put down her spoon. "I see what you mean. I've done the same thing—expecting the worst, then reading it into the situation. For heaven's sake, we just keep making it worse, don't we? How do we stop?"

"By expecting the best. Better still, we assume it. From now on, no matter what, we always give each other the benefit of the doubt. Accept each other the way Jesus accepts us."

Mary smiled and said, "John 15:12. 'My command is this: Love each other as I have loved you.' We don't hide our feelings anymore. If there's a problem we speak up."

"Exactly." Abby scooped a chunk of banana onto her spoon. "So tell me, why are you sitting over there instead of in your usual spot?"

"I . . . The truth is that thing on the fence is unnerving. The bird's body is so artistic, so real, it gives me the willies."

"I'll wash it off after I do the dishes."

"Then you don't think there's anything to worry about?"

"I really don't, although I admit, I can't be certain. We'll be sensible. We'll keep the doors locked and the phone handy."

"You're right. We'll be sensible." Mary put her napkin on

the table and picked up her spoon. "I can't imagine who would draw on my fence. We'll keep our eyes open and catch the culprit if he returns."

"Mary," Abby said slowly, gazing out at the fence, "I think the drawing was intended for me. The bird is larger than life and drawn with meticulous care. I think it's some sort of message."

"For what? The birds you're looking for?"

"I think so."

Mary turned and studied the drawing. "Too bad the artist didn't send you a letter instead."

"Maybe he will." *And put a return address on it.*

Chapter Eighteen

Abby carried a sponge and a pail of water down to the fence. Destroying the work felt strange, almost sacrilegious. However, Mary's peace of mind was far more important than preserving a chalk drawing of a headless bird.

"Whatcha doing?"

Startled by her unexpected visitor, Abby turned to look at Bobby. His little shoulders slumped dejectedly. "I'm cleaning up a mess. What's up with you today?"

"I'm grounded," Bobby said sadly.

"Then maybe you shouldn't be over here."

"Nah. It's okay. I just have to be able to hear Mom call me." Sidling past Abby, he went to the garden, knelt down and pulled a few weeds.

She joined him and tugged at the unwanted growth. "I'm sure your parents had a good reason."

"Did you ever get grounded?"

"Usually we were sent to our rooms." *And Mary hated being punished by the isolation.* Abby smiled. "I'll tell you a secret. I kind of liked being sent to my room. All of my books were there. When I opened them, I'd get lost in the stories. I could explore new worlds and meet interesting people. It didn't feel like I was being punished at all. I liked Nancy Drew mysteries."

"*Ugh*, girl stories."

"I had a friend at school, a boy, who used to read Hardy Boys mysteries when he was sent to his room." Abby tossed a weed onto Bobby's growing pile. "The Hardy Boys were brothers who solved mysteries. One thing about Nancy Drew and the Hardy Boys, they always got into trouble too. Maybe that's why we liked them so much."

"I wonder if the man I saw yesterday read those kinds of stories." Bobby moved to the next section of the garden.

Abby's smile and light mood evaporated. "What man?"

"The one in the woods."

"Where?"

"Near the fence over there." Bobby pointed to the spot where Mary's fence ended against the McDonald's property line.

Had Bobby seen the fence artist? "When was that?"

"Last night, when I was supposed to be taking a bath."

"Where were you instead?"

"In my tree house. I was going to take a bath. Honest. But when I looked out the window, I saw this really cool sailboat. I wanted to see it from up in my tree house, you know, the way we'd looked out for pirates. I was pretending I was a stranded buccaneer." Bobby gave a cluster of weeds a hard yank and broke the stems off above the roots. "Oops."

"Were you in your tree house when you saw this man?"

"Yeah, but then I went down to the ground. I thought he was lost."

Gooseflesh prickled Abby's skin. "You spoke with him?"

"At first he just sorta stayed behind the trees." Bobby sat back on his heels. A big grin spread over his freckled face. "He was catching green tree frogs and letting them jump out of his hand. He showed me how to do it. It was so cool. Now I know where to look for them and how to pick them up. He was really nice."

"What did he look like?" *Please, Lord, help Bobby describe this man so we can identify him.*

"Sad." The grin faded and Bobby resumed pulling weeds.

She needed so much more than a one-word emotion. "Can you describe *sad*?"

"At first, I thought he was an alien from Mars."

Only a ten-year-old would approach someone he thought was a Martian, Abby concluded. Or catch tree frogs with him.

"After a while though, when we were catching the frogs, he looked okay. Mom says I'm not supposed to judge people by their looks. I'm glad I didn't. That guy knows all about critters and trees and stuff."

Abby reminded herself that Bobby was safe. If the man he encountered had intended harm, the boy wouldn't be kneeling beside her now. The trick was getting him to describe the mysterious visitor without letting him know how much the encounter frightened her. "Was he tall? Short? Young? Old?"

"About as tall as my dad I guess, but lots skinnier and older.

Dad has brown hair. This guy had like, patches of white hair and bald skin. I could see it where his cap didn't cover the back of his head. And he didn't have any eyebrows. Some of his face had lots of wrinkles. This part." Bobby raised his hand and pointed to the area over his eyes and the bridge of his nose.

"The rest of his face was shiny and smooth looking, like it was plastic. I felt kinda sorry for him.

"I probably ought to go." Bobby stood up and brushed the dirt from his knees. "Maybe if I stay closer to the house Mom won't be so mad about yesterday."

"Are you grounded because you skipped out on your bath?" It didn't seem that big of an issue, but Abby was certain Sandy had her reasons.

"Yeah. I forgot to turn off the water. It sorta ran over the top of the tub."

"Oh!"

"That's how she knew I went outside and she was upset because the sun was starting to go down." He started off toward home.

"Bobby?"

"Yeah?"

"If you see that man again, call me so I can go talk to him too. It was a very brave thing you did, but you were lucky he wasn't a Martian."

"Or a criminal. I thought about that later."

"That's right. You need to be careful of strange people roaming the woods. So will you call me next time you see him?"

"Yes, Abby. I really want you to meet him. I think he needs a friend like you. He seems awful lonely."

Bobby trudged back through the woods to his house. Moments later, Abby heard the staccato tune of his ball bouncing in the McDonald's driveway. As she collected the weeds and carried them to the compost pile, she pondered the situation. In all likelihood, the tree frog trapper was the same person who had drawn on the fence.

Abby finished scrubbing the fence clean then hurried back to the house. Even as she started up the steps to the deck, she heard music with a familiar, quick tempo and an enthusiastic instructor telling Mary to lift up, two, three, up to the count of ten. The middle of her special exercise video was not the time to tell her about Bobby's experience.

Abby went upstairs, downloaded the pictures to her laptop computer and selected several to print. While the pages moved slowly through her portable printer, she looked out her window at the freshly washed section of fence.

"Who are you tree frog man? If you're the fence artist, why didn't you start with the head or stick around long enough to finish it?" she murmured. "And if you're not, what brought you here?"

Examining the photo prints, she felt sure the body shape and proportion were that of a marbled murrelet. The critical question was whether her search for the bird was interfering with her objectivity. Was she reading more into the photographs than was actually there?

She tucked the pictures into an oversized envelope, and placed it and her laptop into her tote bag. She picked up her purse and went downstairs. The living room was empty, the television off. The sound of water running in the back of the house charged her into action.

"Mary?" she called, entering her sister's bedroom.

The running water sounded louder.

She tapped on the bathroom door, got no answer and, with her pulse quickening, opened it.

"My goodness!" Astounded, she stared at Mary through the translucent shower curtain.

Mary's laughter filled the bathroom. The zing of the shower curtain rings sliding along the metal rack harmonized. Wet-haired, she lifted the shower wand, her face alight with confidence and her blue eyes sparkling in triumph. "You should see yourself."

Abby braced herself against the countertop. "Forget how I look. How did you get in there?"

"It wasn't easy." Mary turned off the water, leaned forward and returned the wand to its holder. "I'm really glad to see you because I'm not sure I can get out of here by myself." She tugged a towel off the bar outside of the high tub.

Abby's shock wore off slowly. "You amaze me. I had no idea you could lift yourself like that."

Mary wrapped the towel around her head, reached over the tub and caught a second one. "I was so pumped up after my workout, I thought I could do anything. The hardest part was undressing. Once I got the tub door open, grabbed the trapeze and pulled myself out of the wheelchair, I had to succeed because there wasn't any place to go but down."

Abby took two of the fluffy bath towels and lined the wheelchair. "The thought of you falling in the tub scares me to death. Next time, call me first. You can still do it by yourself, but that way, if you need help I'll be there."

"Yes, Mother," Mary quipped good-naturedly. "That would be the smart thing to do."

"It most certainly would." Abby stood back. "You want to try to get out by yourself?"

"Want? Yes." Mary flashed a mischievous grin. "However, I know when I've pressed my limit."

Abby helped her out of the shower and into the wheelchair, then kissed her on the cheek.

"What was that for?" Mary touched her cheek and smiled. "Not that I mind, of course."

"For being independent, fierce, brave, strong and stupid, all at the same time," Abby answered. She could have said the same of Bobby.

"Yes. I guess I was. Gracious! Look at the time. I need to hurry. The crafters group will be here soon." Mary released the wheel brake and rolled toward the lighted dressing area where her clothing lay on the countertop.

"What are you going to do while the group is here?"

"Visit Dad. Show him those pictures of the fence and see if he can provide any insight."

"He'll think we ought to hire armed guards."

Abby flinched. Knowing their father, he was more likely to call Henry Cobb. That would be disastrous. The mysterious artist wouldn't return with the San Juan County Deputy Sheriff parked on their doorstep.

Unable to remember the last time she'd talked her father out of anything, she mused, "I'm going to have to tread very carefully."

Chapter Nineteen

THE LACK OF A DIRECT ROUTE to the Stanton Farm—one that bypassed the town of Green Harbor—was something Abby once thought of as an inconvenience. Driving through town today, she now saw the one route as an asset.

Green Harbor's stop signs and restricted speed limit forced her to surrender her customary New York hurry-up mode. In return, the leisurely trip gave her the opportunity to see the buildings and people as much more than just scenery filling the space between one destination and the next. The individuals and their family-owned businesses were the warp and weft of island life.

Bound together by brick and wood, mortar and steel, hopes and dreams, the threads of their lives wove the fabric of community. Some of those strings, the ties of family, kept her attached to that unique cloth, though her long absences had frayed her portion to a meager scrap.

It was more than she deserved, she reflected. She was the one who cut herself out of that fabric. Yet every time she came back to visit, they enfolded her in the blanket of their love and tried to reweave her into their lives. She had simply been too blind to see what she was missing.

"Not anymore," she whispered. "I've lost way too much already."

A hand-lettered sidewalk sign in front of The Green Grocer read: *Kari's Creams: Get them while they last.*

On impulse, Abby pulled into the first available parking space. She had heard about the creams, an all-too-rare offering from the store's eccentric bakery chef. On occasion, Kari could be persuaded to turn out a limited number of the custard-filled puffs slathered in a thick layer of fudge frosting that were her trademark. Hoping she wasn't too late, Abby hurried down the sidewalk.

Upon entering the store, she spotted Frank Holloway in the front section of the frozen food aisle and went over to greet him. Oblivious to her approach, he added a couple of cartons of ice cream to the cans, boxes and produce piled high in his shopping cart.

"Hello," she said when he saw her. She gestured to his cart. "Looks like you and Aaron are expecting company. How nice."

"Nobody's coming. Just stocking up." Frank tucked his list into his shirt pocket. "How are you and Mary? Do you need help with anything? Shelves and such?"

"We're fine. The mini-ramps you installed on the back deck slider are working out even better than any of us hoped. Mary goes over the threshold like it isn't even there."

"Good. Good. Glad to hear it. If there's anything I can do with a saw and hammer to make life easier for you two girls, you let me know."

Feeling a little disconcerted at being called a girl, but grateful for the man's caring spirit, she said, "Thanks, Frank. Mary and I really appreciate your willingness to help."

She glanced at the special display near the checkout counter where several spent bakery boxes nested inside one another. "Guess I better hurry if I want any of Kari's Creams. They're Mary's favorite and I want to surprise her."

"Better get cracking, then. They're a lot of people's favorites. I have to be moving along too. It was good to see you, Abby."

"And you, Frank," she said as he steered his cart farther down the frozen food aisle.

Planning to purchase three or four of the sugary treats, Abby went to the display and reached for a waxed paper from the pop-up dispenser. A delectable yeasty aroma wafted from the last box of pastries, teasing her nose and tickling her tummy. There were only a dozen left.

If they tasted half as good as they smelled . . .

Abby decided to take them all, and she closed the lid of the one remaining box and picked it up.

"I should have gotten here ealier," Rev. Hale lamented. "Everyone loves Kari's Creams."

"They sure do. I plan to give most of these to my family."

"Patricia told me to get here early, but I got hung up at . . .

well, no matter." His dismay showed in the upward lift of his eyebrows and the downward tilt of his lips. "I guess that's just the way it goes."

Feeling a bit guilty for taking the last of the special treats, Abby asked, "How many did you want?"

"Three." His features brightened. "But only if you can spare them. It's my night to make dinner."

"Be my guest." Abby lifted the lid. There would still be plenty for what she had in mind.

"I'm glad I ran into you here." He shook open a white pastry bag and, after saying thanks, carefully put three of the goodies inside. "Will you be staying on Sparrow Island for the summer? The reason I ask is because we could use another mentor in our Skills and Crafts program."

"I don't know," Abby said slowly, feeling like a juggler with too many balls in the air. Between Mary and their parents, the university, the murrelets and now the tree frog man, she was struggling to keep up.

"I hope to be here for the next couple of months, perhaps longer, if the university and I can find a way to make it work. I'm not in a position to make a commitment right now, but what does being a mentor entail?"

"I'll put together a packet of the literature for you. Skills and Crafts is similar to scouting. However, since we're a small congregation on a small island, we don't separate the girls and boys. That's actually turning out to be a good thing. All of the kids feel freer to pursue their true interests."

Recalling Bobby's dedication to the garden plot, Abby smiled. "That *is* good. I remember a time when spiders fascinated me. I got teased a lot, but the webs were so amazing, it was worth it."

Rev. Hale laughed and a lock of sandy hair dipped onto his forehead. He gave it a swipe and adjusted his wire-rimmed glasses. "Funny you should mention spiders. We have one girl—seven-year-old Hillary Storm—who is quite serious about entomology. Thank heaven for Hugo. He's our bug mentor and counselor."

Abby was pleasantly surprised to learn of Hugo's active involvement with the church community. "It's the naturalist and the conservationist in him."

"If you're not checking out," Frank said from behind them. "I'd like to. My ice cream is melting."

"I'm sorry, Frank. I didn't see you there." Rev. Hale stepped aside and held up his pastry bag. "I'm not in line, yet. I need to get something more substantial than this for dinner."

"Toby'd be fine with those for dinner," Frank said knowingly.

Rev. Hale chuckled. "Yes, but Patricia wouldn't agree. See you later, Abby."

After Frank finished checking out, Abby paid for her treats. Abby left the store, started the car and pulled onto Kingfisher Avenue. *What am I doing? Making plans and chatting as though I've always lived here and never intend to leave.*

She made a left onto Primrose Lane and headed out of

town toward the farm. The truck in front of her belonged to Frank Holloway. *How strange*, she thought. *He lives on the other side of town.*

When she put on her turn signal for the Stanton Farm, he continued on as if the conservatory was his destination. As soon as the thought crossed her mind, she dismissed it.

He had two cartons of melting ice cream, so why would he take such a wide detour? Certain she had seen his truck traveling this road recently, she searched her memory. Then it came to her.

The day she received the telephone call at the museum from her father she had seen Frank headed in the same direction he was now. Then, she had been too consumed with anxiety to think much about it. Now, she wondered if there was new construction beyond Hugo's property she didn't know about.

Last Christmas she had explored Primrose Lane to the end. When the pavement ran out, the road turned into packed dirt for several miles before dead-ending a few hundred feet from Paradise Cove.

I'll have to go out there again and see if there's something new—when I have time.

She drove to the farm, parked and got out. As she pulled her tote bag from the backseat, she heard male voices singing. *Dad and Sam?* She straightened and listened.

Sam was teaching George to sing a country-western song. When one of them hit a wrong note or messed up the words, both laughed.

Her insides twisted with the pain of another precious thing she had missed. How many deliriously joyful days had she and Mary spent out in the fields with their father, singing at the top of their lungs and laughing like a raft of loons? *Thank You, Lord, for sending Dad such a wonderful companion. For giving him that fellowship and camaraderie.*

Picking up the pastry box, Abby went into the house. How could she not have seen Sam as a vitally important part of her father's life? Yes, she had been profoundly grateful that the handyman shouldered the heavy work at the farm. However, he was so much more than an employee; he was a true friend.

Abby made a fresh pot of coffee, stashed a cream for her mother in a plastic bag, plated two for the men, then went to the screen door and called, "Break time!"

Sam and George exchanged a glance, dropped their hoes and started toward the house. When they reached the screen door, she said, "I brought Kari's Creams."

"Your mother will be sorry she missed out." George and Sam removed their work boots and left them on the porch.

"I saved one for her." Abby pointed to the bag on the counter.

By the time she finished pouring the coffee and putting out napkins, both men had washed up and taken their seats at the table.

"To what do we owe this culinary honor?" George raised his plate until the pastry was right under his nose and took a deep sniff. "*Ahhh.*"

"I was in the right place at the right time," Abby answered.

Fork poised and eyes twinkling, George asked, "How many do we get?"

"You mean, if you wolf this one down, can you have another one?" Sam chuckled and put his napkin on his lap. "I'd say no, unless you want Ellen to give both of us a good case of what for."

Abby smiled at Sam. "Sam's right. Besides, I want to take some home to Mary. These are her favorites."

George heaved a theatrical sigh. "Okay. I'll make it last."

"This is mighty nice of you, Miss Abby."

"It's my pleasure, Sam. You know, on my way out here, Frank Holloway was ahead of me on the road. It seemed kind of odd because he had ice cream—"

"Lucky man," murmured her father.

"You have Kari's Creams," she reminded him.

"Lucky us," Sam corrected.

"Thank you, darlin' daughter, for the treat. What about old Frank?"

"Do you have any idea where he might have been headed? Is there new construction out that way?"

"No. Nobody's building except Hugo, thank heaven. But I will admit I got curious about old Frank too, 'cause he goes by here often. I asked him about it one day and he took me with him to a spot he likes." George sipped his coffee and swallowed. "It's nothing like your dreaming rock, though I suppose it serves the same purpose."

He put down the coffee mug. "Old Frank will help anyone, but he's a private kind of man and not given to sharing personal information. I think that place had a special meaning to his wife. Now that she's gone, it's special to him because of her."

George's logic made sense. "A good place to eat ice cream," Abby mused, though the idea of someone consuming a gallon of the stuff in one sitting was a bit bizarre. He'd certainly pay for it when he got home. He still had a lot of groceries to unload and put away.

Figuring she had as much of an explanation as possible, Abby changed the subject. "What are you two working on today?"

"We just finished covering the strawberry patch with netting," Sam answered. "Since we're not sharing with the birds, we should have a good harvest this year."

"How long before they're ripe?" The big, juicy strawberries were her favorite food. Nothing in the East measured up to the ones her father grew near the barn. And the netting was the kindest way to keep the birds from eating all of them.

"The first crop ought to be ready in a week or so," George answered. "I'll call you and we'll have fresh strawberries and cream."

"I'd better get busy." Sam pushed away from the table. "After I put the hoes away, I'll get started on cleaning the chicken coop."

"No need to rush off," Abby said, surprised he was leaving so soon.

"Yes, ma'am, there is. If I stay at this table, I'll want to eat those creams you set aside for Mary. Besides, it'll be good to get this task behind us."

"Amen to that," George breathed softly as Sam slipped out the screen door.

Abby refreshed their coffee. "About yesterday," she started. "When I stayed out later than Mary expected, I didn't mean to worry anyone."

"You're a grown woman. You owe no one an explanation about where you go, but you should have called us just to say you'd be late."

"You're right, and I will in the future. If you're ever worried about me, please call me on my cell phone."

"Fair enough." He leaned forward, his arms folded atop the table. "You were out looking for the birds, weren't you?"

Smiling, she nodded and caught him up on what she had and hadn't found. "There's something I should tell you. Actually, it's easier to show."

She took her laptop and the envelope out of her tote bag. As she started the computer, she opened the envelope and withdrew the pictures she had printed that morning. "Take a look at these and give me your best guess as to what kind of bird we're looking at."

His eyes twinkled. "You're asking me?"

"You bet I am." She sat back and folded her arms.

After he had pored over each photo, he sat back and shook his head. "These old eyes need more detail than what is here. Where did these come from?"

She turned the computer screen toward him and started a slide show of the rest of the pictures. While it ran, she gave him a brief account of how Mary discovered the drawings on the fence.

"You girls need to keep your doors locked at all times," he said, his agitation obvious.

Abby swallowed her amusement at his description of his daughters. To their parents, and apparently to Frank, she and Mary would always be "the girls" and forever young. "Please don't worry. We're taking precautions."

"I'll talk to Henry Cobb about sending a regular patrol by the house and checking in on you." George turned his gaze to the pictures arrayed across the table.

"I would have already done so if I thought this was at all sinister." She zoomed in on the faint outline of the bird's head until it filled the computer screen. "See? It isn't finished."

"Do you think it ties into the journals?"

"Yes, but if we involve Henry, he'll camp out on our doorstep and we'll never find out what the connection is."

"I don't know, Abby." Her father shook his head.

"There's more." She proceeded to tell him about Bobby's encounter with the tree frog man.

"I don't like this. He doesn't sound like anyone who lives on the island. From Bobby's description, somebody would have noticed him when he got off the ferry."

"Maybe he didn't arrive by ferry," she mused, picking up one of the photos to study it.

"You think he came by private boat?" George scowled and looked at another of the photos.

"I'm just speculating, because you're right about someone noticing him in Green Harbor. The ferry is all the way across town from Mary's house." The only way to get there was through town.

"You talk to the McDonalds. I'll talk to Henry," her father ordered.

"Bobby promised to call me the next time he spots the man—if there is a next time." She offered the straight-on photo she'd been studying. "I've seen a lot of graffiti. There's nothing malicious in this drawing. Furthermore, it was chalk and washed right off."

"You know, you may be right. There's something familiar about these pictures," he said softly. "But it can't be."

"What can't be?"

"The style . . . I know I've seen this before."

"When? Where?"

"I don't remember right now, but it'll come to me."

Abby sat silently as he stared at the picture.

A long moment later, he said, "The library. At one time, there were illustrations like this hanging over the checkout desk. Of course, those drawings had heads. As I recall, the pictures changed every couple of months or so.

"I remember how amazed I was that the artist could capture so much detail with just a pencil. It was a shock when I found out who drew them." He held the sheet up.

"This could have been done by him and—I got it," he breathed, his gaze darting to Abby as she watched him.

"The bird?" She sat stock still, her pulse quickening.

"No. The artist's name. But it can't be him. David Bowditch is dead."

Chapter Twenty

Content she had persuaded her father not to involve the authorities, Abby left him at the chicken coop with Sam and continued on to the dreaming rock. So much had happened in the last twenty-four hours, she needed time to think and reflect. Grateful for the beauty and solitude of the trees surrounding the clearing, she climbed the boulder and, with the cushions from the storage box, made a comfortable perch.

She settled in with a hopeful sigh. Although her thoughts and emotions were as scattered as the squirrels scampering through the boughs of the stately firs, she was certain her Heavenly Father knew of her turmoil and of her need for His peace and guidance.

She closed her eyes to the restless busyness of the forest around her and opened her mind and heart. Somewhere nearby, a vireo began a languid hymn. Not to be outdone, a wren joined the worship with exuberant trills of praise. Smiling at their songs and the evidence of His hand in all things, Abby added a whispered psalm of thanksgiving.

The restoration with her sister was a precious gift. That it came in a manner she didn't expect only added to its value. Filled with a sudden conviction the Counselor had much more in store for them, Abby rested her forehead on her knees.

There was a connectedness in the events of the past several weeks that she was only beginning to understand. The appearance of those rare little birds in the evening sky when she and her father were walking back to the house was not a coincidence. The Creator continually worked His purpose, even if she didn't recognize it at the time.

Now she saw He had taken her passion for His winged creatures and used it to guide her. Her pursuit of the murrelets had led her to stay out late with Hugo and in turn, to the long overdue confrontation with Mary. If not for that emotional encounter, they might never have resolved the past and made such a great beginning to mending their rift.

Abby found that the river of peace springing from their new start was already flowing into other parts of her life and washing away old misperceptions. Sam was a prime example. From the moment he had hired on at the farm, she had held his checkered past against him. Though his years of faithful service had relaxed her guard, she realized now she had tarred him with the same brush of distrust that had characterized her relationship with Mary.

Tears of sorrow and shame dampened her knees and firmed her resolve to never again let a hurt fester and grow. The poison it generated tainted her view of everything and everyone.

She dried her eyes and looked up at the sky. The warm sun streaming down felt like a benediction and an encouragement to continue her soul-searching. If her quest for the marbled murrelets was meant solely to propel her down the path of reconciliation, then surely that intention had been accomplished.

Yet the more she contemplated it, the stronger her conviction grew that God had a bigger purpose in mind. The sighting, the journals, the drawing on the fence—any one of them would have been sufficient to engage her curiosity. All three of them together clearly demanded her continued participation.

She shifted her position, sat cross-legged and let her thoughts drift with the soft breeze whispering through the trees. The journal had appeared on the back deck, the drawing appeared on the back fence, then Bobby's tree frog man appeared in the back woods on the property line.

Although she couldn't shake the uncomfortable feeling she was overlooking something, the connection between the first two events seemed obvious. They were directly linked to her and her career as an ornithologist. If the tree frog man was the artist, then he too was part of the linkage.

Growing restless, she stretched her legs. Maybe she was going about this all wrong. If she approached it from another angle, perhaps a new explanation would emerge. Her father said that the fence artist had mimicked David Bowditch's style.

Given that observation, where did the information lead? David had passed on a decade ago. Even if he hadn't, and was alive and well today, he'd be more than a hundred years old. It was hard to imagine any centenarian prowling around in the dark, over strange and uneven terrain, just to draw a huge headless bird on the fence. It would have been so much easier to mail the drawing to her.

And why not start the drawing with the head? Saving that portion of the anatomy for last made no sense. Unless . . . it was a test! That was what she had overlooked.

Abby exhaled and stroked her fingertips through her hair, pushing the short, brown locks back over her ears. When she washed the chalk off the fence, she had instinctively felt that doing so was a mistake. Now she couldn't help but think she should have finished the drawing.

It would have been easy enough. Though she'd never seen a live murrelet up close, there were plenty of drawings in the second journal. She could have used any one of them as a guide.

The second realization struck with the force of a whirl-wind. How could she have missed such a vital clue?

The answer came immediately. The previous night, recon-ciling with Mary had been much more important. Then, concern for her safety meant a restless night on the couch. Abby shook her head ruefully. Even this morning, she'd taken dozens of extra pictures. That was so unlike her. She supposed it was an automatic precaution against the fuzzy-headedness she felt.

If what she now suspected about the fence artist was true, he, too, had access to David's artwork. However, so did anyone who frequented the library during the time his pictures had been on display.

"Well, I guess I can exclude most of the world and narrow the field to about twenty-five-hundred residents," she muttered to the trees. "That's only twenty-four-hundred-ninety-nine too many."

Weighing what she knew against the factors of time, opportunity and possibility, the tree frog man was her most likely candidate. He was definitely *not* David Bowditch. In any case, she'd been given a test and a message.

Perhaps the mysterious artist wanted to see how much she knew about the murrelets. Was that why he'd left the picture headless? To test her expertise?

Deciphering the message was trickier and, unless she actually talked with the artist, she might never know the truth. Apparently, he knew the island, who lived where and the most opportune time to draw on the fence while he still had light. There was also a strong possibility he left the journal on the back deck.

Now, the biggest question, the one that seemed to have no discernable answer, was why. What did he want from her?

Knowing she could spend the afternoon running in circles and not getting any closer to the truth, Abby slid off the rock and stowed the cushions.

She would update Mary on her speculations and see how she would feel about a new picture on her fence. Mary might be willing to go along with her idea.

Abby hiked up the long incline toward the house and her car. Speculation was all she had. If her interpretation of the facts was even halfway correct, the artist's return was inevitable.

AT THE MCDONALDS, Abby presented Sandy with three of Kari's Creams before mentioning the tree frog stranger. Fortunately, Bobby had already told his mother all about the man and received the same cautions Abby had dispensed.

As they walked out to the car, Sandy said, "Bobby's a bright kid and his instincts about people are pretty sharp. Having this tree frog guy sneaking around is a little creepy, but I agree with Bobby and with you. I don't think this guy means any harm, though I will lock up at night."

"Good. One other thing. If either of you see him again, will you notify me, right away? I really want to talk with him."

Satisfied with Sandy's assurance that she would most definitely phone her, Abby went home.

Taking off her shoes in the laundry room that separated the garage from the rest of the house, she called to her sister, "Mary? Where are you?"

"I'm on the deck. Come out and join me."

"In a minute." Abby stopped in the kitchen, placed the last three Kari's Creams on a dessert plate, poured two glasses of milk and started toward the deck. Two steps later, she turned back.

She arranged linen napkins and forks on a serving tray before adding the glasses and the pastries. Okay, she was getting the hang of the formal niceties Mary enjoyed. The special touches did add something to the snack.

Abby made it halfway across the kitchen before turning back a second time. She had forgotten the little dessert plates. Mary did not consider desserts of any kind finger-food.

"What were you doing in there?" she asked when Abby opened the sliding screen door.

"I was putting together a snack. I bought the last ones at The Green Grocer on my way out to the farm."

"Ohhh, my favorites."

Careful to avoid disturbing the cat curled up beside her mistress, Abby set the tray on the small table. She circled around and pulled a wicker chair close.

Mary closed her Bible and slipped it into the embroidered denim catchall fastened to the arm of the chair with big-buttoned tabs. "I do love these high-fat, high-carbohydrate, high-sugar treats. Why can't broccoli taste like this?"

"Now there's an idea." Abby picked up a napkin and put it in her lap.

"Thank you. This is really thoughtful of you."

Abby mused, "Thoughtful, that's me. A million thoughts have been running a marathon inside my head all day."

"Let me guess. It has to be your search for the bird. Or whoever did the drawing."

"You're mostly right. But during the past hour, my musings have been about you."

"Me?" Glass in hand, Mary paused in unabashed surprise.

"We started something last night. I know there's a lot more we haven't talked about. And we need to. I very much want us to clear the air and be sisters in every sense of the word."

"I've been thinking about that too. The trouble is I don't know where to start."

Abby blinked twice. She hadn't heard correctly. "*Whew*, boy, we're in trouble now."

Horrified, Mary set down her glass and almost missed the tray. "We can't be."

Abby leaned forward, toward Mary. "You're such a people-oriented person. I've always admired your ability to take charge, handle difficult situations and find solutions." Abby gave her sister a sheepish half smile. "I've often wished I possessed even a fraction of what you have."

"Posh. You came up with the solution. Talking openly has always been one of your strong points. You say exactly what's on your mind." Mary shrugged a shoulder. "Most of the time."

"Except when I'm hurt," Abby reflected. "Words often fail me then."

She placed her hand on Mary's arm. "I really admire how you accept life's trials. What you've been through would have sent me to a corner with my Bible."

"Oh, Abby. I use the same Bible, I just try to accept His will and refuse the darkness in the corner."

"I always have a million questions."

"You're a thinker. That's what makes you such a great

researcher and teacher. Even better, your enthusiasm for what you do reaches out to others and inspires them.

"Even though our core beliefs are the same, we approach life differently." Mary gestured to the tray. "Take this, for example. This is very nice. It's just the way I would do it."

Abby basked in the compliment, then looked at her sister. Their gazes met and held.

"I know it took consideration and lots of thought for you to do this," Mary continued and tilted her head. "Your usual style is to hand me a paper towel and a wrinkled bag."

"Make it a box," Abby admitted.

The smile Mary tried to suppress tugged at the corners of her mouth. "I've visited you in Ithaca, remember? Your home has your, let's say, unique style."

Abby nodded, her gaze traveling to the living room beyond the screen door. "And it didn't suit you."

"Sorry, but yes that's exactly how I felt after the first trip. It seemed a bit bland for me. It wasn't until my last visit I realized you don't really live in your house. Your life is at the lab, trekking out into the field and doing the research you share at conferences and symposiums. If I discovered something important, I'd be terrified to get up in front of hundreds of my peers and give a presentation. Don't you ever get nervous?"

"Not for the last twenty-five years. Jerome taught me a little trick. I pretend the attendees are my first-year students and know less than I do. That's generally true, since I'm usually way overprepared. Still, I always learn something from the questions afterwards. You do the same thing in your shop. People come in not just for the flowers, but for your expertise and artistic talent."

"It's not the same."

"Sure it is. Anyone can go out and cut flowers. It's knowing how to buy the best variety and how to care for the blooms and arrange them and . . . well, you know."

"I see. It's knowing when the artemisia is in bloom and that you don't mist lilacs because it makes the flower petals turn brown. Is that what you mean?"

"Exactly."

"But your work is important."

"So is yours. If God gave everybody the same talents, we would, as my students say, die of boredom. Horticulture is one of your gifts and you're very good at it. You've always had a flair for style and fashion. Remember when we exchanged our bobby socks for stockings—"

"And wore the same shade of lipstick," Mary said with a faraway expression.

"Yeah. Mom's. I think she got mad because it looked better on you."

Mary smiled dreamily. "Remember when she found out we used her razor for the first time?"

"You shaved your legs and I shaved my knees."

"And you looked so, so . . ."

"Dorky?" Abby suggested, laughing because it was true.

"*Dorky* is a good word."

Abby nodded, recalling the moment they had been discovered. "You were right. If I'd shaved my legs too, we might have escaped detection."

"Mom noticed because you just had to wear shorts," Mary said fondly.

"Hey, I was twelve and trying to be a grown-up."

"Grown women don't shave just their knees."

Their gazes met and laughter erupted, sending Blossom out to the yard in disgust over the raucousness.

"No one else shares those memories," Abby dabbed the corner of her eye with her napkin.

"Abby, I hate the distance we've built up over the years. More than anything, I want . . ." Mary's voice trailed and she shook her head. "Well, it's not about just what I want."

Abby leaned forward and touched her sister's arm. "What is it you want?"

"I want us to go back to the way we were when we were kids."

"And go through puberty all over again?" teased Abby.

"I mean the closeness we shared."

"I miss that too. If we both want it, there's no reason we can't have it."

"I'm not so sure. Eventually, you'll go back to New York." Mary sniffed and searched her pocket for a tissue. "As a sister and a mother, I know how distance erodes intimacy . . . the closeness between parent and child and grandmother and grandchild. Nothing replaces a hug when you need one."

Abby stared at her hands as the feelings she once feared she'd never get to share bubbled to the surface. "Those first few years I was away from the farm, I thought I'd die of loneliness. I couldn't wait for the holidays so I could come home."

Mary heaved a deep sigh. "The selfish side of me wants you to quit your job and move back here. Live with me. That's unreasonable and I know it. But I hope you'll at least consider it when you retire."

Amazement held Abby speechless. Of all the possibilities she'd considered over the years, living with Mary had truly never entered her mind. Whenever she fantasized about living on Sparrow Island again, she automatically assumed she'd either live on her own or return to the farm. The latter scenario was the most logical and at the time, the most likely. "Do you really mean it, Mary? You want me to share your house on a permanent basis?"

"Yes. I want you in my life. Mom and Dad do too. Besides, when the time comes and Mom and Dad need us to take care of them, it will be so much easier and better if we do it together. But the bottom line, Abby, is that I love you."

Abby swallowed hard to hold back the tears that threatened. She couldn't remember the last time her sister had made her feel so loved and so valued. Another flash of understanding pierced her thoughts. "Wait. You wanting me to stay—is that why you asked me to handle the remodeling?"

"And the colors," Mary said wistfully. "I want this house to feel like your home too. I thought if you had a hand in the remodeling you might feel more inclined to stay or at least come back. I hoped if you had an emotional investment in it . . ."

"The home you built with Jacob, you want to share with me?" Abby's amazement deepened. She wasn't an afterthought. Her involvement had been planned from the start.

"I'm so honored, so touched. I promise, I'll think about it and explore what's possible."

"While I'm baring my soul, there's something else you should know." Mary twisted her ring, then folded her hands tightly in her lap.

Concerned by the telltale signs of distress, Abby said softly, "Whatever it is, we'll deal with it together."

"It's too late for that. I'm sorry. I don't mean to sound so cross. It's just that . . ." Mary looked up, tears pooling in her eyes. "How can I explain stupidity?"

"What do you mean?"

"The reason I'm in this chair is because of my own stupidity," Mary said in a rush. Tears spilled down her cheeks onto her whitened knuckles.

Alarmed by her sister's pain, Abby blurted, "Please don't say things like that. Accidents happen—"

"Yes, they do. But this is different." Mary thumped her fists on the armrests of her wheelchair. "It's my own fault I'm here. Oh, if only I could go back and change that one minute. Just one second of thoughtlessness."

Abby reached out and enclosed one of her sister's clenched fists in her hands. "Tell me. Help me understand."

"I had my purse on the passenger seat. It fell over and spilled onto the floor." Mary scrubbed at her tears with her free hand. "I was stretched across the seat and reaching for my wallet when the deer jumped into the road."

Shudders wracked Mary's frame. "I was so off-balance, I couldn't recover."

A sickening awareness spread through Abby as she began to see the unwarranted guilt eating at her sister.

"I hit the brakes and jerked the steering wheel," Mary continued. "The momentum carried me farther over to the left. Then the wheel wrenched from my hands. That was it."

Mary pulled her fingers from Abby's grasp, threw up her hands in a gesture of despair and surrender, then crumpled in on herself in a curtain of tears.

Abby wanted the tragic tale to end there, yet if she'd learned anything from the past, it was that nothing healed until it was thoroughly cleansed. As bitter and difficult as this was for Mary, now was the time to drag it all out into the light. Only then could they examine it and deal with it. "And that's when the car . . ."

"Went crashing down into the ravine. It turned over and over, taking down saplings and everything in its path." Mary hiccupped and her tears slowed. "It felt like I fell about five-thousand feet, but it was closer to fifty."

Abby slid off her chair and knelt on the deck at her sister's feet. Leaning close, she took Mary's tear-stained face in her hands. "Why have you kept this locked up inside you?"

"It was so stupid."

"I see. You knew exactly when the deer was going to leap into the road and deliberately picked that moment to get your wallet."

"Of course not! But I could have pulled over and done it right, or waited until I got home. It wasn't urgent. That stuff wasn't going anywhere without me."

"Hindsight is always twenty-twenty. Forgive yourself and let it go. I can tell you from firsthand experience there are no winners in the if-only game. There isn't a soul in the world who wouldn't like to go back and change at least one moment in time. But life doesn't come with a do-over card."

"While I was hanging upside down in my seat belt and unable to feel my legs, I thought about what I'd do differently in my life if I had it to live over. The biggest thing I wanted to change was my relationship with you. I desperately wanted a chance to fix things, even though I didn't know how to begin."

"I'd say we just made a great beginning." Abby wrapped her arms around her sister and felt the last of the barriers in her heart crumble.

Chapter Twenty-One

Aʀᴍᴇᴅ ᴡɪᴛʜ ᴄʟɪᴘᴘᴇʀs and plastic leaf bags, gardening hats and gloves, the two sisters spent the rest of the afternoon working and talking. More important than the perennials in need of deadheading, or the bushes ready for pruning, was the stream of conversation flowing between them.

Like a deep river with eddies of laughing reminiscence and rough rapids of misunderstanding, their honest talk cascaded over the rocky course of their past as the sun moved westward. With a word here and an explanation there, obstacles of estrangement dissolved and washed away in the flood.

"I don't know when I've laughed and cried so much on the same day." Leaning forward, Mary powered her way up the ramp to the deck.

"Me neither." Carrying their gloves and tools, Abby surveyed the yard. "And look what happened. The flower beds are weeded." *Like the gardens of our hearts.* "The bushes are pruned." *Like the hurtful misunderstandings of the past.* "The dead flowers are clipped to make way for new blooms." *Like the new life of our relationship preparing to flower in the next season.*

"And we both need showers." Mary brushed at the dirt clinging to her hands.

"We'll do that too." Abby tucked their gloves under her arm and took Mary's hat from her head on the way to opening the screen door. She bent down and kissed her sister's forehead. "God's timing is perfect."

"I couldn't agree more." Mary clasped Abby's hand and gave an affectionate squeeze.

When Abby moved out of her sister's path, the bare spot on the fence caught her attention again. "You know—" She stopped and closed her eyes. It was time to go inside and clean up. "Later."

"Don't later me. What? Tell me what's on your mind."

Abby hesitated, closed the door and sat on a wicker chair so she was eye-level with Mary. "I was just thinking about what Dad said."

"About the drawing on the fence being a carbon copy of David Bowditch's artistic style?"

"Yes. Of course, he couldn't have done it."

"That's been going around in the back of my thoughts since you mentioned it earlier." Mary ran her fingers through her hair, lifting the sweat-dampened strands as her brow furrowed thoughtfully. "Dad's right, you know. Until you told me about your conversation with him, I couldn't figure out what kept niggling at me yesterday. In the back of my mind, I knew I'd seen something like that drawing before. And in a manner of speaking, I had, every time I went to the library."

"Well, we know the artist wasn't David." Wondering if this was the right time to ask for a rather big favor, Abby paused for a moment before turning to her sister.

"I know that look," Mary said. "You have an idea. What is it?"

"Suppose David's son did it." Even as Abby gave voice to the thought, it sounded absurd.

"Ah, well, that might be a little tougher than thinking David drew it." Doubt softened Mary's words. "I mean, Jonah's been gone for over thirty-five years."

Abby sighed. "I know. It's so odd. Just when I think I'm starting to make sense out of it, my logic hits a wall of impossibility and falls apart."

Mary turned her chair so she could look directly at the fence. "I want to say that the tree frog guy is the artist, but I'm going to take a page from your book and be very objective. Do you know what kind of bird the artist intended?"

"I think so, but I can't be absolutely positive. So much depends on the size and shape of the eyes and beak, the reality is that it could be any one of a hundred."

Mary tilted her head as though seeking another perspective. "Is it possible it was supposed to be the birds you're looking for, the marbled murrelets?"

"As a scientist, I have to say I don't know."

"But as one of us rank-and-file civilians . . ." Mary prodded.

Abby decided to take the plunge and share her suspicions. They had all seemed so clear to her on the dreaming rock, but now she realized she wanted a second opinion. "I'm ninety-nine-point-nine percent certain it was a murrelet. Furthermore, I think it was both a message and a test. I believe I was supposed to complete the drawing."

"Wow." Mary's gaze darted back and forth between Abby and the fence. "You're awfully calm about it. That tells me you don't think our artist is dangerous."

"No. I really don't. That doesn't mean we won't continue to take precautions. We don't know if the tree frog man and the artist are the same person."

"Okay. Safety first is a good rule. But, well, we're already grungy from the yard work. Why don't you go out there and draw the bird? Do the whole thing. Like you think it was supposed to be. Let's find out if it was a test or not. And what the message is. My curiosity is running rampant."

Relieved Mary suggested the very thing she wanted to do, Abby let out a small laugh. "Are you sure? The other one bothered you—"

"Because it didn't have a head. But, hey. It's our fence. We can do anything we want with it, including drawing on it. I know I have a box of chalk in the craft room. Somewhere." Mary opened the sliding door. "I'll find the chalk while you put the gardening stuff away."

Ten minutes later, Abby knelt on a piece of cardboard beside the fence. Bees, intent on gathering the last bit of pollen from the alyssum buzzed around her knees. With Mary watching from the grass and checking Abby's efforts against a drawing in the second journal, Abby sketched a marbled murrelet onto the rough cedar planks. Every now and then, she stepped back and looked at the pages of the leather-bound book. She wanted to imitate as closely as possible the style of the original artist.

"It looks terrific," Mary said, awe in her voice. "You know, maybe you'd like to do the entire fence in something more permanent than chalk. Boy, talk about a color booster in the winter. A bright mural would be just the ticket."

Abby grinned at the idea. "Right. I could have a second career painting fences."

"Wouldn't that be great? We could take bookings at the flower shop. We would probably sell tons of plants. Just think of all those customers wanting to decorate the inside of their homes to blend with the murals outside. What a great theme. I'm excited just thinking about it."

"Whoa!" Abby tossed a surprised glance over her shoulder. "I'm not looking for a business venture."

"I know, but isn't it fun to dream and scheme about possibilities?"

"Yes, it is. Your creative mind pops from one idea to the next. I would have never thought about painting a mural on the fence, let alone opening a business."

Abby collected the chalk and moved beside Mary. "That's it. What do you think?"

"I had no idea you have so much talent. Are you sure you don't want to color it? I brought a box of pastels," Mary said thoughtfully.

"Thanks for the compliment, but no thanks to the pastels. I'm afraid to take that much license. I think I need to keep it on the same plane as the original."

"I get it. If this is truly a test, you don't want him to think you take it lightly."

"Yep. Now, the next move is up to our mystery person. I hope he comes soon."

"I do too. I think."

SATURDAY STRUGGLED TO BRING SUNSHINE. Instead, a dip in the temperature brought fog and the heavy mist familiar to the Northwest. Mindful of the thickening dampness out on the deck, Abby closed her Agatha Christie novel and went inside to the living room.

"I hope this burns off soon," Mary said as she rolled up to the sliding door.

"I don't think it will. It hasn't thinned much since I went out." Fog or sunshine, today was a good day to take Hugo up on his offer and photocopy the birding journals. Much as Abby wanted to hold on to both books, only one of them belonged to her. Once she made copies, she would return the second journal.

"Do you always go outside to read in the morning?"

"I prefer being outdoors. A little misty fog is nothing

compared to an upstate New York winter. Then, I turn up the heat and stay in bed to read. By the time I finish my reading for the day, the house is warm enough for me to get in the shower." Abby put her novel next to her Bible on the table near the sliding doors.

"You are disciplined," Mary murmured softly in a preoccupied tone.

Abby looked at her sister. "Isn't it time for your workout?"

Mary opened the slider. "In a minute."

"Where are you going?" Intrigued by her sister's actions, Abby followed.

Mary wheeled across the deck to the far side. "Yes. I am right. There *is* something different about the drawing on the fence."

"I wouldn't doubt it. Chalk and misty fog are not a good mix. I'm surprised you can still see anything."

"No, it's not that. Come over here and look."

Abby did as instructed. "I see what you mean. From this angle . . ."

"Go check it out. Wet as the grass is, I'll never get this chair down there without getting stuck."

Abby was already on her way down the stairs. Feeling like she was in a race with the thick mist, she hurried across the slick grass as fast as she dared.

The chalk had nearly disappeared into the damp wood when she reached the fence. There was just enough left to see that the mystery artist had indeed returned in the night and added more detail. Ghostly tree limbs and a nest surrounded the feet of the phantom bird.

Although he had not signed his efforts, there was a number chalked on the lower right side. Because of the moisture beading in the cracks and sliding down the wood like a wet eraser, she couldn't determine if the digit was a three or an eight.

"Who are you? What does this mean?" she whispered.

She examined the ground, looking for anything he might have left behind and wondering when he had returned to draw the peculiar nest the murrelets favored. It must have been late, after she and Mary finally locked the doors for the night and closed the shades.

A lump of white in the dark mulch caught her eye and Abby picked up a broken piece of chalk. As a clue, it was too common and ordinary to be of any use. Still, she stuck it in her pocket.

Wishing she could have seen the artist's surprise when he returned and found her drawing instead of his, she studied the strange signature. Or whatever it was. *Why* did he sign the work with a number?

"What are you doing out there?" Mary called from the deck.

Abby straightened and retraced her steps to her sister's side. "He added a nest under the bird. And what might be a signature."

"He signed it?" Mary's voice echoed her astonishment.

"In a manner of speaking."

"So speak. Don't keep me in suspense. What is his name?"

"Either three or eight." Struggling with her own confusion, Abby looked over her shoulder at the drawing. "There's no name, just a number that's impossible to read. The moisture in the fog might, or might not, have washed away part of it. That's why I can't tell which one it is."

Mary wheeled to the edge of the ramp. "Still, it's a good thing you redrew the bird. He put a nest under it. That has to mean you passed the test. It's the right one."

Abby took out the chalk and fiddled with it while her mind played over the possibilities. "There may be one more connection. I copied the image right out of the second journal. That makes me think the artist knows about it. And he's the same person who left the first journal for me by the planter."

"Okay, but what does the number mean?"

"I don't know." Abby opened her hand. Damp chalk coated her palm and fingers. "Why don't I ask?"

"How are you going to do that?"

"Watch." She marched back to the fence and put a big question mark beside the fading number. The wet chalk crumbled as she formed the curve and line. It disintegrated when she put the period beneath the query.

SUNDAY MORNING, instead of going out to her prayer place on the deck, Abby stayed in her room with the blinds closed. Light leaked through the slats and danced on the pages of the

Bible on her lap. Determined not to give in to curiosity or let earthly desires interfere with her commitment to spend time in the Word, she repositioned her chair and returned to her study.

Today, Paul's prayer for the Ephesians to grasp the all-encompassing breadth of God's love seemed particularly apropos. She saw that the ongoing renewal between her and her sister was a result of, and a conduit for, the blessings He wanted to bestow.

The realization astounded her and stayed with her as she prepared to attend the service at Little Flock Church. When she was ready, she checked the time and went down to help Mary.

"Did you look at the fence?"

"No. I thought we'd do it together."

Mary's delighted grin was all the thanks Abby needed for curtailing her curiosity. She opened the closet doors, inviting her sister to select the outfit she wanted to wear to church. Anticipation charged their usual routine. They spoke little and moved quickly. Like long ago Christmas mornings, they wanted to be together and share the unveiling of a surprise.

With the final button buttoned and the last zipper zipped, they went out to the back deck. Side by side, they peered through the morning mist at the fence.

"I'm not sure what we expected to see." Abby couldn't keep her disappointment out of her voice.

Mary didn't even try. "Well, I don't know about you, but I sure wanted more than just a fading question mark."

Chapter Twenty-Two

By Monday morning, the chalked question mark had disappeared into the rough wood of the fence.

"No response to your question." Dressed in yellow and lime green exercise gear, Mary sat at the top of the ramp leading to the yard and gazed across at the empty boards.

Abby sighed dejectedly. *A mystery with too many dead ends and unanswered questions.* She returned to her usual chair on the deck and drank her morning coffee. "Nothing is coming together and I'm beginning to feel completely clueless."

Mary joined her at the wicker table. "Please, explain what you mean."

"It might be easier to show you." Hoping the exercise would help her too, Abby tore a paper napkin into irregular pieces and put them in a pile in front of her. "Think of our mystery as a jigsaw puzzle waiting to be fit together. The first problem is not having a picture to show me what it's supposed to look like."

Mary smiled. "You and Dad. You know, he still digs out

those old puzzles every winter and puts them together while Mom and I knit. She bought new ones for him, but he always goes back to the puzzles you two did together."

Abby sipped hot coffee to melt the sudden lump in her throat.

"I didn't mean to upset you." Mary offered a tissue. "It's just such a sweet thing, I thought you'd want to know."

Abby took the tissue and blotted her cheeks. Only the pain of the inevitable parting that was in her future could make such a beautiful memory hurt so badly.

"Stop now or you're going to get me started too." Mary reached across and tapped the pile of napkin pieces. "Let's get back to these. What were you going to show me?"

Abby met her sister's inquisitive gaze. "Dad and I always started a big puzzle by sorting the colors and doing the border. I'm still sorting here and there's a lot of guessing involved."

She separated the napkin shreds into eight pieces and began with a finger on the first piece. "This is the actual sighting Dad and I witnessed. The second one is the journals. It touches the third—the picture on the fence—because it matches the picture in the book. The fourth piece is the tree frog man."

Mary moved the fluttery piece to one side. "He's over here by himself because you don't know for sure where he fits in. Correct?"

"Yes. Now, number five is the Bowditch family and the property they gave to Whale Riders, Inc. It's the marbled murrelets' most likely nesting grounds. Six represents you, Dad, Mom and Hugo, because you're connected to me and through me to the birds." Abby looked up to see if her sister was still interested.

"Don't stop now. What are the last two?"

"Number seven is the mystery artist." Abby moved that piece closer to the napkin shred representing the journals. "And number eight is Frank Holloway. He overheard Dad telling Hugo about our sighting. Frank reacted strongly. Negatively. He really didn't like the idea of my looking for the murrelets."

Mary tapped her lips with her forefingers. "At least it settles one question. If he doesn't want you to even look for the birds, he isn't the one sneaking around at night drawing pictures on the fence. But, shouldn't that eliminate him altogether?"

"Maybe, maybe not. Dad talked to him the next day and he said he wouldn't tell anybody anything. But who knows? Frank was pretty upset when he left the party and might have said something to someone later on. Or someone might have overheard him grousing to himself."

"I still don't think he's involved," Mary insisted. "He's so not the bird type."

Abby laughed into her cup and sloshed coffee onto her hand. She grabbed the tissue she'd used earlier and mopped up the drops. "What's your definition of the bird type?"

"True birders, like you, have to be patient. We already

know I'll never be one. We found that out the first couple of times we went birding with Dad. Frank isn't one either. No way can I picture him hanging out for hours waiting for some bird to come flying by."

"I can't either," Abby said morosely. "That's part of what makes it so confusing. Somehow, our mystery man learned of my interest in the murrelets. If Frank didn't tell him, then I'm stymied again. All I know for sure is that a few days after the party, the first journal showed up here on the deck."

Mary studied the napkin pieces on the table, then shook her head. "I'm beginning to see this is a lot more complicated than I thought. It doesn't look like there are enough pieces to put the puzzle together."

"If I could just make a few more connections, I might be able to figure it out. Learning the identity of our fence artist is key."

"I really hoped he would return and give you an answer to your question mark," Mary said pensively. "But with the fog . . . Don't give up on him yet."

"No, I won't." Abby gathered up the napkin shreds. "There is something I've been wondering about lately."

"What's that?" Mary asked.

"Can you think of anyone we know who might have attended Jonah Bowditch's funeral service?" Abby paused, her mind whirling.

"Or if there even was a service," Mary said slowly.

Determined to find out, Abby popped out of her chair and went inside for the cordless phone.

"You know, I don't remember there being a service," Mary said as soon as Abby returned. "It was a long time ago, but when something big or tragic happens on the island, folks usually remember. There might have been a small service at the grave site."

"I'm drawing a complete blank too," Abby admitted. "I was so preoccupied with graduation and preparing to go to Cornell that year, I paid no attention to what was going on in Green Harbor." She punched in their parents' number as she paced the deck. After a quick catch-up with her father, she told him the purpose of her call.

"I can't say I recall a service for Jonah Bowditch," George said contemplatively. "Let me ask your mother."

Abby cupped her hand over the phone. "He's checking with Mom."

"She would know." Mary nodded confidently.

Their father returned to the phone. "Sorry, your mother doesn't recall either. That was a busy summer and if there was a public service, we didn't attend. She suggested you check with Janet."

"Okay, Dad. Thanks."

"I'd demand to know what's up if Sam wasn't waiting for me. Give me a call this evening, okay?"

"Will do." Abby disconnected and punched in another number.

"Are you calling Janet?" Mary asked eagerly. "She knows something about everything that has ever happened on the island."

"That's the problem. With all due respect, Mary, Janet has a wider circulation for her news than *The Birdcall*. I'd prefer the whole island didn't know I was asking questions about Jonah."

"*Hmm*, I see your dilemma."

"Hugo, this is Abby Stanton. Got a minute?"

Moments later, she sighed and set the phone on the table. "My two best sources came up with big zeros."

"Then we'll just have to wait and see what appears on the fence," Mary said. "Whoever the man is, he sure seems to be trying to get a message across. I don't think he'll quit now." She leaned forward and placed a hand on Abby's knee. "You know, you can't miss an opportunity with your name written on it."

"I do know." Abby put her hand atop Mary's and an idea struck with the force of a thunderbolt.

"Uh-oh," Mary said teasingly. "You're at it again. What is it?"

"I could go to Friday Harbor and check the county records."

"It's a great day for a ferry ride." Mary glanced at her watch. "If you hurry you can make the next one. It leaves in forty minutes."

"What about you? Isn't today your knitting group?"

"Not to worry. We'll have it here." Mary reached for the phone Abby had laid on the table. "Go get ready."

Abby picked up her coffee mug, glanced at the fence and slid open the screen door before looking at Mary.

"You don't have to say it. I won't breathe a word of where you've gone or what you're doing," Mary promised.

"I trust you, Mary." *Trust.* The precious word settled deep in Abby's heart. *Thank You, Lord.*

"What if you don't find Jonah's name where it should be in the county records?" Mary asked as she wheeled into the living room.

Abby tossed her hands up. "That's the big question."

"Hey, Miss Stanton."

Surprised to hear her name, Abby looked up from the spiral-bound notebook containing the record of her search for the marbled murrelets. "Aaron, it's good to see you."

Aaron Holloway swayed slightly as the ferry left the dock at Green Harbor and he tentatively returned her smile.

Closing the notebook, she welcomed the opportunity to chat with the young man during the ride. "Are you going to Friday Harbor too?"

"Yes, ma'am. It's my day off." He pushed the hair from his eyes and grinned. "I'm going to the big city."

Abby chuckled softly at his tongue-in-cheek reference. "Join me, won't you?"

"Thank you." He slid into the padded booth on the other side of the table. "Grandad said you traveled all around the world. I reckon you've seen most of the big cities." Aaron rested his forearms on the table and curled his long fingers around the brim of his Seattle Mariners ball cap.

"Big cities have their purpose and a special kind of allure," she said, recalling the bastions of culture and commerce she had roamed over the years. "For day-to-day living, nothing beats the peace and quiet of these islands." She tilted her head toward him. "I'm speaking strictly for myself, of course."

"Grandad would agree with you," Aaron said slowly.

"What about you?" Her curiosity about the industrious young man began to simmer. He was trying hard to live up to expectations and fit into the tightly knit Sparrow Island community. She applauded his zeal. If he didn't find happiness though, he wouldn't last.

"I grew up in Seattle. There was always something going on somewhere. I wasn't sure I'd like living out on an island where it takes a couple hours to get to the mainland." He ran his thumb over the brim of his cap.

"And now?" Abby asked, wondering if Frank understood what a tremendous adjustment Aaron was trying to make.

"I read a lot of books." He grinned. "Even so, it wouldn't hurt to have a movie theater in Green Harbor."

Abby laughed. "I hadn't even noticed we didn't have one."

"Then you must not be a movie buff."

"I'm what you might call cinematically challenged. I try to go to one movie a year whether I need to or not. Just to stay current." For the last decade, few movies appealed to her.

"Grandad isn't big on movies either."

"Speaking of Frank, how do you like working at the

hardware store?" During her last visit, Aaron seemed to have a lot to learn.

"I like it better than any of the other jobs I've had. I like the people most of all." Aaron sat back, his arms stretched on the table. "Those old guys who gather on the porch are a hoot. They try to help me out. But I gotta tell you, when Grandad isn't around, sometimes they confuse me a lot more than they help me."

"I understand your grandfather wants you to take over the store when he retires."

"It better not be for a very long time. Heck, I haven't figured out why he carries half the stuff he does, let alone what to do with it. He knows so much. I've worked heavy construction, driven a delivery truck, worked in a bakery and even bussed tables. Nothing I did before coming to Green Harbor was like running a hardware store."

"If you've done all that, you know more than you think. Sometimes it's a matter of perspective."

"What do you mean?"

"You didn't do all those jobs at the same time, did you?"

Aaron laughed. "No, ma'am. I just sorta drifted from one to the next, not going anywhere."

"I have an idea. Let's start with you telling me what you did on each of the jobs you had."

"Uh, well, okay."

Aaron revealed a wide range of responsibilities. Gradually, a pattern emerged. Every time the young man switched jobs, he went to the library and checked out books germane to his new job. When he washed cars at a dealership, he read Henry Ford's biography and everything written by Lee Iacocca. Very quickly, Abby realized that behind the wall of hair drooping into his eyes, the shy twenty-five-year-old had a brilliant mind.

"Let me see if I understand this," she said. "You're struggling with what might be called the minutia of the stock on Frank's shelves while searching for the big picture of how it all goes together." *Now there is a situation I relate to completely.*

"I hadn't thought of it that way, but yeah, you could say that. Did you know our town library doesn't carry any books on hardware stores?"

Suppressing a smile, Abby nodded. "I doubt there's much demand."

"Nope. There isn't."

"You know, Aaron, Frank was raised in the hardware store business. What he knows took a lifetime to learn."

"Yeah, well he can fix plumbing, build a house, run electrical wiring, overhaul a lawnmower and everything else all at one time. I'm beginning to think I'll never get there."

"Frank doesn't expect you to pick it all up overnight." Abby put a strong note of reassurance in her tone. "You might want to start with his weaknesses."

"I don't think he has any."

"When I was at the store last, you didn't know how to do computerized inventory."

"I do now. Joe Blackstock showed me. It was a piece of

cake. Now, Grandad wants me to do all the computer work, which is fine by me." Aaron suddenly sat straighter in the booth. "Hey, you're right. Grandad *does* have a weakness. Computers kind of scare him, but they're something I understand and like."

"Think of the hardware store like a computer."

"Huh? You lost me, Miss Stanton."

"Most of us know which buttons to push and what programs to run to do things like accessing the Internet or writing a letter. We don't have any idea of how the machine actually works and don't care as long as it continues working the way we expect."

Aaron gave an agreeing shrug. "That's true."

"The shelves at the hardware store hold all the pieces and parts. Think of them as the inside of the computer. The store is the case. The cash register is the keyboard. Do you see how the information flows?"

He leaned forward. "I get what you're telling me, Miss Stanton. If I think of the inventory as a database and the part numbers as the keys, I can pull out what I need. After a while, it will all make sense. If I have a good picture of the whole, it'll be easier to understand the pieces. At the same time, I'll be picking up stuff from Grandad and the guys."

Aaron's hair bobbed over the bridge of his nose as he nodded, more to himself than to her. "That's cool. I can do that."

"You might also want to consider checking out a few books on small business management."

"Yeah. I'll stop at the library in Friday Harbor." He grinned. "By the way, I have learned the difference between standard and metric."

"Did Frank teach you?"

"Sure did. Good thing too. Lately, he's gone more than he used to be."

The opening was too blatant for Abby to ignore. "Where does he go when he's away from the store?"

Aaron shrugged. "Out."

Familiar with the monosyllabic answers many students gave when they didn't want to explain something, she kept quiet. Silence was often a better prod than a hundred questions.

"The past couple of months he's gone to Bellingham more than he used to." The way Aaron lowered his head and stared at his hands betrayed his concern. "All he says is that there's something he has to do for a friend."

Whether it was Aaron's tone or the simplicity of his statement, Abby saw the possibility of a new angle on the mystery she sought to solve. "Do you know the name of the friend he's aiding?"

"Nope. Grandad tells me about all his friends, but he doesn't talk about where he goes on the mainland or who he's with." Aaron raised his head. "He just seems kinda sad, you know?"

Abby nodded. Considering Frank's volatile reaction at the homecoming party, something weighed heavily on his mind. If he wasn't sharing with Aaron or her dad, he was keeping his troubles close to his heart.

Aaron turned in his seat. "Man, I can't believe we're at Friday Harbor already. Thanks, Miss Stanton. The time flew while we were talking. I'll work on what you said."

"You've changed my perspective too." She gathered her things and put them in her tote bag.

Wanting to time her arrival at the courthouse for after lunch, Abby browsed the little specialty stores along the way. A yarn shop with a bright display of multicolored cardigan sweaters caught her attention.

Mary would love some of the soft, vibrant yarn for a sweater of her own. Although more expensive than most of the skeins in the store, the textures and hues suited her personality.

On an impulse, Abby spoke with a saleswoman eager to share her expertise.

By the time Abby left, she carried another bag stuffed with the special yarn and had to hurry to get to the courthouse. She found a friendly clerk who dealt with public records, explained what she was looking for and chatted while the elderly woman searched the computer databases.

Two hours after arriving in Friday Harbor, Abby boarded the ferry for home with a light step. She had learned a great deal more from her trip than she expected.

Chapter Twenty-Three

THAT EVENING, ABBY rummaged around in the coat closet in the foyer. An old mackinaw, probably left by her father, was her first find. Not caring that the dark brown coat almost reached her knees, she put it on and rolled the sleeves up to her wrists. Invisibility was her goal. This was a good start.

In the living room, Mary looked up from her knitting. Her eyes widened with dismay she tried valiantly to conceal. "Where, uh, are you going?"

"Why? Don't you like my outfit?" Abby tucked her hair into a navy blue watch cap.

"Since you asked, I have to say no. It's nearly sundown." Mary's fingers twitched in the new yarn on her lap and the soft wool shimmered like a rainbow of confetti. "Well, if you're going out, I have a closet full of blazers and jackets. You're welcome to any of them. There's a lovely tweed that—"

"Sorry, I was just teasing. I'm going outside to watch for our mystery artist."

Mary's shocked expression softened into wry amusement.

"I should have known. What makes you think he's coming this evening?"

Abby fished in the jacket pockets for a pair of gloves. "If the number on the fence was a three, it could have meant he planned to return in three nights. That's tonight."

"What a pity he won't come to the front door and ring the bell."

"I doubt that will ever happen," Abby said sadly. "I've been giving this a lot of thought. The tree frog man Bobby described was somewhat disfigured. The boy used the words *alien* and *Martian*. I believe that may explain his reluctance to be seen."

"Just like our artist doesn't want to be seen." Mary tapped her chin. "So what you're saying is they might be one and the same person."

"It is possible. Children are more open and accepting of appearances than many adults."

Mary began folding her knitting. "I'll come out and sit with you."

"Normally Mary, I'd love to have you with me." Abby glanced at the long shadows filling the backyard. "It's just that I've nestled a chair against the rhododendrons so I can't be easily seen."

"Ah, a woman with a real plan. You'll be able to see him, but he won't see you unless you want him to. And it would be hard to miss a wheelchair bogged down in the impatiens." Mary smoothed the yarn on her lap. "This is a one-woman stakeout. Go get him, Miss Marple."

Abby smiled at the comparison with Agatha Christie's legendary sleuth. "I'm not certain my deductive abilities are as good as hers, so I won't hold my breath."

"Good. I'd hate to have to explain to anyone why you fainted out in the bushes."

Leaving Mary in the comfort of the warm house, Abby went out to the deck. A cool front had moved in with the twilight, carrying a sweet scent, heavy with moisture. It promised night dew would soon coat every leaf and twig, and also bring the penetrating damp that stiffened joints. Abby descended the stairs, crossed the grass and settled in to wait and watch.

"I can't see you out there," Mary called from the screen door.

"I'm here." Abby waved a white handkerchief.

Mary lingered and Abby realized with a little more effort in the setup, she could have included her sister.

Abby rose, went to the edge of the deck and said to Mary, "If our guy doesn't show tonight, we'll do this together next time."

"I'd like that."

"It's a promise. Call if you need me."

"I'll be fine." Mary wheeled away from the screen, looked back with a tender smile and added, "Now."

A moment later, Abby heard her close the vertical blinds, then turn on the TV. Bless her heart; she was helping in the only way available.

As the sky turned lavender, gold light gilded the edges of the long, high clouds stretched above the trees. Flying west, a murder of crows squawked at the sun as though chastising it for setting before they finished playing their soaring games in the sky. Abby returned to her perch in the bushes.

Thanks to today's trip to the county courthouse, the pieces of the puzzle were beginning to come together. If she had guessed the true nature of the picture correctly, tonight several of the pieces would slide into place. Two minutes with the stealthy artist was all she needed for confirmation.

Gradually the sounds of the day turned into night. Many species, bold and saucy in the sunshine, quieted down quickly as stars filled the sky and the owls came out to feed. Dark on dark against the trees, with great wings stretched wide, they glided silently inland leaving nothing behind but a fleeting shadow.

Listening for any disruption to the normal ebb and flow in the foraging of the night creatures, Abby slouched back in the chair. The air grew still as though waiting with her and she turned her face to the sky. The brilliant swath of the Milky Way glittered overhead, filling her with awe.

God's blessings were even more bountiful than the stars. This time on Sparrow Island with her parents and Mary was a treasure far in excess of Abby's wildest expectations. She'd hoped, dreamed and prayed for restoration and reunion. He'd responded with an abundance that still boggled her mind.

Wondering which was more complex, a human being or a star, she smiled as the answer came even before she could finish the thought. *God never sent His Son to save a star.*

His purposes stretched far beyond what she could imagine. He had created the peace flourishing between her and Mary. On it, they were building a positive, open relationship free from the clouds of guilt and the storms of distrust. "Dear Lord, what a brilliant master planner you are," Abby murmured. "You brought me here to—"

Words suddenly refused to form on her lips. She sat in stunned silence, waiting on Him.

Fresh from the sea, the wind began whispering through the trees, rustling the rhododendrons and showering her with pink petals. *Stay, child*, she thought she heard Him say.

Could it be? Amazed and breathless, she watched the pale petals float onto her lap. Who was she to put limits on the Lord? She had asked Him to attend the cry of her heart. That He was also attuned to the groaning at the innermost depths of her soul should not be surprising. Opening the storehouse of His love, He gave her the reunion she sought and the promise of so much more.

Too overwhelmed to move, Abby considered the future He offered. Watching movies and eating popcorn, doing jigsaw puzzles and telling corny jokes—these were just part of the glue binding a family together. Being there when a family member needed help or encouragement, offering a tangible shoulder to cry on or rejoicing together—all of these could be hers in the truest sense.

All she had to do was accept His gift.

"Thank You for showing me there is a time for all things,

a time to leave and a time to return. Thank You, Lord, for bringing me home. Not just for a visit, but for a new season of life."

A peaceful rightness settled over Abby, bringing a deep contentment. As she considered the richness of the new path before her, a giddy joy made her laugh and glance up at the heavens.

Judging by the position of the stars, it was well after midnight and time to go inside. Somehow Abby knew the elusive fence artist wasn't coming tonight. But that was okay. Tonight, she'd been given something far more important than the answers he might provide.

With a light heart and a head swimming with ideas, Abby picked up her chair and headed for the deck. Today was a new day, the first day of her permanent return to Sparrow Island. In the morning, she'd tell Mary.

HENRY COBB KNOCKED on the front door just before breakfast and Abby tucked away the news sparkling inside her for later. She liked Henry and was glad to see him. Given the tender manner in which he regarded her sister, it wasn't a big leap to believe he had arranged his schedule so he could drop by for a visit.

Abby decided to get a head start on her agenda for the day. Leaving early would allow Henry a little personal time with Mary. Later, when she and Mary were alone, would be the time to reveal her change of plans.

As soon as Henry agreed to share breakfast with them,

Abby cut up the rest of the fresh pineapple and added a couple more eggs to the bowl for scrambling. While her sister and Henry lingered over the meal, Abby took her plate to the sink. "I leave you in good hands, Mary. I have an errand to run. If you need me, call my cell phone."

Mary raised her hand, her thumb and forefinger forming a circle of acknowledgment. "I memorized the number. I'll be fine."

"Sure she will," Henry said as he poured fresh coffee for the two of them.

Moments later, Abby backed the car out of the driveway and headed across town to the conservatory. The moment she turned into the parking lot, she spotted Hugo. Heartened because not all of her previous rejections had dampened his enthusiasm, she angled the car into a parking space as he strolled down the flower-bordered walk toward the lot.

When Abby turned off the ignition, he opened the car door and said, "You picked the perfect day for a tour and my sales pitch."

"I'm at your disposal," she said, climbing out of the car. "And I don't have a completely unbiased mind."

"Ah, that was part of the bargain," Hugo reminded.

She gave him a bright smile. "I came prepared to be impressed." *And if possible, accept the job.* "I want to see and hear it all, Hugo, the pluses and the minuses."

"Excellent. Where would you like to start?"

"Inside." She accompanied him up the steps to The

Nature Museum and waited while he opened the door for her to enter.

Near the children's area, Rebecca stood chatting with a couple of junior high school girls. Abby returned the teenager's happy wave. Although still early in the day, a group of Japanese tourists moved slowly among the exhibits.

"Business is good," Abby commented, wishing she knew what the patrons were saying. Their conversation was certainly animated. "They look as though they've discovered a gem in the hinterlands."

"With your assistance, we can make it sparkle."

As they moved from one area to the next, Hugo provided a detailed explanation of the logic behind the content of each exhibit along with the message he intended the observer to take away. By the third stop on his "tour," he had attracted several of the tourists. After the fourth, most of the visitors were tagging along and asking questions.

A font of knowledge, complete with anecdotes and the authority of experience, he spoke just loud enough for the growing group to hear. Abby was pleased to see he didn't miss a beat even when the construction crew working on the addition to the museum powered up their heavy equipment. The noise had no effect on his presentation. His unflappability impressed Abby.

Hugo's audience turned expectantly toward the sign touting The Wonderful World of Wings. While he explained it was under construction and gave them an overview, one of the Japanese women approached her.

"Excuse, please," the woman said with a slight bow. "I am wondering if you are Dr. Abigail Stanton."

Surprised, Abby answered, "Why, yes, I am."

Beaming, the woman with silver threading through her short black hair extended her hand. "I am Dr. Miko Okamoto from University of Tokyo and most pleased to make your acquaintance."

"Ah!" Delight buoyed Abby's already high spirits. "Dr. Okamoto, I am familiar with your efforts to preserve the *Sterna albifrons* on Atsugi, Kanagawa."

"Yes, the little terns. Thank you for taking notice. We fear the birds will become extinct if we are not successful in our work."

With the attention of the entire group focused on them, Hugo stepped in smoothly and asked, "What threatens them?"

"The little terns migrate from Australia and nest in Japan in the spring. The largest of the colonies numbers a little over three hundred." Dr. Okamoto shook her head sadly. "Roadwork planned for the island threatens their habitat."

"I would love to speak with you further," Abby said as she shot a questioning glance at Hugo.

Grinning, he gave a nod of approval and said, "I'll continue the tour and we'll finish our discussion later."

Grateful for the opportunity to chat with a colleague, Abby smiled at him and motioned to the back room. "May I?"

"Certainly." Hugo went over and opened the door labeled "Private."

Abby and Miko discussed the impact of habitat loss and pollution and the efforts of their respective countries to contain both. The minutes passed much too quickly, and all too soon Hugo and the Japanese group crowded into the room, explaining they had to hurry to catch the next ferry to Lopez Island. After exchanging business cards, Miko joined her traveling companions and bowed farewell.

"Well, that was very unexpected," Abby told Hugo when they were alone.

"It is just one of the benefits of working here, Abby. You meet people from all over the world."

"I'll keep it in mind. How about showing me the conservatory grounds?"

"This way." He gestured to the door. "When we're finished, we'll have a soda and I'll show you the architect's drawings for the construction we're doing."

"From what I've seen so far, you think big," she mused appreciatively.

"What I think is that with your expertise, we can make the museum and the addition of The Wonderful World of Wings very special, not just for Sparrow Island, but for the entire Northwest."

"Maybe the nation," she teased.

"Could be," he said seriously.

"The world?" she asked, trying to suppress her incredulity.

"Why not?"

"I admit you do surprise me, but I wouldn't put it past

you. The planning and execution I see here use technology at its best. I see a fine example of vision and efficiency."

"Meaning I'm someone you would enjoy working with, I hope."

As they walked along the path leading to the woods where yellow warblers sang from the red branches of madrone trees, Abby nodded and gave Hugo a sideways glance. Although he was somewhat a man of mystery himself, he knew exactly what he wanted and had the persistence to succeed. "Let's get down to basics."

In a flash, she realized that was exactly what this job would be—a return to basics and the rapt wonder of her childhood. Rather than cold charts, clinical facts, stark diagrams shown and endlessly discussed, her new position would take her back to the fundamentals. The glories of flight—dipping, whirring, climbing, wheeling, turning—in all its enormous freedom. The heart-stopping rush of wings as a flock of Canada geese lifted off as one. The sheer pulse-pounding joy of fledglings learning to fly.

How long had she been removed from that? When had those true joys of her profession escaped her grasp? She felt like she stood on the edge of a tall cliff ready to leap out into the unknown. Yet, it was familiar territory. She was coming home.

Chapter Twenty-Four

WITH A DOZEN IDEAS for her new position tumbling through her mind, Abby carried bags of groceries into the house shortly after three o'clock. She hoped she hadn't forgotten anything they needed.

Mary rolled into the kitchen. "You were gone so long," she teased, "I figured you went shopping in Friday Harbor."

"What did I miss?" Abby rushed over to the calendar of Mary's appointments.

"Relax. I hadn't planned on going anywhere today." Mary opened the refrigerator and unloaded the fresh produce from one of the bags into the vegetable bin.

Abby handed her a carton of orange juice, then another one of milk. "*Whew.* For a moment there, I thought I'd missed something."

"You didn't." Mary retreated and closed the refrigerator. "It won't be long before you can retire from your chauffeuring duties."

Alarms went off inside Abby. "Uh, why is that?"

"Talking with Henry today was a real boost," Mary continued. "He agrees I should search for the right vehicle and start driving again."

"Well," Abby said slowly, her mind racing. The van would be here soon. Somehow, she had to thwart Mary's plans to find transportation before then. "Uh, what else did he say?"

"He knows a man in Bellingham who might be able to help me find exactly what I need. I was thinking about calling him and setting up an appointment. We could take Mom with us and make a day of it. It would be fun."

"The Stanton women explore Bellingham. We'd have a blast. You're right. We have to pick a time when all three of us can go." Hoping to clue their mother in first so she could come up with reasons to stall Mary, Abby mentally counted the days until the Dennys would deliver the van.

"So, how about tomorrow?"

"Tomorrow? So soon?"

"It doesn't seem soon to me," Mary said. "Although Dad thinks I should wait a couple of weeks. But I can't see his point."

Abby filled the kettle with water and turned on the stove. "Let's have some tea and talk."

"As long as you're not going to try to talk me out of getting a car I can drive," Mary said warily, stacking several cans in the pantry.

"Nope. You have your mind made up. You'll do it. Furthermore, I've already agreed it would be good for you to drive again." Abby set the teapot on the table. "The immediate impediment is the timing." She picked up a container of assorted melon chunks. "Put out the placemats. I'll get a plate for the fruit."

Mary laid out placemats and napkins.

Abby sat at the table, settling her inner self before she poured the tea. "Last night while waiting for our no-show fence artist, I did a great deal of thinking and praying about our situation here."

Mary reached for her sister's hand. "We need to give this new relationship of ours time. Please don't let the past cloud the future."

Abby turned her hand over and laced their fingers together. "Actually, I came to a decision. I'm going to take you up on your offer of a place to live." She hadn't realized she was nervous until Mary squeezed her clammy hand. "I'm staying on Sparrow Island. Permanently."

"Really?"

"Really."

"Thank you, Jesus, for answering my prayers." Mary laughed joyously. "Only He could put such a big change in your heart."

"I suppose I was a tough case. He's been working on me for a while. Everything just came together last night."

"Praise the Lord." Mary's eyes widened and she shook their hands. "Why didn't you tell me this morning?"

"I was planning to, then Henry came by." Abby released Mary's hand. "You two had a good visit, right?"

"Yes," Mary conceded. "He's easy to talk with."

Silently, Abby agreed. "He likes you, genuinely likes being around you."

Mary seemed to weigh the meaning of that statement before responding noncommittally, "He's a good friend."

"Yes, he is." *And that's all I'm going to say. Henry will have to press his suit for your heart on his own. I will not be a buttinski in matters of the heart.* "We have another good friend, my new boss, Hugo Baron."

A cry of sheer glee escaped Mary. Blossom went running for the back of the house. "No kidding? You're going to go to work for Hugo?"

Abby's mirth joined her sister's laughter. With each revelation, she felt better and better about her decision to stay on Sparrow Island. "At my age, I never kid around about a career change. Part of me can't believe I'm doing this."

"All of me is thrilled you are. I can't wait to see Mom's and Dad's faces when you tell them. They'll go bonkers." Singing "Oh, Happy Day," Mary speared a piece of melon with her fork. "How about calling and having them over for dinner tonight?"

"Great idea." Abby bit into her melon.

"Having you here permanently is going to be so good, Abby. For all of us." Mary sipped her tea. "Mom and I will start planning the garage sale tonight."

Abby paused mid-bite, her mouth full of fruit. "Huh?"

"We need to clear out the upstairs to make room for your furnishings. You can change anything you want, just make it yours. I'll even get Frank to paint the walls beige if you like."

Abby looked at her fork and put it down. "I don't know how I forgot about that part. Moving will be a pain. I've been so caught up with this decision and how I'm going to handle Cornell—"

"Uh-oh." Mary paled.

"Are you all right?"

"Your department head, Jerome, phoned earlier. I told him you'd call when you got home. I'm so sorry. I forgot to tell you the moment you came in."

Abby shook her head dismissively. "It's not a problem. If it had been urgent, he would have called my cell phone. Knowing Jerome, he doesn't have good news."

"Does it matter now?"

Abby thought for a moment. "I don't intend to abandon my search for the marbled murrelets. Especially now. And there is nothing that will change my mind about staying on Sparrow Island. You call Mom and Dad. I'll phone Jerome at home."

Mary backed away from the table. "You're going to have your hands full for a while, aren't you?"

"The next several days I'll be living on the telephone. I'm going to try to move without making a trip back to Ithaca." Abby shook her head as images of dear friends and lifelong colleagues crowded her thoughts. "Going back right now would entail more emotional upheaval than I want to take on."

"You can always go for a visit."

"Yeah, maybe next year, in the spring."

Mary reached for the telephone as Abby took hers from her pocket. "You know, I'd really like to have you with me when I talk about cars and financing. I'll hold off until you have time to go with me before I speak with Henry's friend in Bellingham."

"It would be a big help." Relieved to have dodged another complication, Abby smiled and punched in Jerome's home number. "I need to take one thing at a time."

The phone rang twice before he answered. "Mixed news, Abby," he said after an exchange of pleasantries. "The funding I'd hoped to tag for your murrelets has been reallocated. One of our big alumni contributors is concerned about the little terns on one of the Japanese islands."

Lord, You have such a unique sense of humor. "Dr. Miko Okamoto's project from the University of Tokyo," Abby said, pleased for the dynamic ornithologist.

"You know of it?" Surprise raised Jerome's voice.

"Yes. In fact, I met Miko here on Sparrow Island. She has an excellent grasp on the problem and the stakes if she doesn't succeed. I'm afraid she has quite a battle ahead. This is people and progress against the little tern's natural habitat. She'll need all the resources and influence she can muster. Having Cornell on her side will certainly help."

Abby elaborated on her conversation with Dr. Okamoto and answered Jerome's questions on her own search for the marbled murrelets. Without the funding from Cornell, she would have to find another way to protect their nesting grounds, although Jerome offered to lend his prestige to the project when the time came. Perhaps one day, the two of them would get to see the elusive little birds nesting high in an old tree.

"There is one more thing, Jerome. I'm formally asking you to withdraw my request for a leave of absence."

"You're coming home?" he asked excitedly.

"No. I'm resigning." The heart-thumping emotion she had anticipated while making the announcement failed to occur. The decision was so right, so rock-solid, not a qualm quivered. Eyes closed, she envisioned an enormous scissors poised at the cord tying her to Ithaca.

"You're what?"

"I'm staying on Sparrow Island." *I'm home for good.* "I'll mail my letter of resignation to you tomorrow so you'll have it in writing." In her mind, the blades of the giant scissors closed.

"I don't know if it makes any sense, but I'm stunned, yet not surprised, considering your family is involved. You're irreplaceable there and here."

"No one in academia is irreplaceable," she said softly.

"True, however, friendship is another matter."

Elbow on the table, Abby rested her forehead on her hand and silently agreed with the man who had been her friend and mentor for thirty-five years. Tears dripped onto the placemat as she thought of the dear ones she would leave behind.

THE ELDER STANTONS received the news of Abby's decision to stay on the island with joyful tears and a profusion of gratitude for the way the Lord answered prayer. Humbled by the realization that her entire family had been praying for this change of heart, Abby tried to take things in stride over the next few days.

The rest of Tuesday—keeping her emotions at bay and giving her logical side free rein—she attacked the mountain of tasks like a general organizing a campaign. She made lists. These spawned more lists. She sorted them by order of importance, made a master list of her lists, then finally retired for the night.

The three-hour time difference between the West and East Coasts required her to set her alarm clock and rise with the sun on Wednesday morning. While the rest of Sparrow Island awakened, Abby worked her lists by telephone and through the Internet.

Fortunately, the contacts she established over the years in Ithaca became a gold mine. They yielded a mother lode of recommendations for moving companies, realtors and resources to handle the odd jobs necessary for her home to sell quickly. Through multiple phone calls and references, she sifted the ore repeatedly until she found the nuggets—the companies and the right people for the tasks.

Making the temporary change of address permanent with the post office was a simple matter of filling out a card and placing it in the mailbox. If only the rest was half as easy. Contacting her credit card companies, utilities, subscriptions and the multiple associations in which she held a membership would take far more than the time frame she'd allotted and she decided to save those calls for next week.

Breaking the news to her friends, the graduate students she

had nurtured and above all, to Francine, was the most emotionally draining task. Yet, she was not alone in this. Christian music played softly in the background. A refreshing pot of tea and a tray of nourishing snacks appeared on the table. Through it all, she felt His presence and constancy.

Mary arranged her own transportation in order to visit her shop after lunch. After spending an afternoon at Island Blooms, she had Henry bring her home along with an armful of faxes sent to the store for Abby. He also carried in dinner from the Springhouse Café.

In a concession so huge Abby didn't bother to ask, Mary told her to leave her things on the dining room table and instructed Henry to set up trays in the living room. To be sure, they all had placemats and linen napkins. But the stacks of handwritten notes, estimates, printouts, quotes and lists remained undisturbed on the table.

Long before the sun went down Wednesday evening, Abby fell into bed exhausted. The mountain that God said a believer could move by faith felt as though it had actually budged an inch. She had a packing and moving company. They had an opening and enough space on the truck to accommodate the household goods she chose to keep. Packing would begin on Monday and they would load on Tuesday.

Francine, bless her heart, would oversee the move and the sale of the unneeded furnishings. *Dear Lord, how I will miss her.* A silent tear slipped onto Abby's pillowcase before sleep whisked her away.

AT THE SOUND OF LIVELY CHATTER and a horde of people entering the house Thursday morning, Abby closed the folder holding the offers for real estate representation on her home. She set the file aside and hurried from the dining room.

"Okay, ladies, now is your chance. I'm prepared to entertain offers when you're ready to make them."

Half a dozen women filed through the foyer. The little parade headed upstairs, talking excitedly in disjointed conversations.

Bewildered, Abby gazed at the backs of the women ascending the staircase. "What's going on, Mary?"

"I quashed the idea of a garage sale. My new idea is to auction everything off. I already have sealed bids from Janet and Margaret." She nodded toward the stairs. "These ladies are also interested in my antiques, so I'm giving them the opportunity to participate."

Abby placed a hand on her sister's shoulder and squeezed. "Are you sure? I know how you prize those pieces."

Mary waved her left hand dismissively, winked up at Abby and said sotto voce, "What good do they do me now? It's not as if I can suspend monkey bars from the ceiling and go up and visit them periodically. It's best to get rid of them and make room for our new lives."

"But what's with the sealed bids?"

"You told me I have a good head for business and I'm taking you at your word. I thought I'd have a little bidding war and make a few dollars in the process."

Abby regarded her sister and the happy new light in her features. "What an ingenious idea. Give buyers a preview and an opportunity to bid what they're willing to pay."

"And against each other," Mary added in the same hushed voice. "Call it open market competition. An item always assumes greater value when more than one person is interested in it. This way, everyone gets a chance and we reap the benefit."

"What do you mean *we*?" Abby asked, impressed by Mary's business savvy.

"You and me. We're tithing the top ten percent and splitting the money. I'm putting my half toward a vehicle. You can use your half to help defray the cost of the move."

"No way, Mary. Those are your antiques. Your furniture. I couldn't—"

"Possibly refuse," Mary finished for her. "The way things worked out, you had no chance to go through your household and lighten the load you're moving. I know Francine is doing it for you, but I'm sure she'll err on the side of caution. If there are pieces you don't want when it all gets here, we'll repeat the bidding process."

Mary adjusted her chair. "This is our home now. Yours and mine. We both have to be comfortable. I can think of no better way than to make the upstairs completely yours."

Abby's cell phone rang on the dining room table. "You are amazing. Just don't let anyone take the bed until I'm done with it."

"Not a chance."

Abby hurried to her work area, answered the phone and spoke to the realtor she had hired twenty minutes earlier.

"Enough," Mary said late in the afternoon. "Everything is closed in New York. You've been at this nonstop. It's time for a little diversion."

"You're right. I've done as much as I can for now. Give me a few more minutes and I'll relinquish the table." The papers strewn over the surface for the last couple of days now resided in neatly labeled folders.

"Just in time. We're about to have company."

Abby glanced at the clock. It was almost five-thirty. "Goodness, where did the day go? It's my turn to cook and I haven't defrosted anything."

"That's okay. They're bringing dinner."

"Who are they?" Abby collected her things.

"Janet and Margaret. We'll do a girls night in. We'll eat everything they bring and play Scrabble." Mary shook her finger at Abby. "No esoteric bird words, got it?"

Abby laughed. "No exotic flowers either."

"Fair enough."

Abby carried her papers and files upstairs. Pausing at the window, she looked down at the fence. Counting tonight, there were three more until the eighth night. "Will you come then?" she whispered. "I'm keeping your secret. I haven't told anyone."

Chapter Twenty-Five

Y OU'RE WELCOME TO COME with us, Abby." Henry Cobb, in pleated dress trousers, white shirt and summer sport coat cut a dapper figure. Beside him, Mary fairly beamed. Earlier, she had attributed the glow in her features to the bold floral print of her dress. Though the blue, green and yellow silk shimmered with every movement, Abby suspected Henry was the real cause of her sister's happy smile. A Friday night dinner date at Winifred's was a special occasion, one Mary acknowledged by abstaining from her afternoon snack.

"Thank you, but no," Abby replied. "Please go enjoy dinner and each other's company. I want to spend some time outdoors. The last few days of doing paperwork and making phone calls have used up my sitting quotient, so I'm going birding."

"Well, we won't be out late." Mary carefully tucked her purse against her hip and smoothed the silk to keep it from wrinkling.

"I probably will be," Abby cautioned. Having someone interested in her day-to-day welfare was still taking getting used to, but she liked the feeling of belonging. "I'm going to the northern part of the island, past Paradise Cove, so it may be well after dark before I get home."

"Okay," Mary said with a note of concern. "But please, take your cell phone."

"Absolutely." Eager to get started, Abby ushered the couple out the front door, then called Hugo. She had promised to include him in her searches and they only had a few hours of light left. After six rings, his recording came on and she left a message telling him to meet her at the trailhead parking lot. If she wasn't there, she told him to look for her near the barbed wire fence enclosing the Whale Riders' land.

Hoping Hugo would get the message in time to join her, Abby changed into her birding togs. She tucked her camera into her vest pocket and a pair of binoculars in another pocket. Upon double-checking her gear, she added a notebook, the map from Hugo and a pencil. The rest of the pockets bulged with orienteering tools.

On the drive to the trailhead, she weighed possible search routes against the remaining daylight. A smile lifted the corners of her mouth.

The marbled murrelets preferred the idyllic, out-of-bounds area, but they were not confined to it. She might see them flying in. Excited by the possibility, she determined to explore the full length of the Whale Riders' property line.

It wouldn't be easy or quick, but with enough diligence and fortitude, she might meet that goal in the next few weeks before she ran out of time. They were well into nesting season and when it was over and the chicks matured, the birds would exchange the forest for the sea.

To prove they had indeed returned to the island, she needed pictures of them in the nests, in identifiable trees, in a verifiable habitat. She needed to find them soon or she'd have no choice but to shelve the project for a year, until the next nesting cycle began.

The hiking trailhead leading into the woods was deserted and disappointment dulled her excitement. She had half-expected, half-hoped, to find Hugo waiting beside his car. Without him to act as her ground man, she wouldn't be climbing any trees tonight. Reluctant to give up on him, she parked the big Lincoln where he could see it from the road.

As she strode down the trail, vireos and nuthatches flitted from tree to tree. The crisp scent of fir blended with the earthy aromas from the moss-laden forest floor and renewed the sense of wonder and joy she always found in the wild. An appreciative audience of one, she drank in the majesty of her surroundings.

A cluster of wood violets bloomed in the lee of a large boulder near the boundary fence belonging to Whale Riders, Inc. A Stellar's jay perched on the barbed wire above the no trespassing sign and squawked a caustic warning to keep her distance.

"I hear you," Abby murmured. "For such a pretty bird, you sure are noisy."

Turning right and paralleling the fence, she threaded her

way along a deer trail. Several hundred feet into the sparse growth beneath the lush canopy, the track veered off into a dense thicket of blackberries. Temporarily stymied, she glared at the fence, the one constant companion to her quest.

Squirrels darted over, under and through it. Their little freeways in the branches and atop the deadfalls ignored the barrier that thwarted her. The sharp tapping of a woodpecker proclaimed his industry and determination and renewed her resolve.

After checking her position with her compass, she wove through the trees, making her own trail until she came to a sharp drop-off. On the far side of the ravine, she spotted a fencepost and the hint of a path. Navigating cautiously down the steep slope, she tested her footing with each step and when needed, held onto the hardscrabble shrubs for stability.

From the bottom of the ravine, the climb up the other side appeared much steeper than she originally thought and she paused to catch her breath. Insects buzzed lazily and a little brook burbling a few feet away reminded her to quench her thirst.

She took a long pull from her water bottle and as her gaze played over the opposite bank, she realized the post she had spotted from above was no longer visible. A look back the way she came quickened her pulse. There wasn't a recognizable landmark anywhere.

She tried to remember when she'd lost sight of the fence, the primary reference point leading back to the hiking trail. It had to have been after she left the deer trail, when she started making her own path.

Taking several calming breaths, she pulled out her compass and map and set to work approximating her position. The calculations left her heavyhearted with dismay. Not only was she trespassing, she was a long way from the trailhead. She'd traveled much farther than she intended.

The shadows were thickening quickly, too fast for her to retrace her steps and make it back to her car before dark. Her best option was to take the trail of least resistance along the winding brook. According to the map, it was a shorter and easier hike.

Just as she turned upstream, a faint *keer-keer-keer* came from the sky to her left.

Adrenaline shot through her. Fumbling her compass from her vest pocket, she took a direction heading on the cries. Hoping to catch another glimpse of the rarities, she scrambled up the slope, setting off mini-slides of rock, dirt and forest debris that tumbled down into the ravine.

The birds called again, louder.

Grabbing handfuls of shrubs, tree limbs and protruding rocks, she pulled herself to the top of the steep slope.

And saw nothing except the spreading branches of ancient timber.

She waited, her heart pounding with exertion and excitement. The mated pair called again and she followed the sound, scrambling over and under and around the obstacles in her path.

When all she could hear was the sound of her labored breathing and the racing of her heart, she stopped. Bending at the waist, she braced her hands on her quaking knees, struggled to catch her breath and chided herself for her foolish behavior.

Several moments passed before she could draw a deep breath and she tottered on shaking legs to a nearby deadfall to rest. Instinct born of experience warned her to keep moving. The massive trees were blotting out the sun, which would set all too soon.

She reached for her compass once again, only this time the pocket was empty. With growing alarm, she searched her vest, taking everything out and checking thoroughly. When the search proved fruitless, she scanned the ground where she had bent over to catch her breath. Her last hope that it had fallen out there crashed into disappointment.

The compass was gone.

Knowing she'd gotten herself in a royal pickle and wondering whom to call, she retrieved her cell phone and turned it on. While it searched for a connection, she rose, tilted her head back and strained to see the direction of the setting sun. It was no use. The dense forest canopy hid the sky as effectively as the terrain blocked the signal from the phone in her hand.

She was on her own. Even the old axiom of moss always growing on the north side of a tree was no help. These giants had moss all the way around.

Mentally retracing her steps to the last place she had the compass, she started walking. In all probability, the trusty direction finder she had relied on for more than twenty years lay somewhere on the steep slope. With it, she could find her way out.

She had covered a few hundred obstacle-riddled yards before the shadows closed in. Switching on her flashlight, she began to pray, "Merciful Lord, please, please don't allow me to become a source of worry for my family."

As she moved, the girth of the trees changed perceptibly. Even so, the Sitka spruce and Douglas firs were at least fifty years old with thick branches that still blotted out sky. She prayed aloud for guidance and nearly shouted with relief when she came upon a deer trail.

"Not that way."

Abby stopped and swung her flashlight in an arc. Thick shadows danced in the gloom. Had she imagined hearing a voice in the trees?

Imagination or not, the message was too clear to ignore and she skirted the trail, her heart beating a bit faster and her senses sharpened.

In a small clearing, she took comfort from the purple and gold sky overhead and quickened her pace to the far side.

"Not that way."

Gooseflesh rippled across her body and she froze. She wasn't imagining the voice. She had company.

The instinct to run set her scanning the trees for an avenue of escape. Seeing none, she took a deep breath and squared her shoulders. *God is with me. I have nothing to fear.*

"'Be at ease, without fear of harm,'" the voice said.

Her fears quieted, but did not settle completely.

"W-who's there?" Abby intended to sound strong and demanding. Instead, her voice came out thin and frightened.

"A friend."

"Who are you?" She shined the flashlight beam all around and turned in a circle.

"Someone who will leave you if you don't keep the light pointed at the ground ahead of you."

Reluctantly, she complied.

"That's better. Turn to your left and keep walking."

Try as she might, she couldn't pinpoint where the voice originated. Keeping the beam on the ground ahead, she set a brisk pace. The terrain gentled, yet the pull in her calves signaled she was headed uphill.

"How did you know I was here?" she asked, feeling braver.

He didn't answer. And he moved so quietly that if not for an occasional command to turn one way or another, she would have assumed he had left her to her own devices. Alternately questioning the wisdom of following his instructions and praying he was guiding her to the trail, she quietly obeyed his directions.

After what felt like a long silence, he said, "You are aware you are trespassing on private land."

"I lost the boundary marker, the fence, when I climbed down a ravine." He seemed to know every rock and tree on the Whale Riders' property. Thus far, he had taken her by a much easier route than the one she had chosen earlier.

"My name is Abby Stanton," she said, climbing over a deadfall.

"I know who you are," he said softly from what seemed very close behind her.

The temptation to whirl around and shine the light on him gnawed at her. In the same instant, she knew such an act would be wrong. The feeling didn't make much sense. Then again, neither did his sudden arrival just when she needed help. "How do you know me? Have we met?"

"In a sense, we have. Everyone on the island knows you as the Bird Lady."

Abby nearly laughed. "Well, I suppose that's appropriate. It was chasing birds that got me into this situation."

The sweep of her flashlight beam revealed familiar territory. "How did we get back to the trailhead without ever seeing the barbed wire fence?"

In the last ribbons of light vanishing from the sky, she saw the Lincoln. She turned off the flashlight and peered over her shoulder into the darkness. "Thank you for guiding me out of the woods."

There was no answer. Her rescuer was gone.

Chapter Twenty-Six

"Henry is quite a conversationalist." Mary grasped the trapeze and hoisted herself onto the bed.

"So you said." *Three times already.* Abby straightened her sister's blue nightgown over her legs. The little help wasn't necessary, but the need to be close, even in a small thing, was particularly strong. Getting lost, then rescued in such an extraordinary manner had heightened Abby's awareness of what truly mattered. "I'm delighted you two had a good time."

Mary yawned and struggled to keep her eyes open. "Since you got home, all we've done is talk about me. How about you? Did you enjoy your bird walk?"

"It was . . . interesting, but it'll keep." Abby turned off the light on the nightstand. "I'll tell you about it in the morning, before I leave for work."

On the deck, with a proper breakfast tray on the wicker table between them, Mary listened raptly while Abby related her unusual experience in the woods.

"Weren't you scared?" Mary's wide eyes held alarm and amazement. "I would have been petrified."

"I was at first. But then he said, 'Be at ease, without fear of harm.' The phrase sounded so familiar, yet so old-fashioned . . . my fears lessened considerably. I looked it up this morning. It's from Proverbs 1:33."

"Wow." Mary reached for her tea. "You certainly are a magnet for mysterious men. First our fence artist, then Bobby's tree frog man and now this. I sure wish you could have seen his face."

"He was quite firm about me keeping the light ahead of my feet. After I started following his directions, I knew if he left me, I'd have to wait until morning to find my way out. That doesn't mean I wasn't sorely tempted."

"I'm glad you found the strength to resist." Mary nibbled a bran muffin and nodded thoughtfully. "I would have been all over Henry to call out the Coast Guard and every deputy in the county."

"Sometimes it's difficult to keep my curiosity from burning a hole in my good judgment." Abby wrinkled her nose and tried to appear mischievous instead of secretive. There was so much more she wanted to share, yet a growing sense of restraint kept her quiet. These weren't her secrets to tell.

She owed the man in the woods, or the Whale Rider as she now thought of him, much more than simple gratitude. Without his intervention, she would have been on a collision course with disaster. She knew very well that fumbling around in the dark, in unfamiliar and hazardous terrain was asking for trouble. Yet, she had let her eagerness at possibly seeing the murrelets again override her good sense.

At the very least, the Whale Rider had saved her from a miserable night in the ravine and spared her family unnecessary grief. Keeping his secret, letting him play it out on his own timetable, was only fair. For the time being, as much as possible, she would keep her speculations to herself.

Mary wiped the last crumbs of muffin from her fingers with her napkin and said, "Before you arrived on the island, I thought my life was full. I was so wrong. I have so much to do today. And tonight we may discover the identity of our mystery artist."

Remembering her promise to include Mary on the next watch, Abby gulped her orange juice. Surely, the mystery man was aware of her sister and her involvement. It was, after all, her fence. The vow notwithstanding, she had a right to be present.

Oblivious to Abby's hesitation, Mary continued, "The number on the fence was supposed to tell us something. If it means how many nights until he plans to return, like you thought, then we know it wasn't a three. If it was an eight, then tonight is the night."

Blossom leapt from Mary's lap, freeing her to collect the remnants of their breakfast and return the dishes to the tray. "Are you excited about starting today at the museum?"

Grinning, Abby opened the slider and led the way inside. "You know, I really am. And I'm glad I'm starting on Saturday, the museum's busiest day.

"I have a feeling I'm going to find it quite liberating and

more diversified than at Cornell. Initially, we'll be developing the exhibits for The Wonderful World of Wings and expanding the museum. I'll be conducting the bird walks and Hugo wants my input on the feasibility of an ornithology lab."

"You'll be busy, won't you?" Mary closed the door, and followed Abby to the kitchen.

Abby picked up the tote containing her lunch. "Yes. On top of all that, he said my first assignment is to locate the murrelets' nesting grounds."

"No wonder you're so eager to get started."

"This is a big day for you too. It's the grand opening of the bids this morning, right?"

Abby followed her sister's glance. In the living room, a large crystal bowl in the center of the coffee table held an assortment of envelopes. Plain white, eye-catching colors or cleverly decorated, each one assigned a monetary value to the things Mary treasured.

Certain it would be a difficult process, Abby offered, "If you like, we can do it together when I get home."

"Thanks, but the ladies are coming over at one o'clock and we are opening the bids then." Mary squared her shoulders. "It's all right. Truly it is."

"It should be interesting." Abby picked up her purse. "There are a lot of envelopes in that bowl. By the way, I took the apple crisp out of the freezer. It should be thawed just in time for your bidding party."

Pleased by Mary's sudden smile, Abby headed for the garage.

ABBY'S NEW STATUS as associate curator of the conservatory allowed her to examine the financial aspects of Hugo's present and future operations. What she found vaporized the last of her reservations over leaving Cornell for a small island conservatory.

Many men had big dreams. Hugo was making his a reality, but his well-ordered plans didn't stop there. He was building a legacy meant to last far beyond his lifespan.

Late in the afternoon, after working through lunch, Abby was ready to call it a day. She picked up her tote and her purse.

"Come, let me show you another route to the parking lot." Hugo held the door for her. "On the way we can see how the construction is going."

"Great. By the way, I can help with the paperwork on those grants you spoke about earlier. I've done so many of them, I'm sure we can get funding for two of the projects scheduled for next year. Maybe even three."

"Excellent." Hugo toed aside a two-by-four lying across the path.

The framing for the exterior walls rose above the concrete slab, giving it dimension. The finished addition would be much larger than she had originally thought. Impressed, she said, "This crew has done an amazing amount of work in a short period of time."

"The project will be finished by the end of summer. If we need to expand in the future, we'll start earlier so we don't have to turn office space into exhibits or a workroom."

"What did you do with the things you moved out?" she

asked, splitting her attention between where she put her feet and the conversation.

"All that stuff is sitting in a room at my home."

"I'm sure you can't wait to get it back where it belongs."

"I just keep the door closed. Most of the time I forget it's there. Until I need a file or something. Then, I revert back to my safari days and go hunting."

Abby's cell phone began to ring and she stopped to dig it out of her purse. Seeing Mary's number on the display, she said to Hugo, "I'm sorry, but I have to take this."

"No problem."

When she put the phone to her ear, a nearly inaudible voice whispered her name.

Alarm spread through her. "Mary? Are you all right?"

"I'm fine. Come home. Now."

Instantly, Abby turned around and headed for the parking lot. "I'm on my way. Do you need an ambulance?"

"No," Mary said in a harsh whisper. "I'm *fine.*"

"Why are you whispering?" With Hugo hard on her heels, Abby rounded the back of the museum and cut across the lawn.

"He's here. I don't want to be overheard."

"Who?" A bolt of fear nearly caused her to stumble. "Mary, is someone in the house with you?"

"No. The fence artist is out there again."

"He is?" Abby stopped so short that Hugo bumped into her. The force propelled her toward the car at an even faster pace. "Where are you?"

"I'm in my bedroom, peering around the draperies and blinds, trying to be invisible."

"Is he still there?"

"Yes."

"What's he doing?" This didn't seem right. Why would a man bent on hiding his identity and preserving his anonymity come out in the afternoon? It might be a feasible idea during one of their thick fogs, but not when the sun was shining and there wasn't a cloud anywhere.

"I can't tell. I can barely see him from this angle."

"I'm coming home."

"Good. Hurry before he leaves." The phone went dead. Mary had hung up without even saying good-bye.

"What's wrong? Is it Mary?" Hugo lengthened his stride, and his much longer legs easily matched Abby's power-walking gait.

"No, she's fine, Hugo." Abby glanced up at him while feeling through her purse for the car keys.

"I'd be able to let go of my anxiousness if you'd tell me what's going on."

"The fence artist is in the yard. I told Mary to call me if she saw him." Abby unlocked the car door.

"I'm coming with you."

Although she felt the seconds tick by, she stopped and faced Hugo. "Please don't. We don't want to scare him off. He may be the only avenue to the birds."

"He may be a madman too. You don't know one way or the other."

Rather than argue, she opened the car door and got in behind the wheel. Hugo dashed around to the passenger side and knocked on the window as she turned the ignition key. Seeing no escape short of driving off with him holding onto the door handle, she released the lock and let him in.

He drew the seat belt across his body and fastened it while she pulled out of the parking lot.

"Stay out of sight when we get there," Abby warned.

"Not unless I'm certain you and Mary are safe."

ABBY PULLED INTO THE GARAGE and practically ran from the car as though it was on fire. She raced through the laundry room and stopped short. Hugo grabbed her shoulders to keep from knocking her down.

Mary met them in the door to the kitchen. "He's gone."

"I'm not surprised." Crestfallen that the opportunity to speak with the man had slipped away, Abby caught Mary's hand and managed a smile. "Of course, we want to hear every detail."

"I'm a little light on those." She wheeled into the living room and motioned for Hugo to have a seat. "Nice to see you, Hugo."

"Did you call Henry Cobb?" he demanded and remained standing.

"Why ever would I do that?" A puzzled expression knit Mary's brow.

"You have a stranger prowling around your yard and you

don't think you should phone the authorities?" Hugo thrust his hands into his trouser pockets and shook his head.

"He was just by the fence," Mary explained. "He wasn't coming toward the house or doing anything menacing. What would I tell Henry or any of the deputies? There's a man in my yard who isn't doing anything wrong, come and arrest him?"

"He shouldn't be in your yard," Hugo said emphatically.

"We invited him," Abby said softly, hoping to end the discourse she considered pointless. More than anything, she wanted to know why their visitor broke his nocturnal pattern and came to the yard during the day. Surely, it was important to him. And to her too.

"Invited him?" Hugo raked his hair back with both hands. "How so?"

Mary lifted her eyebrows and looked expectantly at Abby.

On the spot and searching for the right words, Abby took her time placing her purse and keys on the coffee table. "I washed the first drawing off the fence, the one he drew, the morning after it appeared. The fact it was headless was somewhat alarming at first. We reconsidered and I redrew the image. This time, I added a head so it wouldn't look so bizarre."

Hugo straightened and touched his mustache.

"We, Mary and I, wanted to open up a dialogue with him. So, you see, he was invited."

Hugo opened his mouth to speak, but Mary quickly interjected, "Abby's right, you know. We were hoping to learn more." She angled her wheelchair to face Hugo. "If this man intended us harm, he would have already acted."

"How does he get here?" Hugo settled onto the silk damask couch. He seemed calmer now, as though his presence provided all the protection they needed.

"I don't know," Abby admitted. The question cropped up often, demanding an answer she had yet to discover.

"It doesn't really matter." Mary brushed it off with a shrug. "He just . . . shows up. I had several ladies over today. After they left, I opened the sliding door to let Blossom in and a movement caught the corner of my eye. I looked up and saw him approaching the fence."

She glanced from Hugo to Abby, then back. "I don't expect you to understand, but honestly, if this man had been a threat, Blossom would have either headed for the brush or come running when she saw me at the door. She did neither, just laid in the sun and watched us."

"There's no question animals have instincts about danger," Abby thought aloud. "They flee for higher ground before tidal waves hit a beach and act strangely before earthquakes or tornadoes strike. Birds in particular have been observed fleeing an area in giant flocks shortly before an earthquake."

"Those are occurrences of nature. They're not the same kind of danger posed by a man prowling about your backyard," objected Hugo.

"Perhaps not, but the presence of danger is what the animals and birds are running from," Abby said.

"You know, there's no need to worry anyhow," Mary said cheerily. "He's gone now."

"But he may come back. Will you call Sergeant Cobb if he returns?" Hugo asked Mary.

"Trust me, I'll be on the phone to Henry so fast it'll make your head spin the instant I feel I'm in danger. I'm not foolish or foolhardy." Mary smiled apologetically. "No one knows my limitations and vulnerabilities better than I. Thank you for your concern, Hugo. You're a dear friend and brother in Christ looking out for our welfare. I'm privileged to be the recipient of your heartfelt concern."

Abby watched Hugo melt under Mary's flowery compliments. The remarkable thing was that they were all true and the sincerity in her expression undeniable.

"As you can see, all is well here." Abby picked up her keys and purse. "Come on, Hugo. I'll take you back to the museum so you can lock up. No doubt Rebecca is getting a little nervous, wondering when you'll return."

Hugo rose and for a moment appeared torn and irritated. "You two are quite a pair."

A pair of what, Abby wasn't brave enough to ask. Instead, she said, "Thank you. My sister is amazing."

When Hugo started toward the garage, Abby risked a glance at Mary.

"Hurry back," she mouthed, with a pointed look in the direction of the fence.

Chapter Twenty-Seven

ABBY SET HER THINGS on the telephone table. "All the way to the museum and back I've been thinking about your 'hurry back' message. Now tell me what you didn't want to say in front of Hugo."

"Bless his heart. He takes his duty as a Christian friend so seriously. I'm thankful for it, but he would have gone ballistic if I'd mentioned why our mystery man paid us a visit."

"You know what it was?" Abby viewed her sister with a new respect. All the time Hugo was in the living room, Mary had harbored an enormous secret. Although she must have been bursting to reveal it, she had not only controlled the urge, but also hidden her excitement. "Speak."

Mary was already rolling out of the kitchen toward the living room and the sliding door. "Our surreptitious artist left something in the fence. I couldn't get to it without parking in the alyssum. I was afraid I'd get stuck and the bees would build a hive in my chair." Mary glanced over her shoulder at Abby. "Believe me, I considered taking that risk."

Abby hurried outside. If her suspicions were correct, and the mystery artist, tree frog man and the Whale Rider were the same person, he was getting ready to reveal himself. Soon, she hoped, she'd learn the reason behind his visits.

Watching for any sign of movement in case he lingered in the woods near the fence, she followed the faint tracks of Mary's wheelchair across the grass. Fortunately, Hugo hadn't noticed them or he'd still be here—with a deputy sheriff as added company. And he'd still be lecturing Mary on the need to be cautious and security-minded, and not expose herself to potential danger.

Abby reached the fence. There was no new drawing, no new numbers, just a piece of paper folded small and inserted between the weathered boards.

"Shoo. Go away," she told the bees gathering pollen from the clusters of tiny white flowers. "I only need a minute. Just pretend it's dark and you're going home to your hive."

They didn't pay any more or less attention to her than the last time she encroached on their territory. She placed one hand on the fence and leaned across the flowers. Pinching the paper between her thumb and forefinger, she worried it free and beat a hasty retreat from the buzzing alyssum.

On the way back to the deck, she opened the first of what appeared to be many folds.

"Don't you dare," Mary called.

Startled, Abby looked up at her sister. Even from the top of the deck ramp, her "don't make me come down there" expression was unmistakable. "Okay."

Once on the deck, Abby kept moving until she reached what had become her favorite chair. Taking a seat, she waited for Mary to wheel up beside her.

"Okay. You can open it now. I'm dying to see what it says." Mary leaned over the side of her chair until her shoulder touched Abby's. "You can't imagine all the things that have run through my mind since I saw him."

"Did you get a good look at him?"

"Unfortunately, no. His back was to me the entire time. All I know is that he's thin and tall."

Slowly, carefully, Abby unfolded the one-inch packet. Initially, all she could see was white space and she began to wonder if that in itself was the message.

Not until the standard sheet of paper opened all the way did the message come into view. Abby read the tiny line in the middle of the big piece of paper aloud, "Proverbs 27:8."

"A Bible verse?" Disappointment softened Mary's question and she gave a disconsolate sigh. "Why does everything have to be a test of some kind?"

"Let's find out." Abby handed the paper to Mary and quickly rose. She retrieved her Bible from the table inside the door and returned to her seat. Opening it to the Book of Proverbs, she turned the pages until she found the right chapter and verse. "Here it is. 'Like a bird that strays from its nest is a man who strays from his home.'"

"What do you think it means? Don't leave home?"

"Possibly. In the general context, I think it means that

God has given each of us gifts and He has a particular place for us to exercise those gifts. Those places become the nest He designed for us." Abby reread the scripture several times.

"That's a lot of words to say 'bloom where you're planted.'"

Delighted with her sister's keen insight, Abby laughed. "I should have known gardening terms are the best way to relate. So, dig deeper."

"What other way is there to look at it?"

"Let me think about it a moment." God's Word, although clear, often held deeper meaning. So many times she had read a passage and found a message applicable to a specific situation. Later, when she read the same passage again, the same words provided insight and answers to a totally different set of circumstances.

She read the passage aloud again, then said, "We know one more thing about our mysterious artist."

"We do?" Mary sounded surprised.

"Yes. We know he's a Christian. He knows we are too."

Mary's eyebrows pinched together. "Just because we are Christians doesn't mean we speak a different language than the rest of the world."

"In a sense, it does," Abby said absently, still trying to view the whole picture.

"Even so, he could have just written what he wanted us to know instead of using a Bible quote, right?"

"I think he expects us to investigate and find the meaning in the context of the current situation."

"Please, you're giving me a headache."

Abby reached over and touched Mary on the shoulder. "You had it right from the beginning. It's another test."

AFTER DINNER, as the long shadows of evening filled the backyard, Abby asked, "How did the bidding party go this afternoon?"

Mary stroked the cat nestled in her lap. "Blossom considered the envelopes a new toy. I let her play with them until the ladies came at one o'clock. Then she went outside."

"Who were the big winners?" Abby watched the petals of the geraniums flutter in the gentle sea breeze.

"I can't say there were any big winners." Mary spoke reflectively as though remembering the early afternoon from the perspective of distance. "More important, there were no losers."

Amazed, Abby shook her head. "You mean to say everyone who bid got what they wanted for the price they were willing to pay?"

Mary stroked the cat's uplifted head. "Well, not exactly."

"I'm having trouble following you. Explain, please."

"In a sense, everything went to the highest bidder, just as I said it would."

"Now I'm really confused, Mary."

"Well, not everyone's bid consisted solely of money." Mary scratched behind Blossom's ears. "Some things are worth more than money. I carefully weighed many factors before making some decisions. Others were no-brainers. For instance, Janet put in a heart-stopping bid for the entire suite of furniture in your bedroom. She got that, but not the armoire Jacob made."

Good, Abby thought. She couldn't imagine Mary parting with that precious piece, though she didn't know where they'd put it. When her things arrived, space would definitely be dear.

"Patricia got the antique secretary. Candace got the bookcases in the upstairs study. It all worked out. Even the armoire. Especially the armoire."

Her heart sinking, Abby said, "Tell me."

Even now, she recalled in detail the Christmas when Jacob unveiled the exquisite piece he had spent six months building and polishing. At the time, Mary was pregnant with Zack and Nancy was a precocious three-year-old.

"It was the most difficult choice. I had always thought I'd give it to one of the children. Nancy lives so far away, I can't see shipping it to Florida. Besides, she has no place to put it."

"What about Zack?"

Mary laughed. "My talented nomad son. Right now, he shares a house with four other musicians in New Orleans and is home barely long enough to do his laundry and get acquainted with a new roommate. Whenever one person moves out, another young man moves in."

"That leaves out Zack and Nancy. So who got the armoire?"

"Sandy McDonald."

Abby sat back in her chair and gazed at the woods separating their property from the McDonalds'. "How on earth did you work that?" There was no way Sandy could have outbid any of the women vying for Mary's treasures.

"She promised to make a Chocolate Wonder for our birthdays every year until we tired of them. Along with the cake baking, she bid a small amount. I doubt she really expected to get the armoire, but she bid as much as she had. It was her nest egg. I know she's been scraping and saving for months because she wanted one nice piece of furniture. Ironically, if I had known how much she wanted the armoire because Jacob made it, I would have given it to her. She regarded Jacob as a second father."

"That's so sweet. You accepted her bid and cake promise in exchange. I'm really touched."

"Don't be. I rejected Sandy's bid."

"What? You're talking in circles and I'm trying to follow you to the point of getting dizzy. I thought you said Sandy got the armoire."

"She did." Blossom jumped off Mary's lap and arched in an elaborate stretch. "Sandy got the armoire because I accepted Bobby's bid."

Abby held her forehead. "I didn't even know Bobby knew how to bid. Why would a ten-year-old who would rather have a telescope to watch for pirates put in a bid on a piece of furniture?"

"He loves his mother," Mary said softly.

"What was his bid?"

"The next eight years of weeding my garden during

summer break. He wrote a note explaining why his mother wanted the armoire. That's when I learned how much Sandy loved Jacob and why she was willing to spend her nest egg."

"I love that kid," Abby breathed, drawn even closer to the boy because of his tender heart.

"Yeah," Mary agreed. "No one could outbid Bobby. His bid was priceless and the only one that focused on someone other than himself." She sniffed and brushed at a tear. "It closed the circle. Love made the armoire and love found it a new home where it will be treasured long after I'm gone."

Abby took Mary's hand and held on in the darkness. There was nothing more to add.

They sat quietly, waiting for their nocturnal visitor, hoping he'd return. With the exception of Mary's bedroom light, the house was dark. Seated just outside the sliding door and dressed in dark clothing, they blended with the night.

Abby watched the fence, her mind drifting to the Bible story about a widow woman who gave two mites at the temple offering. A gift from the heart, she gave all she had and God was very pleased with her.

Abby felt certain God was pleased with Mary too. Though she didn't know it yet, He had blessed her mightily in advance. Her new van would arrive next week.

Motion in the shadows against the fence caught their attention. Mary squeezed Abby's hand, then let go.

A man walked along the alyssum border. His purposeful stride carried him to the spot where Abby had removed the folded note.

Her heartbeat quickened with excitement. At last, she would close a circle of her own.

"Sir, please come up on the deck," Mary called out, startling Abby and the man in the yard.

He looked around, then turned away and began a retreat.

Abby dashed across the deck, down the stairs and across the grass. "Jonah! Please. Don't go."

Chapter Twenty-Eight

THE MAN HESITATED, his lean, tall frame poised for flight. Beyond the copse of junipers by the shore, Abby glimpsed the mast of a sailboat and her heart sank. If he left now, she had no way to follow him and no assurance he would return.

"'Be at ease, without fear of harm,'" she said softly, hoping he'd find the same comfort in the Proverb as she had when he said it to her in the woods.

Tugging his ball cap down, he twisted stiffly and looked over his shoulder. Moonlight softened the taut burn scars distorting his features and seemed to magnify his reluctance to reveal them. Then, as if he'd lost some inner struggle, he turned away.

"A child of the Most High is beautiful in His sight."

"But not in the eyes of the world," he said.

"What is seen is temporary, what is unseen is eternal."

Slowly, Jonah turned to face her, the evidence of the agony he had endured visible in the moonlight. She put her empathy and admiration for his courage into her smile and extended her hand in welcome. "Please. You set this time for us to meet."

"Your persistence is an admirable trait, Bird Lady." A lopsided smile quirked briefly and he touched his fire-ravaged hand to hers. "Take care that it does not lead you astray in the dark again."

"The Lord provided, Whale Rider. He sent you."

With a raspy laugh, Jonah said, "And you. You are more than I hoped for. How did you know it was me?"

"There was no death certificate on file in Friday Harbor. Please, come up on the deck. We can talk there and my sister is waiting."

He remained rooted to the ground like one of his ancient trees. "I am not accustomed to an audience and I have much to say."

"Mary is not a spectator. You made her a participant with the headless bird on her fence. It gave her quite a scare."

"It wasn't my intention. Please, give her my apologies."

Abby cast a pointed look at the stairs to the deck. "I trust her to keep our confidences."

He seemed to consider, then sadly said, "My appearance may add to her fears."

"I've learned not to underestimate her."

"I'm learning not to underestimate you. In this then, it shall be as you wish."

Thin clouds glided through the moonlight, casting wispy shadows as Jonah and Abby went up to the deck. After an introduction and Mary's warm welcome, Jonah took a seat on the edge of the chair that put his back to the moon. With his features obscured, he seemed more at ease.

"You know, everyone on the island believes you died years ago," Mary said gently.

"That was my intent." Jonah turned to Abby. "And the reason for Whale Riders, Inc."

"The corporation was very effective," she agreed with a smile. "Why did you choose that name?"

"It seemed fitting for a man who found himself while he was engulfed in a whale of pain and pity."

Her curiosity burning so brightly she suspected she glowed in the dark, Abby struggled to contain her questions. She sensed any attempt to push him or rush him might send Jonah scurrying back to his sailboat. His slow and deliberate actions over the last weeks spoke of a purpose he would reveal in his own way and his own time.

She poured a cup of hot chocolate for him from the service on the table and silently thanked Mary for her foresight in providing it.

As Jonah sipped the steaming cocoa, he settled more comfortably onto the chair. "You have questions, I'm sure. If you'll permit me to tell my story, I believe you will find the answers you seek."

Abby nodded and Mary folded her hands on her lap.

"Dr. Stanton, I learned of your interest in the marbled murrelets through a friend. He sang your praises so loud and long, I became doubtful. Forgive me for being skeptical, but the honesty he spoke of is a rare commodity and I determined to test you."

"With the journals," she murmured as that piece of the puzzle locked in place. "May I ask who was singing my praises?"

He tilted his head as if to say "in due time," and continued, "When you kept the first book confidential, I was heartened. I arranged for the second journal to be included in the boxes sent to Hugo Baron and again you honored our unspoken pact. I couldn't learn this about you over the telephone or the Internet. Actions *do* speak louder than words."

Abby nodded her agreement, sipped her hot chocolate and studied her visitor. In speech, bearing and style of dress, he was a mix of the old world and the new. The cashmere scarf at his neck was as functional, subdued and comfortable as the baseball cap shielding some of his scars.

He turned to Mary. "Mrs. Reynolds, it was I who drew on your fence. Please accept the apology of an old man who has lived alone too long and forgotten his manners. I had no wish to frighten you. I should have paid attention to how such a thing might be perceived."

"Apology accepted." Mary refreshed Jonah's mug and blurted, "Are you Bobby's tree frog man, too?"

"Ah, the smart lad from next door. I'm pleased he thinks of me that way."

Jonah looked at the sky and Abby followed suit. The wispy clouds were thickening.

"The fog will come and there is much to tell. The property

you are interested in, Dr. Stanton, belonged to my grandfather. He gifted it to me at my birth. A long time later, I learned why he didn't bequeath it to my father, David. Grandfather considered him too ambitious, too much of a wheeler-dealer, to use his words. Ironically, my father would have been a better steward than I was. He loved the birds and the old trees.

"When I was thirty-five, they were the least of my concerns. I wanted to leave the island, to move beyond my father's sphere of influence and power. We hadn't been close for some time."

Jonah hesitated as though debating how much of his past he should reveal.

Recalling her father's description of David Bowditch, Abby could only guess at how difficult life might have been with the dogmatic and self-righteous politician.

"He wasn't present when my mother died. She left this world calling his name." Jonah turned his head toward the fence as though contemplating the memory. "Afterward, finding a way to retaliate and leave the island permanently became an obsession."

Abby nodded. Few things in life were as complex or emotional as family relationships.

"I found several buyers for the property who were willing to pay me twice, once for the land, more for the timber. Rashly, I underestimated my father and his cronies in Olympia and bragged about my pending success. They pushed a bill through the legislature, protecting old-growth timber. I was furious when I learned how he had thwarted me."

Jonah sighed heavily. "I took my boat and went roaring through the feeding grounds of the birds he loved. I was determined to destroy them. In my blind anger, I crashed into the rocks. The boat exploded and . . ."

Gooseflesh rippled over Abby. The dire consequences of Jonah's rage had been swift and catastrophic. Yet the growing ease with which he spoke revealed an acceptance.

"As far as I was concerned, my life was over. I asked my father to let me die. Instead, he let everyone believe I'd succumbed to my injuries. When I was able to travel, he brought me back to the island in secret to our estate in the woods. Everything he failed to do for my mother, he did for me.

"In the beginning, I could scarcely bear his company. Instead of conversation, I communicated by quoting verses from Mother's Bible. In time, the Word led us to forgiveness."

Jonah finished the hot chocolate, cleared his throat and said, "I haven't spoken so freely since Father went to join the Lord."

Mary leaned forward. "I don't understand. If you hated the birds, why . . . ?"

A hoarse laugh escaped Jonah. "Father kept saying 'Not a sparrow falls.' In my zeal to prove him wrong once again, I began studying the winged creatures outside my sickroom. That interest gave me a reason to live. Eventually, I came to see them as Father did, though I didn't acquire his taste for recording my observations."

"I see," Abby said, putting another piece into her mental puzzle. "The journals were his but you shared the same passion."

Jonah nodded and rose from his chair. "Many thanks for your hospitality. It's been a very long time since I've had the privilege of conversing with two charming ladies."

"You're not leaving," Abby cried. "We've just started. I have so many questions."

"The fog grows thicker. I must go now."

Unable to deny the gathering mist, Abby tempered her disappointment. "Will you come back?"

"Tomorrow evening, before sunset, you come see me, Bird Lady." He started down the stairs.

"Where?" She had no idea how to get to the Bowditch estate.

"I'll watch for you in the car park at the trailhead where we last parted. Be ready."

As the darkness closed around him, Mary looked up at Abby and asked, "Be ready for what?"

"I don't know."

Chapter Twenty-Nine

On Sunday, Abby went about her day, attended church with her family and tried not to think about her sunset appointment with Jonah. Knowing it was hours away only made her more conscious of the time she still had to wait. The minutes seemed to stretch out in front of her, as innumerable as grains of sand in the desert.

Rather than count them one at a time, she drove over to Stanton Farm to visit her parents. Mary had begged off, saying she had things to do. Abby and her father decided to take a leisurely walk down Primrose Lane. Throughout their trek, whenever she was tempted to divulge even a hint of her exciting secret, she thought of how much Jonah valued his privacy and expected her discretion. Honoring his trust was a challenge she could handle.

To keep her mind off the impending visit, she hummed songs of praise and concentrated on the words.

Her father didn't press her for an explanation, nor did he comment when she missed a note or three. He did send curious looks in her direction. By the time they reached Cross Island Road, he began humming along with her, gaining volume when necessary to keep her on key.

On their way back to the farm, George said, "I won't ask what prompted all that humming, but I believe I will try it this evening."

"Really? Why?"

"Your mother has invited her friends from the senior center over for dinner tonight. I won't get a word in edgewise."

"Ahh." *I wish I could tell you I'm meeting with Jonah Bowditch.* "Enjoy."

After a few moments of companionable silence, Abby asked her father, "Have you heard from Victor Denny about the van?"

"Yes, I have. It was delivered to the dealership yesterday and Sherry took it for a test drive. She's eager to visit Sparrow Island and give Mary a few pointers."

"She'll love that. When are they coming?"

"In a couple of days. Right now, the van's in the paint shop in Seattle."

"Wonderful. I just know Mary's going to ask me to take her to Bellingham next weekend. She's been very patient and I'm out of excuses."

"We just have to make sure she holds out a little longer, Abby. Victor and Sherry say it's even prettier than the brochure. Mary's chin will hit the floor when she sees it." Her father laughed as though visualizing the event. "I'll have to take my camera and get a picture."

"You always did like to catch us at our most flattering moments," Abby said, rolling her eyes at the memory of those awkward photos.

"It's a father's duty. We're supposed to capture the special moments in our children's lives."

"Right. By the way, what about insurance?"

"Marvin's got it covered, literally and figuratively."

"All of you are making this too easy on me."

"Abby," her father said seriously, "no one expects you to handle everything by yourself. We're all in this together. If everyone does a little, then it's a piece of cake."

Abby turned and gave her father a hug. "I love you, Dad."

"I love you, too. I'll be sure to let you know when Sherry and Victor are coming. Now let's get inside and see what your mother is up to."

Relieved by his thoughtfulness, Abby and George entered the house. After some lemonade with her mother and father around the kitchen table, she headed home.

As she entered disaster central, formerly known as the kitchen, she stopped in her tracks. A disheveled Mary looked over from the dishwasher that held half the mixing bowls she owned.

"What on earth . . ." Abby caught a whiff of something baking in the oven. ". . . smells so delicious?"

"I figured you were too keyed up to eat today, but I knew you'd need fuel for tonight, so I made dinner." Mary placed the bowl that wouldn't fit into the dishwasher rack on the counter. "Ignore it. I'll get it on the next cycle."

"You're a jewel." Gratitude thickened Abby's throat. Mary must have spent most of the afternoon preparing a meal just for her. "I'll fill you in on every detail when I get back tonight."

"Ah, there's nothing like appreciation. And a little food bribery." She closed the dishwasher and turned it on. "You've got twenty minutes before we eat."

"I'll go wash up and then I'll set the table."

"Good. Because I need a favor."

Abby feigned innocence. "You do?"

"I want to go to Bellingham next weekend and look at vehicles. I really need transportation."

Abby grinned. "We'll go whenever you like." *Thank You, Lord.*

A KNOCK ON THE SLIDING GLASS DOOR startled Abby as she carried the last of the dinner dishes to the sink. She shot a questioning look at her sister.

Mary returned a mystified glance, then wheeled her chair into the living room and opened the slider. "Frank. What a surprise."

"Sorry to come without calling first." The hardware store owner entered the house with an abashed shuffle of rubber boots and his Seattle Seahawks cap in his hand. "Hope I didn't scare you."

"No. What can I do for you?"

Pinning Abby with a meaningful gaze, he said, "There's been a change of plans."

"Excuse me?"

"We have a mutual friend. He said to give you this—" Frank reached into his raincoat. "—and that you're supposed to come with me."

One look at the compass Frank put in her hand was all she needed. The direction finder was hers, the one she had lost in the woods. *Jonah sent Frank Holloway? Was he the one who sang her praises to the sky?* Abby felt her chin drop. *Why not?* an inner voice insisted. *Dad said Frank was proud of me.*

It was almost too big to take in. She had been quite certain Frank was part of the puzzle, but had not expected him to be so deeply involved. He had delivered the materials from the San Juan Islands Birding Society. How easy it must have been for him to slip the second journal into one of the boxes at Jonah's behest. The Whale Rider knew Hugo would show it to her once he discovered it.

"Bring a waterproof jacket," Frank ordered. "You're bound to get wet. And no lollygagging. The tide's going to turn in an hour."

Abby ran upstairs for her birding vest, then fetched the mackinaw she'd worn the other night and returned to the living room.

"It's obvious you're going by boat, Frank," Mary said in an exasperated tone. "Otherwise when the tide turns wouldn't matter. Just tell me where you're taking her."

"I can't. I'm sorry, Mary, but it's not up to me to give out that information. All I can tell you is not to worry. I'll bring her back safe and sound." He opened the slider and went out to the deck.

Abby bent, hugged her sister and whispered, "Don't worry. Old Frank's bark is worse than his bite."

Mary chuckled. "Don't mind me. I thought if I got a rise out of him, he'd satisfy my curiosity. Now go, before he leaves you here."

Frank was already halfway across the backyard and showing no sign of slowing down. Abby hurried to catch up. "Is something wrong? You seem upset."

"Don't like leaving your sister there, but she can't come where you're going."

"Where *am* I going?"

"You'll see."

Resigning herself to his strangely morose mood, Abby climbed into the Day Sailer.

With the familiarity that came with years on the water, he shook loose the mooring rope he'd looped over a branch, pushed off and jumped in. Although she sat facing him, he ignored her attempts to engage him in conversation. Instead, he sat silently, handling the sail and the tiller and staring glumly at the sea.

The course he set kept them a safe distance from the shoreline and carried them around the southern end of the island, then northward along the eastern shore. Gulls and crows wheeled and squawked at the sail, the water and each other. A fitful breeze misted Abby with salt spray and she hastily donned the stocking cap Frank offered.

Some time after they passed the broad entrance to

Paradise Cove, Frank said, "You need to watch, now. It's a little tricky here."

She swung around on the seat. The huge rocks and boulders lining the shore seemed to race toward them. "Fr-a-ank! What are you doing?"

Dumbfounded, she clutched the seat and stared at the steep cliffs. If he didn't change course immediately, they'd crash into the jagged stones. She braced for impact.

"Relax. It's an optical illusion." Frank collapsed the sail and leaned hard on the tiller. "See where the two slopes look like they meet? They don't. Watch."

The sailboat glided through an opening in the cliff that just a moment ago didn't exist. While he secured the sail and started the little outboard motor, she marveled at the nearly perfect bowl of the hidden cove. Steep cliffs rose on every side.

A hundred yards ahead and to the right, a short pier jutted out above the water. Frank motored to it and moored the boat next to a small platform by the stairs. After helping her climb out, he said, "Go on up, Jonah's waiting for you."

She took off the watch cap, gave it back and shook out her hair. Leaving Frank busily stowing the sails, she climbed up to the pier and through the gate on the chain link fencing that denied access to the uninvited.

In a broad brimmed hat, pulled low on his forehead, Jonah leaned against an unusual conveyance that reminded her of an amusement park ride. It had two seats, one behind the other, and sported cartoonish balloon tires.

"It is good to see you again, Bird Lady."

"And you, Whale Rider." She swept a glance down at the boat and back to the cart. "You're full of surprises."

"If you mean Frank, he's a true friend. Without him, the life my father and I chose would not have been possible." Gesturing for her to take the back seat, Jonah climbed stiffly into the front.

A glimpse of his damaged hands revealed enlarged knuckles and fingers angled at the joints, and explained the tiller that served as a steering wheel. After she took her place behind him, he put the cart in motion and rolled quietly away from the steps toward the land beyond.

"As for our chariot," he continued, his amusement clear, "a friend of my father's made the first one from a battery-powered golf cart. This is number seven and has several modifications. I trust you are comfortable?"

"Very." Abby watched in amazement as he drove up a narrow passageway cut into the cliff face and invisible from below. A low wall on the downhill side proved reassuring, especially when they rounded several switchbacks. Halfway up the mini-mountain, the rock road flattened out and a series of stone pillars came into view.

Supports for the upper story of the stately wood and stone structure were built partway into the rock; the pillars framed the entrance to the lower floor.

"My home," Jonah said somewhat apologetically, "though not our current destination."

He steered the cart onto another path that led into the forest and wove around the massive trunks of ancient trees. Overwhelmed by the beauty of the natural cathedral, Abby tried to look at everything at once and finally just sat back and enjoyed the magnificence.

"Oh, Jonah," she breathed. "Do you think the Garden of Eden looks like this?"

He gave his peculiar raspy laugh and said, "I certainly hope so."

Abby lost track of time until he stopped at the bottom of a steep incline. Evening shadows were lengthening and with a start, she remembered the birds. Sighting the murrelets had launched the journey that brought her to this place. As she thought of them, hope quickened her pulse.

Motioning her to be quiet and to follow his lead, Jonah extricated himself from the cart. He moved so slowly, so painfully, she doubted the wisdom of proceeding. He stood for a long moment with his eyes closed, visibly stretching his joints as if willpower alone could make them more mobile.

With a heavy heart, she recognized the sufferings of a man stricken with arthritis and in the midst of an excruciating flare. She touched his arm, shook her head and motioned that they should go back.

Smiling, he mimicked the motion, but pointed upward and mouthed the words, "I must." He set off, favoring his right side, his left arm swinging as if the movement helped propel him up the slope.

Realizing he intended to proceed, with or without her, Abby followed close behind. The way was obviously familiar, for he took the easiest and quietest path. When they finally reached the top of the slope, the surrounding growth thinned and they could see pieces of the purpling sky. A few feet in front of them, the land fell straight down into darkness.

With his twisted right hand, Jonah gestured for her to look back. The panorama took Abby's breath away. Against the twilight color streaming across the western sky, the ancient trees stood regally, giant guardians of a magnificent domain.

What a privilege to view God's splendor from what felt like the top of the world, where night chased day from the sky in a glaze of color. In the distance, the sea mirrored the sun's surrender to starlight.

Overjoyed, Abby raised her face to the heavens with a prayer of thanksgiving for the beauty around her. Someone had once said a person could find diamonds in their own backyard if they only had the courage to look. Right here on Sparrow Island was a piece of heaven and she was thrilled with the privilege of viewing it.

Keer-keer-keer.

Jonah touched her arm and pointed toward the trees growing up from the base of the cliff. The cries of the marbled murrelets grew louder. Acting quickly, she retrieved her binoculars from her vest and studied the boughs of the upper story canopy in front of her.

Even the breeding plumage of the marbled murrelet was

designed to help it hide. Their compact bodies were less than a foot long, marbled in muted tones of brown and buff that blended into the forest background. Streaks of white marked where their wings joined their backs.

Although the mated pairs were unique among alcids in their preference for three hundred- to eight hundred-year-old trees, they didn't build traditional nests and the locations they chose were hard to find. High in the canopies of ancient hemlocks, spruce, cedars and firs, the nondescript birds selected a needle-choked crotch in the branches, or a protected mossy depression where the limbs joined the trunk. There, hidden as much as possible from natural predators, they laid a single egg per breeding season.

A pair swooped in from Abby's left, landing on a branch that seemed close enough to touch. They appeared too small and vulnerable to live so much of their lives on the harsh sea.

Scarcely daring to breathe, she fingered the focus on the binoculars. The pair fluttered closer to the tree trunk. The faint cry of a hungry chick brought tears to her eyes.

Here, the cycle of life continued for the rare little birds. She watched in awe as the murrelets fed their solitary chick, conscious all the while that she was a privileged spectator to an event most people would never see.

When darkness reigned over the forest, she lowered the binoculars and put them back in her vest. Only then did she realize she had not taken a single picture.

Chapter Thirty

I CAN'T BELIEVE IT," Abby said through the growing sense of wonder that made her skin tingle. "I didn't take a single picture and I'm glad. The birds are here. Right here on Sparrow Island and they're safe! That's all that matters."

Laughing, she turned to look at Jonah and found him resting on a stony outcrop, wearing such a warm lopsided smile, it added to her joy. "Thank you. From the bottom of my heart, thank you."

"It is I who should be thanking you, Bird Lady."

"Why? You and your wonderfully frustrating corporation made this possible, Whale Rider. I'm so tickled I feel like a dozen Fourth of July rockets are going off inside me."

His raspy laughter floated out to the horizon. In the distance, she heard another pair of marbled murrelets calling and she hugged herself to contain her explosive joy. "Oh my. I'm so overwhelmed. Give me a minute and we'll start back down."

"The moon will rise soon. The journey will be easier in its light, and we still have much to discuss."

The note of sadness in his voice drew her close and confirmed what she had suspected since she read the note he left in the fence. Suddenly heavyhearted, she sat on a stone next to his perch. "This is about Proverbs 27:8, isn't it?"

Nodding, he quoted, "'Like a bird that strays from its nest is a man who strays from his home.' I am that man, Dr. Stanton. I must leave the Northwest. As you may have noticed, this is not one of my better days. Along with the arthritis that plagues me more frequently now, my infirmities are doing what nothing and no one could. I can no longer tolerate the cold and the damp. To stay means to surrender the rest of my mobility."

Abby held her head in her hands. "Dear God, what a hellish choice."

"It was, until He sent you. I have always known my residency here was temporary. Yet I couldn't leave the land without a caretaker. That's you, Dr. Stanton. With your expertise and your contacts, you can ensure all the birds in this little piece of Eden are protected."

She sat very still, recognizing this as a defining moment for both of them. It was a passing of the torch, the giving of a precious and beloved responsibility into her hands. In her heart, she knew Jonah was right. The True Owner, the Eternal Caretaker, had sent her and was putting her in charge. Yet her position would also be temporary. Her replacement would come when the time was right.

"Where will you go, Jonah? How will you live?"

In the rising moonlight, the scars on his cheeks were wet

with unabashed tears. He attempted a smile and said, "Whale Riders bought a place outside Tucson, Arizona, next to a National Forest. The property has a goodly number of trees."

Lifting his head, he stared at the regal giants around them with a hunger she could feel. After a long moment, he said, "The trees there aren't like these, yet they too come from the Creator's hand. I trust He has something for me to tend."

Jonah pushed slowly to his feet.

Abby quickly scrambled up to stand beside him. "Would you mind if I gave you a hug?"

He closed his eyes and when they opened again, he wore a new air of contentment. "On the contrary. I would like that very much."

She stepped into his arms, into a brotherly hug that carried the weight of the world and the joy of Christian fellowship. Holding her like spun glass, he said, "Thank you, Bird Lady. It's been a very long time."

He touched his cheek to the top of her head. "This is a greater gift than you can imagine." He released her and stepped back. "A word of advice. Bring your father and make it soon. The chicks are nearly ready to test their wings."

"If you'll give me your number, I'll call and let you know when we're coming." The last thing she wanted to do was intrude on the time Jonah had left in this little paradise. Just the thought of leaving was breaking his heart—and hers.

"As you wish." He turned on his flashlight and pointed it downhill. "If you would be so kind as to go first and let me use your shoulder for balance, I'd be most appreciative. The descent is difficult for me."

"Certainly." After readying her own flashlight and mindful of his frailty, Abby slowly began retracing their steps. Except for directions and cautions, they didn't speak. Even with the added light of the moon, it was a hard trip. He struggled not to lean too heavily on her and she concentrated on every step, determined to provide the stability he required.

At the base of the incline, he rubbed his knees and winced. "Perhaps you wouldn't mind driving back? There's a shorter route."

"I'd be delighted."

His instructions were as clear and precise as the beam of the headlight and soon they were back at the estate. Subdued lighting cast golden pools on the ground. Frank waited in one of them by the second pillar. He helped Jonah alight and told her where to park.

Jonah waited for her by the entrance of his home. Fatigue and pain dragged at his scarred features, but an inner peace seemed to shine in his green eyes. "Thank you, Bird Lady. This evening has been a rare pleasure I will cherish."

"For me as well, Whale Rider."

"Until we meet again." He tipped his hat and went inside.

"Come on, Abby. We're driving back. Let's get you home before your sister calls Henry Cobb and tells him I kidnapped you," Frank jested as he took her elbow and steered her to his truck.

Emotionally spent, she managed a weak smile. Frank had known Jonah and his father for years. Surely, there were a hundred questions she should ask. None that mattered came to mind. She was mentally stuck in neutral, contentedly replaying the incredible evening.

Tomorrow, or thereabouts, she'd talk with Frank. For now, she just wanted to keep watching her mental movie of the marbled murrelets in Jonah's piece of paradise.

Chapter Thirty-One

THE FOLLOWING EVENING after dinner, Abby carried a cup of herbal tea out to the back deck and gazed at the fence.

The clack of Mary's knitting needles slowed, then stopped. "Is there anything I can do for you? I'm sure you're tired."

"A little, but last night was worth every minute of lost sleep." Abby took her seat at the wicker table. "It was so amazing. I just wish I could have put you inside my head, inside me, so you could've experienced what I felt."

An enigmatic smile quirked Mary's lips. "In a way, I did."

"How so?"

Mary put her knitting on her lap and said softly, "Jonah came to see me today."

"He did? I mean, I'm surprised he came during the day."

"Frank brought him by. I fixed lunch for them."

Perplexed, Abby asked, "Why didn't you tell me earlier? What did they want?"

"Jonah asked me to wait until after dinner to mention his visit." Mary reached out and clasped Abby's hand. "I'm still digesting everything we talked about. He's every bit as wonderful as you said. The birds were his gift to you. His gift to me was of a more personal nature."

At a complete loss, Abby asked, "What is it?"

"Perspective." Mary rested her hands on her knitting. "We spoke for a long time, about his accident and mine. I told him everything, including my foolishness for trying to collect the stuff that spilled out of my purse. I wish I'd met him sooner. He knows every peak and valley on the road I've been traveling.

"We both were solely responsible for what happened to us. We both paid a price and have come to accept there's a much greater purpose to the outcome than we saw originally."

"He helped you find a way to forgive yourself," Abby said softly, smiling. Jonah Bowditch, once the worldly rebel, had grown into a tenderhearted man of compassion.

"Yes." Mary pointed to her temple. "I've always known that all things happen with God's knowledge, for ultimately He turns the bad things into good for His children." She laid her open hand on her chest. "Jonah helped me know it here. That was the tremendous gift he came by to give me."

"A gift from the heart is one of the greatest treasures we can receive from anyone," Abby agreed.

Mary reached into the denim bag hanging from the arm of her wheelchair and withdrew a large brown envelope. "He asked me to give this to you."

Her heart breaking, Abby took the legal-sized packet and stared at the painstaking handwriting. "He left today, didn't he?"

"He and Frank are spending the night in Seattle. Jonah has an early flight. Frank's handling everything on this end and Jonah has someone to meet him."

"I thought we'd have more time . . . that he'd stay at least through the summer." Remembering how he'd looked at the old trees with such hunger and the tears scalding his cheeks, she realized he'd been saying good-bye. He told her he was leaving—just not that it would be today.

Mary adjusted her yarn ball to keep it from rolling off her lap and onto the deck where Blossom waited for just such an opportunity. "Aren't you going to open it?"

Abby broke the seal, opened the envelope and removed the contents. A letter from Jonah in his pain-filled hand rested on top. She read aloud:

Dear Bird Lady,

Your decision to remain on Sparrow Island is a reflection of God's perfect timing. The land and the old trees now belong to you. I have enclosed the deed. You may convert the house into anything you like, except a resort. Live in it, if you so desire. It, too, is yours. There is also a trust fund for the preservation of the land and to cover the upkeep of the house for the next several generations.

The papers you need to sign and their respective contacts are included. These are good people, like you and Mary. They will help you.

Trust in the Lord.

Jonah Bowditch

Tears blurred Abby's vision. Last night, when he said "caretaker," she had assumed he wanted her help to protect the land and its secrets. He did, but not in the manner she expected. He *gave* it to her along with something just as precious—his trust.

Her chin quivered. Jonah's awesome generosity and the faith he showed in her ability to preserve what he had guarded so zealously for more than three decades humbled her.

Mary produced a handful of tissues from her pocket.

Abby reached for some and her sleeve caught the edge of an envelope. It fell to the deck with a clank. "Those must be the keys to his house."

"Your house."

Abby retrieved the keys and wondered how many days it would take for any of this to mesh with reality.

"Your furniture is coming this week," Mary began warily. "Will you have it delivered . . . ?"

"As Dad says, 'don't even go there.' I live here. With you."

Mary breathed an audible sigh of relief.

"Hey," Abby said brightly, as she grabbed the arm of Mary's chair and shook it. "You're stuck with me. We had a great thing going in our first childhood. I can't wait to see what we're going to do in our second one."

"Watch out, Sparrow Island." Grinning, Mary leaned over the papers. "Did Jonah leave us his new address?"

Abby checked through the documents. "Here it is, along with a phone number and e-mail address. Guess he knew I'd hunt him down eventually."

"Or torture poor Frank until he talked," agreed Mary. "You know, old Frank's really a great guy. It must have been terribly hard to keep Jonah's secret when he overheard your conversation with Dad and Hugo."

This explained Frank's irascible moods. The last of the jigsaw puzzle pieces fell into place.

"Well, it's been a full couple of days. I hope tomorrow slows down for both of us." Mary stuffed her knitting into the denim bag.

Abby smiled and kept her own counsel.

Shortly before lunch the next day, Abby hung up the phone and called, "It's here, Hugo. Time to go."

He tucked a file in a desk drawer. "I'm ready."

Ten minutes later, she led a convoy of vehicles down Primrose Lane, through Green Harbor and finally onto Oceania Boulevard.

When she turned into the driveway, she pressed the garage door opener. Careful to leave plenty of room, she pulled over to one side.

Next came two shiny vans. Behind them were the Stantons' pickup truck and Hugo's car. Marvin Sherrod parked on the street and quickly exited his car.

"Mary," Ellen called into the house through the laundry room. "Can you come out front for a few minutes?"

"Mom," Mary exclaimed from somewhere in the house. "I didn't expect you. I'll be right there."

Abby hung back, privileged to play spectator. This time, it was appropriate. She glanced at her father and smiled. He lay in wait with his camera ready.

At twilight tomorrow, she'd close another circle in the cycle of life and take the last step to complete her homecoming. She and her father had begun the adventure of a lifetime in the fields behind the farmhouse when she was a child. His patience and enthusiasm had launched her flight into the winged world. Now, she'd take him with her to Jonah's piece of Eden and share the best adventure of all, high in the canopy of the old-growth forest.

Whispers through the Trees
by Susan Plunkett & Krysteen Seelen

Flight of the Raven
by Ellen Harris

Meet Abigail Stanton, an ornithologist, bird watcher and keen observer who brings a sharp eye to bear on the secrets that lie hidden on Sparrow Island, a place of extraordinary natural beauty in the San Juan Islands. Fate has brought Abby back to the island—and the life she thought she had said farewell to forever. But Abby, inspired by hope and faith, soon discovers that life on Sparrow Island is full of intrigue and excitement when she opens her eyes to the mysterious ways God works in our lives.

Susan Plunkett and Krysteen Seelen are sisters and neighbors in Manchester, Washington. Susan is a RITA finalist and the winner of the National Readers' Choice Award. Krysteen, when not writing, works as a part-time bookseller. They both enjoy gardening, reading and traveling with their husbands.